FATAL DISTRACTION

FATAL DISTRACTION

OR HOW I CONQUERED MY ADDICTION TO CELEBRITIES AND GOT A LIFE

Emmi Fredericks

THOMAS DUNNE BOOKS ✖ ST. MARTIN'S PRESS

NEW YORK

THOMAS DUNNE BOOKS.
An imprint of St. Martin's Press.

www.stmartins.com

Book design by Jonathan Bennett

ISBN 0-312-31294-6

First Edition: February 2004

10   9   8   7   6   5   4   3   2   1

For Joan Fredericks,
who always let me stay up to watch the Oscars

FATAL DISTRACTION

CHAPTER ONE

A **WARNING TO** *the reader . . .*
This story is not for the faint of heart. While mine is ultimately a tale of triumph, it is also a harrowing chronicle of a trial of the human spirit. So, if you're not in the mood for peril and heartache, just put the book down. You can find enlightenment and self-awareness some other time. It's okay by me.

All right. Now that we've sorted out the players from the poseurs, let's continue.

A plague is sweeping America. An addiction that afflicts the unsuspecting citizen without warning. Early symptoms are often missed. Denial leads to postponement of treatment—or, indeed, failure to seek help at all. Inexorably, the sufferer is gripped by a state of near delusion. Relationships suffer. Isolation sets in. Normal, everyday life as most people know it becomes unbearable. Larger and larger cash outlays are required to sustain the habit.

What is the plague I speak of? The disease that enslaves and weakens millions around the globe?

Celebraholism.

Yes, you read right.

Celebraholism: a complex psychological disorder characterized by an excessive, compulsive need for exposure to celebrities.

To further illustrate the affliction of our age, I present two scenarios.

In the first scenario, you and I pass each other on the street. What happens?

Nothing. (What did you think, I was going to run up and assault you with a hammer?)

Second scenario: You and a celebrity pass each other on the street. What happens?

Your mind explodes. You think . . .

Oh My God, it's So-and-So! (Reader, feel free to supply the celebrity of your choice.) *I can't believe it. So-and-So—on the very same street that I am walking on.*

You hope maybe they notice you, that your eyes meet, and they say, You. Yes, you. Come to me. Be my costar, my sperm donor, my slave . . .

Or you start wondering if maybe they've had a little surgery since you last saw them. You sneak a look to see if the difference shows.

Or you think, Gee, he's shorter than I thought.

But whatever you think, however you react, *these thoughts are not just passing impressions.* These thoughts have far greater significance than, say, if you walked by me and thought, My God, that's an ugly sweater.

Skeptical? In denial? Let's take another look at Scenario Two. Maybe you pass a celebrity, and you don't think very much at all about it. But it's a good bet that at some point in your day you're going to say something like, "Hey, you know who I ran into today? So-and-so. He's shorter than you'd think." And someone will say,

---

THE AEROBICS OF *Celebrity* SPOTTING

THE EYE SLIDE
The most basic exercise in celebrity spotting. Keeping the head still, simply slide your gaze in the reported direction of the celebrity. Keen celebrity spotters should practice this at least two minutes a day to keep ocular muscles toned.

"Oh, no, I knew he was short . . ." And so on. You are now engaged in conversation, connecting with another human being. *All because you ran into a celebrity.*

Fact!

A celebrity encounter can make you a more interesting person for at least five minutes of your life. For that five minutes, you are a lot more interesting than someone who did not encounter a celebrity.

Celebrities say they are just people like anybody else. This is a lie. In our world, celebrities are conversation, connection. They are walking, talking, breathing Opportunities. They are conduits to happiness. I'm anybody else, and believe me, I've got nothing like that to give out.

How do I know this? What makes me an expert? It's very simple. My name is Eliza H, and I am a celebraholic.

It takes enormous courage to open this book. It means that you are ready to take that first step. To look beyond the veil of your pain to a brighter future.

That's good.

HOW TO KNOW IF YOU ARE A *Celebraholic*

This is not always easy. Celebraholism is a socially acceptable disease, covertly and overtly encouraged by a number of societal norms. The key is to know how much you can handle and then ask yourself, Do I indulge within my limits?

1. You read *People* magazine and *Entertainment Weekly*. One or the other is more or less safe. The combination indicates addiction to toxic levels.

2. You are always one of those people caught in the hall discussing Not That Fucking Trial/Scandal/Divorce again.
3. The word *overexposed* means nothing to you.
4. Pleas for privacy strike you as self-indulgent.
5. Next to the gossip column, the obituaries are your favorite part of the paper.
6. You are willing to listen to self-styled "experts" with no credentials, as long as they're not discussing politics or economics.
7. You feel the people on E! are the only ones who understand your needs.
8. Who wins a presidential election matters far less to you than who wins, say, the Oscar.
9. In spite of all rational, adult thought processes to persuade you to the contrary, you feel you have no life because it's not played out on the pages of a magazine or on film.

Some of you might ask, Well, what's the problem? Why shouldn't I obsess about celebrities if that's what turns me on? It's a free country.

The fact is, celebraholics are not happy people. At certain levels of exposure, famous people become toxic. Real life in a world of celebrities has a way of getting you down. You know that the good life is out there and you know it ain't yours.

Celebraholism: ACTIVE AND PASSIVE FORMS

There are two forms of celebraholism: the active and the passive. The active form (or stage I) involves a serious psychosis: to wit, the actual desire to *be* a celebrity. Later stages of the active illness involve several unpalatable symptoms: depression, alcohol abuse, and, of course, actual celebrityhood.

The passive form (stage II) is more common. (For the obvious reasons that out of all the deluded schmucks who yearn for fame, very few actually achieve it.) Often, they become passive celebraholics, people who simply want to know every detail about celebrities' lives—no matter how trivial or disgusting.

For years, I was in the grip of the active form of the disease. Yet inexorably I sank into the deepest depths of stage II celebraholism. My life became dedicated to watching other people have lives.

Which brings us to a crucial point . . .

There is no cure for celebraholism.

That's right, just like any other addiction, celebraholism cannot be cured, only controlled. You will never look at the cover of a glossy magazine without wanting to know the contents. You will never not care if a famous person gets married, dies, or switches gender. You will never not be in thrall to the power of celebrity.

So, I hear you say, what's the answer? If it's all hopeless, why should I bother giving up my subscription to *People*? Why should I pretend that the activities of ordinary people are as fascinating as those of the rich and famous? *Why should I give up my dream of one day becoming a celebrity?*

You will never be a celebrity.

It's time to realize that. Take a deep breath and say it to yourself.

I will never be a celebrity.

I will never be a celebrity.

I will never be a celebrity.

Good. Now, take a moment, cry it out.

Take your time. It's a big step.

Done?

Okay. You have faced the fact that *you will never be a celebrity.* (It's okay if the idea still causes you pain. You're just starting the process.) You have acknowledged your loss of control over your own identity, admitted your infatuation with and addiction to the identity of others.

You will never be a celebrity.

But you can be a Great Bit Player.

This book will show you how.

CHAPTER TWO

CELEBRAHOLISM—THE EARLY YEARS

A **VERY IMPORTANT** factor in your recovery process will be to understand how the events of your childhood have contributed to your illness. In fact, the first rule of all addictions is . . .

Blame your parents.

Now, I'm not saying it's *all* my parents' fault. I'm not saying that if they had been, say, an investment banker and a dermatologist, I might never have known the torment of addiction. I'm just saying that, given who they were, it wasn't a big fat surprise that I did.

My father was a serious Stage I celebraholic. He was, of course, an artist. He was, of course, untalented. His chosen course to fame and fortune was Broadway. He dreamed of becoming a lyricist. To my father, nothing was a complete sentence unless it rhymed. Love songs were his specialty, reality his weak point.

The funny thing is that my father's belief in musicals was justified by his meeting my mother, because there is no other way these two people would have come together on life's great stage. It happened at a performance of *Man of La Mancha*. My mother's date had stood her up, and she was standing outside the theater, hoping to give the ticket away to the first likely slob that came along. My dad was that likely slob.

He thanked her profusely, even obnoxiously, until the lights dimmed and the curtain rose. Then at intermission, he made up a song for her: " 'Rosie, with the free seat. Rosie, who you'd like to meet . . .' "

My mother hated the name Rosie, but she was really pissed off at her ex and really sorry for anyone who rhymed *seat* with *meet*, so she agreed to have dinner with my dad. During that dinner, they learned that they had some things in common—well, at least two. They had both come to New York hoping to make it in the arts. My mother had wanted to be a dancer, but she taught ballet to pay the rent. Not to worry, said my father. One Day he was going to Make It Big, and then she could go back to the dancing that she loved. The fact that my mother liked teaching more than she ever liked dancing was something that went right over his head—as most things did.

For his proposal, he wrote a song: " 'Rosie, the most important thing . . . Rosie, for you I have a ring . . .' " My mother probably said yes to get him to shut up before the neighbors called the police.

The marriage was the first and last dumb move of her life. I imagine when my dad asked her to marry him, it was like that moment when you look down from a great height and you have the strange impulse to jump. You know it's crazy, you know it's going to end with your guts splattered on the pavement, but some-how you want to test the good will of the cosmos. To prove that, no matter what, it all turns out for the best.

Well, it didn't. The marriage lasted seven years, surviving big dream after big dream, one child, and a number of songs involv-ing Rosie. It even survived my mother's hysterical confession that she hated the name Rosie. That was okay—my father just switched to *rose* and *blows* and *nose* and *hippos,* and they carried on for another year.

My father was also responsible for my name, which he got, yes, from *My Fair Lady*. All in all, I consider myself lucky. I mean, with his predilections, I could have been an Evita. Or a Mame.

But then the Broken Leg Theater Company blew into town and brought my parents' idyll to an end. The Broken Leg Theater Com-pany was a dinky little troupe, run by an old college buddy of my dad's. They were doing *Godspell*, and the chum asked my father if he would mind reworking the lyrics to take the Jesus references out. It was such a great show, they hated to ruin it with the religion thing.

For three months, our home was in the grip of *Godspell*, as my father devoted himself to the epic task at hand. He would sit in the kitchen, rhyming to himself (*Lord, gourd, fijord,* and *Judas, screwed us*) deep into the night. He and my mother stopped speaking around that time, but I don't think it was out of animosity. She had probably just given up any hope of getting a coherent sentence out of him.

Then, finally, the big night—the premiere of the Broken Leg Company's new and improved *Godspell* now known as *Rising Sign*! The whole dismal endeavor played in a basement of a local church, squeezed in between AA meetings and bingo. The audiences were just as dismal: friends, sleeping partners, and irritable parents who couldn't believe that theater was a better career choice for their daughter than, say, dentistry.

But to my father, the show was a revelation. Here, for the first time, were real live people listening to his words. They didn't clap, and they might have even booed a little when my father took a bow at the curtain call. Nevertheless, when the Broken Leg Com-

THE AEROBICS OF *Celebrity* SPOTTING

THE HALF RISE

Performed most often in restaurants where fellow diners may be an impediment to celebrity viewing. Rise from your seat as if you were adjusting your skirt. Keep your head lowered during this part of the exercise. Then, as you start to sit back down, raise your head in order to gain a clear view of the celebrity.

pany took to the road, my father decided he could defer the dream no more. He did leave my mother and me a note—and yes, it rhymed.

Ah, ha, you say. *So, your father's abandonment led you to worship remote celebrities who would never notice you.*

It's a neat theory. It wins points for tidiness. But I have to admit, in my heart of hearts, it never really takes.

⌐ Fact!
Not every dysfunction can be attributed to a single childhood trauma.

Sorry, guys.

It's hard to miss someone who was never really there. My father's chronic dippiness was his most damaging legacy to me. I think my mother was relieved more than anything else. For starters, she didn't have to listen to any more songs that rhymed *adore* with *matador*. But there was one problem: child care.

Now that my father was no longer part of our domestic profile, I was minus a minder. My mother had to take on a lot more classes, and God forbid I should be left alone. Who knew what could happen to me? I could fall in with the wrong crowd . . . become an addict or something.

Now, my mother is a good woman, and at that time she was in a tough spot. But in light of what happened, she might have taken a little more care in choosing a baby-sitter. How much care did she take? Well, I imagine that some of the interviews for prospective sitters went like this:

"Oh, you drink to excess? Well, as long as you don't carry firearms."

"You moonlight as a prostitute? Just not in front of the child—nudity makes her anxious."

"You look familiar. Did I see you in the Zapruder film?"

And so on.

I suppose I should be grateful that I wound up with Arthur and Lloyd. Arthur and Lloyd lived in our building. They were lawyers, but Arthur had recently given up the law to pursue the perfectly reasonable dream of becoming a concert pianist. Lloyd was getting testy over the family income being cut in half with nothing but a Chopin polonaise to show for it. And it was just good luck that my mother happened to be in the elevator when the two men were trying not to argue over money—and failing.

Desperation had made my mother bold, and between the third and fifth floors, she proposed a scheme that would have me covered for two of the nights she had to be in class, while providing income for Arthur and Lloyd.

And so it came to pass that on Tuesdays and Thursdays, I listened while Arthur wrestled with his beloved polonaises. Arthur's great hope, he confessed to me, was to one day play in an atmosphere of complete silence that would last exactly five seconds after the final note had sounded, then explode into what he called the Perfect Applause.

"Not frenzied, but not tepid, either. Ordered, but with a sort of madness to it. A storm of love that's directed solely and utterly at me. Does that make any sense?"

I nodded.

Tuesdays and Thursdays with Arthur was only the beginning. My mother also arranged for Mila on Wednesdays, and Rodney on Mondays. Mila lived on the third floor, and she was a poet. Her poems were composed of one word, sometimes with flute accompaniment.

"This is 'Wind,' " she would announce. Then she would dance around the living room waving a scarf, and chant, "Wind, wind, wind, wind . . . wind! Wi-i-i-i-ind. Wind? *Wind.*" Other poems included "Ocean," "Sunlight," and "Sewage."

Monday was Rodney, on the second floor. Rodney was an actor who studied with Uta Hagen, so we usually spent the day with Rodney transforming himself into an array of household items that would have done *The Price Is Right* proud. One week he was a chair, the next week a potted plant. Then when he felt he had fully grasped the essence of furnishings, he moved on to animals. One week I found him mewling under the couch. He was trying to see what it felt like to be a guinea pig.

Here was creative endeavor undertaken for the pure joy of self-expression, and it was complete hell. This is not to say that Arthur, Rodney, and Mila weren't all very nice people, but their antics scarred the mind of a young child who would forever gag at the phrase "art for art's sake."

Given my captive state as Member of the Audience for a bunch of loser no-talents, it should come as no surprise that when I was just nine years old, I had my first Celebraholic Episode.

THE FIRST *Celebraholic* EPISODE

For some, it was the first time they ever heard the opening strains of *Gone With the Wind*. For others, the time Elvis swiveled on *The Ed Sullivan Show*. Many people in the world, I'm sure, have seen *Gone With the Wind* or happened to watch Elvis on *Ed Sullivan* that night. They did not become celebraholics. But other people did.

Why?

Because they had an Episode.

Your first Celebraholic Episode. As maddening and intense as first love, it's that original flash of brain-blanking passion for a larger-than-life person you will never, ever meet in the flesh. It's the moment you know you are capable of dedicating your life to the ingestion of any fact or rumor concerning this person, no matter how small or immaterial.

My first celebraholic experience occurred in the summer of 1979.

The first celebrity I became obsessed with was cruel, inhuman, and parasitical—but from the second it burst, squealing and shrieking, from John Hurt's stomach, it changed my life forever.

Before I even saw the movie, I was hooked. One day, walking home, I passed by a boarded-up storefront, and there it was: in a long row of posters, repeating as far as the eye could see, like one of those old flip books. The strange, cold, dead bodies, the ominous green sac hanging above them. The word in futuretype: *Alien.*

I stared at those posters forever, struck dumb with frantic curiosity.

What was this? Where was this? *Where could I see more?*

It was my first real megablast of hype. Never in my life had I seen an individual personality make such an impact. As far as I was concerned, that creature was what was happening in the world, and I wanted to be a part of it. I begged my mother for weeks to take me to the movie. She said, No. I said, Why. She said, You're too impressionable.

"What does that mean?" I asked.

"It means that what you see has far too much power over you."

And, as is often the case with addictions, when faced with a choice between obeying my mother and pursuing my self-destructive ways, I pushed the self-destruct button without a second thought.

What happened was that one afternoon, Rodney had gotten tired of being a goldfish or whatever, and decided to take me to a movie. I said I wanted to see *Alien.* We argued for maybe . . . two seconds. Because, let's face it, Rodney wanted to see *Alien* a lot more than he wanted to see some doofy kids movie. In line, he said, "Don't tell your mother. And don't blame me if you have nightmares."

But while the rest of the theater screamed and cowered, I was simply . . . transfixed.

What amazing power. What awesome presence. Throughout the entire movie, the only thing you wanted to see was this creature, this metallic, toothy Garbo, that only appeared briefly—a claw here, triple-rowed teeth there—to crunch and munch its way through the cast.

Rodney kept hiding his eyes. But I kept my eyes wide open. And they've been wide open ever since.

The Alien and I were having a child's version of a doomed love affair. I knew that one day it would vanish from my life altogether. Remember, we're pretty much talking PVE, the Pre-Video Era, and my mother refused to get cable TV, which then we called HBO. At that time, once a movie left the theater, it was gone forever, until it showed up in its hacked-up version on TV four years later.

So, in the way of all doomed lovers and celebraholics, I became obsessed. I bought and read everything I could that had anything to do with the object of my obsession. I read the books; I read the magazine articles. Anything having to do with the movie, I bought. For the first time, I was aware that people were producing goods and disseminating information *just to meet my needs.* For the first time in my life, I felt in tune with the world.

By the time I had outgrown that alien, there was *ET.* By the time I had outgrown *ET,* there was Chuck and Di. J.R. got shot, Michael Jackson moonwalked, and Madonna got touched for the very first time.

From that point on, I was aware that a far more interesting world than my own existed. A world exciting enough to get itself

THE AEROBICS OF *Celebrity* **SPOTTING**

THE SUDDEN SWIVEL
When the Eye Slide proves insufficient, turn abruptly at the waist. Try to make it seem as if this is an involuntary movement, caused by gas or other.

---

written about, talked about, and put on television.

The year of my first Oscar telecast—a seminal event in the lives of all celebraholics—was 1980. At the Oscars, I saw for the first time what I would spend the next two decades pursuing: a glimpse of the celebrity out of character. A glimpse of the celebrity as a normal, neurotic human being—albeit with ten thousand dollars to spend on a dress. On the Oscars, you see celebrities cry, you see them drunk, you see them really pissed off. It's live, they're wired, and the potential for embarrassment is enormous. Every year, I sat riveted, hoping for someone to fall out of her dress, make an obnoxious political statement, or forget his wife's name. You learned who had drug problems, who was fat, who was nice and classy, and who was rude and tasteless. It was famous people au naturel, and it was even more exciting than their movies.

To the Oscars, I quickly added the Emmys, the Grammys, and the Tonys. Even the Daytime Emmys, which gave awards to people I didn't know. I read all the speculation about the nominees, and what everybody had to say about the winners and losers the next day. I started watching the Olympics, election campaigns, Kennedy Center Honors, even the occasional telethon. If a show had one famous person walking down the aisle to music, I watched it.

My mother didn't get it. Like so many parents who see their

children in the grip of an addiction, she dismissed it as a phase. An annoying phase, but a phase.

"I don't know how you can stand to read that stuff," she would say over breakfast as I pored over *People*. "I mean, why do you *care*?"

Even now, I don't know how to answer that question. People do ask it a lot—usually after they've gotten every last scrap of dirt out of you. "My God, why do you care?" I don't know. Why eat? Why go to the beach? Why masturbate? Because it's fun. Because it's interesting. Because doing it is a lot better than not doing it.

"I want you to think about what you're going to do with your life," my mother said.

Oh, I knew what I was going to do with my life. I had it all planned out.

Age 13-18: Develop the creative talent that would be my launchpad to celebrity.

Age 18-22: Go to college. Belong to a small, select circle of highly talented and charismatic individuals. Become well known and envied.

Age 22: Receive a generous offer to do something artistic. Accept.

Age 24: Be nominated for an Oscar. Lose. Graciously contradict people when they say the winner got the sentiment vote.

Age 26: Get nominated again. Win. Make the kind of speech that gets shown on Oscar documentaries.

Age 27: Write play. Let Meryl Streep star.

Age 28: Win Tony. Look modest when people tell you you are the youngest person ever to win a Tony *and* an Oscar. Remember to say nice things about Meryl.

Age 29: Move to the Dakota. Exchange witty banter with fellow celebrities in the elevator.

My thirties I saw as one instance of fabulousness after the next.

By my forties, I might descend into a depression and decide that my work was just too popular to be taken seriously. I would do very dark, cerebral pieces that people would fail to understand at the time, but would later be accounted my best work. The fifties was the time for retrospectives, my second Barbara Walters interview, maybe a volume of memoirs. I didn't think too far beyond that because I was fourteen and anything after fifty meant wobbly necks and too many jewels.

I would get dressed up and walk down the aisle to music. Some girls have that fantasy and call it a wedding. But weddings only last one day, and then you're just an ordinary person. I wanted my walk down the aisle, all eyes upon me, to last forever.

I wanted to be a celebrity.

CHAPTER THREE

PORTRAIT OF THE CELEBRAHOLIC AS A YOUNG WOMAN

Age 13-18: Develop the creative talent that would become my launchpad to celebrity.

I **WAS IN** every school play—admittedly as the stage manager, but who raided the burned-out building for the *Stage Door* scenery? Who borrowed her mother's bathrobe for the sophomore production of *Cabaret*? And who caught hell when Mom saw it prancing around a mock thirties Berlin? I wrote for the school newspaper, worked on the yearbook—I even sang in the choir. Five performances of "You Light Up My Life" have got to count for something in this world.

I began to worry a little; with so much talent, it was going to be tough to choose my field of expertise. I began to think in terms of second careers.

> BARBARA WALTERS: It's very unusual, isn't it, to win the Nobel Prize in literature after such a successful acting career?
>
> ME: Limitation is not a word in my vocabulary, Barbara. I believe in fulfilling your potential to the fullest.

Age 18-22: Go to college. Belong to a small, select circle of highly talented and charismatic individuals. Become well known and envied.

I did get into college. I even got into a college I wanted to go to. Why? I was just so damned psyched to go, and I think the admissions people sensed this. "So, why do you want to come to XU?" "Because I love it." "What you think about XU so far?" "Love it." "What do you expect to get out of XU?" "Everything. I love it here."

"You need to think about what you're going to do with your life," my mother said as she drove me up to the campus.

I smiled, and made plans to buy her a nice big house far away from me.

So, I arrived at college ready to meet my destiny. Only destiny wasn't so ready to meet me.

I took Freshman Theater, tried out for every production, and failed to get even a walk-on part. No problem. I painted backdrops, hemmed costumes, went to the mall for extra fuses, and swept up backstage. I wasn't worried. The way I saw it, I was paying my dues.

In my sophomore year, I met Dinah Sharlip.

$Fact!$

Anyone who wants to pursue a career as a celebrity should avoid people like Dinah Sharlip. Anyone who wants to do anything productive with her life—ever—should avoid people like Dinah Sharlip.

The first time I met Dinah, she was pointing a nail gun at me.

We were working on the set for *Antigone*, a very avant-garde design that involved huge quantities of garbage bags. Dinah had been nailing the bags to wooden flats when she made her opening statement: "This sucks."

"Point down," I said. "Please."

She did. The nail gun launched its projectile into the floor.

"Doesn't it?" she demanded. "Suck? Completely?"

She's not a person you argue with now, and then she had a weapon in her hand. With tact, I inquired what sucked specifically. At which point, she dropped the nail gun and proceeded to verbally shred the college, the department, and the students.

But it was the professors who really pissed her off.

"Have you ever heard of any of these phonies? They're pedophiles with voice lessons. Strictly amateur hour. Forget it, amateur *minute.*" She lit a cigarette. "I tried out for this show. I went in with this completely rip-ass monologue. And they say to me, Oh, well, dear, maybe you'd like to focus on the character roles. I was like, you mean the parts for *dogs.* The asexual. The geek and freak patrol."

Well, Dinah's look was not exactly what you'd call ingenue-friendly. Her hair looked as if she had cut it with toenail clippers, and she had a stud in her nose, but even though she was sort of the ugliest person I'd ever seen, she also made you feel it was a failure of nerve on your part that you didn't look like her.

"I'm an artist, I don't need this shit."

I asked what kind of artist she was.

She shrugged. "I'm not into labels."

"Oh."

"My art is me. It's whatever way I express myself."

"Oh."

"They try and put limits on you here. They put you on these tracks."

"That's true."

"I can't put limits on myself."

After a year of sweeping up after thin people with great cheekbones, I was intrigued by this person who was in the same rotten position as I was but who, instead of blaming it on herself, blamed it on everyone else. I asked her if she wanted to get a cup of coffee.

"Nah, I hate coffee. It makes me twitch."

Well, as I was to learn, a lot of things made Dinah Sharlip twitch. She didn't avoid most of them—in fact, she sought them out. When I finally did get to see her act, I was struck by her glaring lack of talent. The same was true of her singing, her poetry, her paintings, and her mime. (She was the Shadow Strangler. She would stalk people on the pathways, pretend to grab their shadows and choke them to death. Once in a while she forgot it was a mime exercise. Eventually, she was asked by the campus police to find another outlet for her creative expression.)

Dinah never really showed any talent for any artistic endeavor. What she did show was a willingness to ruthlessly exploit every asset—no matter how negligible—in her pursuit of fame and fortune. Like her appearance, her performance style was so off-putting, so completely wrong, that you had to pay attention to it.

Talking to Dinah, I came to realize that my earlier visions of celebrity had been painfully naive. I had thought of celebrity and its rewards in very childish, sentimental terms: awards, adulation, attention. But Dinah really had it figured out. She knew exactly why she wanted to be a celebrity.

Power.

"I wanna be fat and have people say I'm beautiful. I wanna be obnoxious and have people say that I tell it like it is. I wanna step on people and have them say, She knows how to get what she wants. I wanna be really dumb and have people love me because I'm so unpretentious."

One drunken night, Dinah and I made a list of questions for the future celebrities we were certain we were.

And until she was famous for her art, she would be famous in every other way: dating only the most spectacularly awful men, throwing up through the railings of stairs, attacking a romantic rival with a Bic pen, and doing mushrooms before speaking the most amazingly convoluted Chinese in an oral exam . . . for French. For all of these performances, she needed an audience. And that audience was me.

FUTURE *Celebrity* QUESTIONNAIRE

Would you ever appear nude either on-screen or in a magazine?

Would you marry someone just because it was good for your career?

Would you donate your time and name to charitable functions? If so, which ones?

East or West Coast?

Would you have servants, even though it was undemocratic?

If your costar was sleeping with the director, how far would you go to ensure you got equal screen time?

If a president you didn't vote for invited you to the White House, would you go?

White, silver, or black limousine?

How nice should you be to the paparazzi?

Who would you thank first when you won the Oscar, your parents or your friends?

What would you wear to your first big awards show?

What would you not do to be famous? (Dinah couldn't think of anything; I pretended I could.)

A typical conversation with Dinah went something like this:

> DINAH: I cannot believe that fucker. I mean, he invites me
> and his fiancée to the show, then he sits in between us, and
> then asks me to give him a hand job at intermission. And I
> was like, forget it, because Alan was sitting two rows ahead
> of us, and I didn't want him see to us . . .
> ME: Dinah, I have two days to live.
> DINAH: And he's like, who's that guy, and I'm like, what guy,
> and . . .

STAGE II *Celebraholism* (CODEPENDENCY)

I think that it's safe to say that my shift into stage II celebraholism began around this time. When you spend all your time with someone who talks nonstop about herself, it's easy to lose sight of the fact that you exist beyond your ability to see and hear. With Dinah, I was slowly transformed into a passive receptacle of horror and melodrama. As I listened, I would find myself in a strange half-conscious state, bored, numb, yet transfixed, hungry for the next detail. Some people in my position become psychotherapists. I became a stage II celebraholic.

So, inquires the rational reader, why remain friends with such a selfish, distracting person? Focus on your own goals. Attain your own dreams.

It's a good question, one I occasionally put to myself at four in the morning. The truth was that my ideal incarnation was still a little late in manifesting itself. I was beginning to suspect that I didn't really have it in me to be an actress. Or a director. Or a playwright. I don't know . . . it all seemed to require so much energy.

In my junior and senior years, I sank deeper into celebrity watching. There was absolutely no question about it. On a steady diet of magazines, tabloids, and TV shows, I was growing addicted to celebrity news.

Fact!

A good, juicy piece of gossip has ten times the energy jolt as caffeine.

I had only to inhale one rumor, and my mind instantly grew sharper, my thoughts clearer. A single glance at a headline could jolt me awake in the morning. The lead statement would spark my first reaction, and by the time I had reached the end of the piece, I had formed a fully cogent thesis on what had really happened—and how it differed from the official story.

The downside, of course, was that if I was deprived of headlines, rumors, and gossip, my mind didn't work very well at all. In fact, it often flatly refused to exert itself in pursuit of any kind of knowledge not related to celebrity—say, literature, history, or any of those things they give you a college degree for.

In my senior year, I came to an important conclusion: faces are indispensable to our way of life. We use people, real and imagined, to sell everything from cat food to movies. Do you buy a dessert or Sara Lee? Spaghetti sauce or Newman?

And at some extremely drunken point, I had a miraculous vision of the future, of a society divided into two classes: the Seen and the Unseen. The Seen—maybe two percent of the population—would be an elite group of individuals whose image was reproduced for the purposes of selling and/or entertainment. The Unseen—all those other losers—would be reduced to the status of nameless drudges who possessed just two meaningful assets: the ability to labor and a credit card. As they labored ten hours a day, the credit card would effect the transfer of funds, also known as tithe or tribute, from their accounts to that of the Seen.

I didn't want to be a nameless drudge. I didn't want to be Unseen.

What I was going to do to get Seen, however, was a complete mystery.

Dinah and I decided to get an apartment together after graduation. (The Sharlips knew what they had on their hands. After twenty-two years, they felt it was time to give Dinah her freedom. So they moved to Florida and said she needn't feel obligated at holidays.) We anticipated great futures for ourselves. Once free of the narrow constraints of college, we would be able to develop our creative talents.

My mother drove up for the graduation, and after the ceremony, she took me out to dinner.

"So," she said, "have you decided?"

"Decided what?"

"What you're going to do with your life."

"I'm keeping my options open," I said, and then, because I felt in the mood for a change of subject, I asked her about a married actor who had been caught in a motel with not one but two women.

"He's claiming he's a sex addict," I said. "Do you think it's true, or you think it's just something he's saying to cover in front of his wife?"

"Is this someone you know?" my mother asked.

"No."

"Oh," said my mother, and asked the waiter for some more water.

As we drove back to the city, my mother said, "Honey, can I give you a piece of advice?"

I said yes, because I figured that having dropped tens of thousands of dollars, she was entitled to give a little advice.

"Don't depend on other people to do things just so you have something to watch."

I said I had no intention of doing any such thing.

And for those readers who are muttering things about thousands of dollars down the toilet and four years wasted, I have this to say: It wasn't a waste. I drank a lot, fucked a lot, and had a lot of fun, thank you very much.

So, at the age of twenty-two, with a degree in drama you could use as toilet paper, I returned to the Big City, and became just one more loser thinking if I could make it there, I could make it anywhere.

'⌐ Fact!

New York has more celebraholics per square mile than any other city.

Not only is New York home to the best and brightest, it's home to everyone who thinks they are the best and brightest—despite all evidence to the contrary. All those crazy people wandering the streets? Bet every single one of them came to New York to be famous.

Ms. Sharlip had a lot to say about our prospective domicile.

"Location," she said. "Location is the most important thing."

"How about running water and an indoor toilet?"

"Don't get bourgeois on me."

"I like running water and indoor toilets."

She fixed me with a Prepare-to-Be-Squashed-Like-a-Bug look, and said, "Look, we can live someplace really nice for a long time as nobodies, or we can live in a crummy place for like *two seconds* before we get the megaloft in TriBeCa. It's what they call a *choice*."

Well, I didn't want to choose, frankly. But if you've been paying attention at all, you can guess that Dinah got her way, and we moved into an awful apartment that no one in her right mind would live in—situated in a neighborhood people would kill to call their own.

Age 22: Receive generous offer to do one of the following: acting, writing, directing. Accept.

Not one offer. Not a single, blessed phone call. I knew I was a little behind on my life plan, so I wasn't entirely astonished that Stephen Spielberg did not call me the minute I received my diploma. So I went in search of a job that would get me maximum contact with celebrities.

Oh, says the reader, you mean like an agent's assistant, or a script reader, or studio gofer?

No, I mean—in chronological order—a messenger, a waitress, and catering staff.

My reasoning ran something like this: obviously I was lacking a certain something I needed to become famous. If I was in a position where I could see celebrities, get a good look at them up close and personal, I could find out what that something was and acquire it. Call it celebrity through osmosis. Also, if the old saying "It's not what you know but who you know" (or that verb that rhymes with know) was true, it seemed entirely possible that a casting director would be more likely to hire the girl who served him his scallops than, say, an actress with actual talent.

I did meet a lot of celebrities. Lousy ones. Soap stars. Theater has-beens. And a lot of celebrity wanna-bes. When you work in the service sector, you learn to spot incipient celebraholism. In

New York, everyone who gets something from somebody else, served with a smile, decides they are a special person, entitled to that smile, and anything else you can give them—like extra limes, a free drink, brand liquor at generic prices, entree replacements, and a second scoop of ice cream. In short, they all think they're celebrities. I had one customer when I was a waitress, and I swear, this is the God's honest truth. She ordered a grilled cheese sandwich. When it arrived, she said, "Excuse me, miss? Miss? I can't eat this—it's got cheese in it."

"You ordered a grilled cheese sandwich, right?"

"Yeah, but I didn't want cheese on it. You'll have to take it back."

What did she want? Two grilled slices of bread? No, what she really wanted was to demand the impossible and then throw a fit when her request wasn't satisfied. Celebrities can get away with it. Normal people can't. This is why normal people want to be celebrities.

There were opportunities, job offers. But all of them required more work and dispensed less glamour and riches than I thought were due to me.

At the same time, Dinah was doing everything in her sometimes scary power to make sure the world stood up and took notice of her—at gunpoint if necessary. She lasted an even shorter time than I did as a waitress, but she was an enormous success as a bartender. The surliness and willingness to inflict bodily harm that is so frowned upon when you are a waitress is considered quite a plus in the bartending profession.

Naturally, bartending (and earning money) took a backseat to her art, which was expanding its parameters all the time. Dinah floated from bands to theater troupes to stand-up and then cycled through again when failure looked imminent. One month, she was a white and tone-deaf Billie Holliday; the next month, she was performing a completely unintelligible routine based on the poetry of Sylvia Plath and four cans of pink Silly String.

But at every event, at every venue, I was there. Nobody was there for Dinah back "when" more than I was. I attended endless stand-up, heard "I Fought the Law and the Law Won" one hundred and eighty-three times, and spent a fortune on cheap beer. If that's not support, I don't know what is.

"Dinah, when you win the Oscar, you'll thank me in your speech, right?" "Sure."

She didn't ask if I would thank her in my speech.

Age 24-27: Be nominated for Oscar and lose. Get nominated again and win. Write play.

Wasn't nominated. Didn't win. Didn't write a play. I was twenty-five and nobody when it occurred to me that I might not be one of fate's chosen people.

Why was I so unproductive? Simple. I was now firmly in the grip of stage II celebraholism. And if you were a stage II celebraholic during the '90s, then those years passed in a state very similar to blackout. Because in the '90s, celebrities just went . . . nuts.

A *Celebraholic* TEST

If you know the answer to two or more of these questions, it is possible that you have celebraholic tendencies.

1. Which comedian was caught playing with himself in a movie theater?

2. Who did Julia Roberts dump at the altar? Who did she later marry—and also dump?
3. Where did Woody take Soon-Yi on their early dates?
4. Which is more painful? To be Gillooleed or Bobbitted?
5. How much per boob was Demi Moore paid for her soul-baring scene in *Striptease*? (Bonus question: Real or fake?)
6. Which part of Sarah Ferguson's body was being sucked in the photos taken prior to her divorce?
7. Who or what is an Ito?
8. How old was Michael Jackson's accuser?
9. What did Prince Charles wish to be in order to be closer to his beloved Camilla?
10. True or False . . .
    a. Madonna and Warren Beatty
    b. Madonna and JFK, Jr.
    c. Madonna and Ingrid Casares
    d. Madonna and Madonna

Blame it on the money, blame it on the drugs, famous people were getting stupider and stupider by the second. No sooner had they pulled themselves out of one scandal then they were embroiled in the next. Just keeping track of the trials—Remember those cute Menendez boys?—took up vast amounts of my time.

I spent my weekends in celebrity-dense neighborhoods, haunted movie premieres, peered into the windows of the best restaurants, and kept my eyes peeled for celebrity joggers in Central Park.

I couldn't stop. I was helpless.

But one good thing did come out of my celebrity watching.

I met Danny Beale.

I met Danny Beale outside the Belasco Theater during one of the worst rainstorms of 1996. Fuzzy Winterspoon was playing Stella in *A Streetcar Named Desire*, and I was lying in wait at the stage door after the show. While I was waiting for Ms. Winter-spoon to emerge, I noticed Danny. It wasn't hard. We were the only two out there. I did a quick analysis and identified one fabulous-looking, unfamous guy. He was alone, ergo, he was waiting for someone. He was good looking, ergo, he was possibly an acquaintance of a famous person.

Maybe he was Fuzzy's new beau.

When it's raining and you're waiting, it's only logical to strike up a conversation. As Danny had no umbrella and I had come armed, I offered him shelter, which he gratefully accepted.

"So," I said brightly. "Waiting for Fuzzy?"

"I'm sorry?" The beautiful eyes opened and closed. On anyone else, you would call it blinking. On Danny, you'd describe it as something like waking from a hundred years' sleep to see wood nymphs and fairies cavorting around your head.

"Stella. Fuzzy Winterspoon."

"Oh, no. I mean, she was great." He smiled. Shy. Nice. The prince just before he slides the glass slipper on Cinderella's foot. "But I'm actually hoping to meet Joe Beergarten."

"Oh, Joe Beergarten." I nodded, wondered if we'd seen the same play. Joe Beergarten?

He took his playbill out of his pocket and opened it to the cast list. "He played Walt."

"One of the guys who plays poker with Stanley?"

"Yeah." He smiled. "He's an amazing character actor. Did you see the revival of *The Iceman Cometh*?"

"Yeah."

"He was fourth stool from the left? Made kind of a gesture, like this?"

"Not recalling, sorry."

The smile dimmed just slightly. "Anyway, I just wanted to tell him how much I admire his work."

"You're an actor?" It was barely worth asking.

"How'd you know?" He looked pleased.

"You're just a little too beautiful not to be."

He looked disappointed, and because I really did not want to disappoint such a sweet young man who thought the world of an actor who looked like a baboon's backside, I said, "So . . . if Beergarten doesn't show, you want to have a cup of coffee, hash over the production?"

Danny hesitated—no doubt worried, as he should have been, that I was an ax murderer or worse, a lonely single person.

I explained. "I just hate seeing something and then having no one to talk to about it. I like to discuss, critique, quibble . . ."

I got the smile back. "That'd be fun," said Danny.

Joe Beergarten actually did turn up just a few minutes later. Danny heaped effusive praise on him, compliments the poor guy probably hadn't heard from his own mother. Some more praise, a few more thank-yous, and we were off. Fuzzy, in case you're interested, never showed.

So, all right, he wasn't Fuzzy Winterspoon's secret amour. But as we walked down the street, a little voice kept telling me that this was someone who had an extremely good chance of becoming a you-know-what. By all rights, Daniel W. Beale should have been one of the most nibbled pieces of beefcake going. The guy was better than beautiful. Shaggy brown hair, strong, real-guy nose, full mouth that turned adorably self-deprecating when he smiled. Not pretty, but those kind of unassuming great looks that let every person he meets think they're the first person to notice— and the first to take advantage of them.

Whisking him off to the nearest bar, I proceeded to question Danny about his acting career. When had he first caught the acting bug? When he was seven, Danny's mother had taken him to see a local production of *Death of a Salesman*. This instilled in him a burning desire: (a) never to be a salesman, and (b) to be an actor.

As the evening went on, Danny talked. I listened, trying desperately to think of where I might have seen him.

"*All My Children,*" I said finally.

"I'm sorry?" The huge eyes widened. Really, he was faint-making, just the type to appeal to that cross section of Americans in possession of a pulse.

"That's where I've seen you, right? The young doctor who just came to town, and he's the secret son of mob boss Gino Santone, only he doesn't know it yet?"

"I don't do soap operas."

"Oh. Oh, God, I'm sorry. I'm so stupid. That cat food commercial, where the guy meets the woman in the elevator, and she's just run out of cat food and he says, 'Some tempting salmon sampler . . . ?' "

"Not commercials either."

"Then . . ."

"Yeah?"

"You're independently wealthy."

"No." He shook his head and changed the subject.

One thing Danny wanted made clear that first evening: he was involved. He was not only involved, he was living with someone. He was not only involved and living with someone, but he was deeply in love with that person. That was fine. It had taken me a big fifteen minutes to figure out that Danny was gay, and anyway, I had my sights set a lot higher than love (i.e., close, personal, financially remunerated friendship with a celebrity).

But to make it clear to Danny that my intentions were honorable, I asked him a lot of questions about the man in his life.

"What's his name?"

"You've probably heard of him," said Danny, shyly. "Roger Kelton. The director."

I made big eyes. "Wow."

"Yeah."

"That's so great."

"He's an amazing person."

I said I was sure he was. Just because I had never heard the man's name didn't mean he couldn't be an amazing person. It just meant his name wasn't up in lights anywhere outside of Piscataway.

"So, does he help you? Introduce you to people?"

"Well . . ." Danny smiled. "Roger has something in the works now."

I started fantasizing. Maybe Roger was assisting on some low-budget action flick, and was angling to get Danny the part of the innocent bystander who dies when the bank gets blown up by terrorists. Better yet, the *blind* innocent bystander who dies, and everyone heaves a big "Aw" when his Seeing Eye dog whimpers and licks his face. Better yet . . .

"*The Idiot.*"

"I beg your pardon?" I emerged from my vision of a swooning American public weeping over Danny's tastefully blood-spattered face.

"*The Idiot.* The Dostoyevsky novel. On stage."

"Amazing," I said, swiftly picking up Danny's vocabulary for Danny's lover.

"I might be playing the part of Prince Myshkin."

"The . . . lead, right?"

"Right. But it's only a maybe. Roger hasn't decided. Anyway, we don't even have funding yet, so . . ."

Then he looked at his watch and said that Roger would be wondering where he was. As we waited for taxis, I asked if he had seen the revival of *Candide*. He hadn't, as it turned out. Roger, surprise, surprise, didn't think much of musicals.

"Would you like to?"

"That would be great."

So Danny and I became friends. We split two-fer tickets and dinner. Roger was a very busy man (after all, the man who can think up a theatrical *Idiot* is going to have more than one iron in the fire, right?). As a result, Danny had some time on his hands, and not a lot of friends. He and Roger had been involved for three years, and apparently not everybody *understood* Roger, and what with one thing and another, Danny had found it easier to keep friends at a minimum.

Questioning Danny further on the subject of Roger, I discovered that Roger was: (a) older, (b) a genius, and (c) a big fat asshole.

"You know what it's like with people who are . . . gifted." (Yes, Danny. They're called assholes.)

"You're gifted, Danny. And you're a really nice guy."

Danny smiled and said, "Well, sometime you'll see me act, and decide."

He talked to me about his dreams for the future: the community projects he and Roger would do on the strength of *The Idiot*, performing Ibsen in Norway, children's theater for children of every background. And all the while, I was making plans of my own: namely, steering this lovely boy into the next big action trilogy.

Then funding for *The Idiot* came through. Roger graciously allowed Danny to play the lead. (Only after auditioning several other people for the part. Danny thought it was only fair; *The Idiot* should have the best cast possible.) Danny couldn't stop talking about the production. Roger was brilliant. The show was brilliant. The current script was running a tad long at five and half hours, but Roger was just so brilliant that everything would work out in the end.

Danny might be thrilled, but I wasn't. What Danny needed was exposure, and no matter how brilliant Roger was, *The Idiot* wasn't going to do that as quickly as, say, a good soap. His looks weren't going to last forever, and he might as well exploit them while he had them. Once he had the American moviegoing public at his feet and millions stashed in the bank—well, then he could do Ibsen in Norway.

One evening, I asked him. "Danny, have you ever thought of doing something more . . . accessible?"

"Not really. Roger doesn't think a lot of commercial entertainment."

I didn't think a lot of Roger, but one doesn't say things like that about the love of someone's life.

"It doesn't have to be your whole career, you could just . . ."

". . . 'use it as a launchpad.' My agent said the same thing. I told him to get lost."

I didn't want Danny telling me to get lost, so I dropped the subject. I even apologized for bringing it up.

"It's just that you're so ridiculously good-looking, and it's such a tough business, I keep thinking you should use every advantage you have."

He was quiet a little while, then said in a low voice, "I know."

"So?"

"It's personal."

As it turned out, Danny simply could not stand having people pay attention to him on account of his looks. It made him unbearably anxious, and once he was anxious, he couldn't act. Once, when he first came to New York, he had done a commercial. The whole thing was a complete disaster, and ever since, he had sworn off commercials, and everything that came with them (like money, recognition, contacts, security in your old age). Even now, he still got offers; agents begged him to sell everything from soap to laxatives—Danny could have made constipation attractive—but he wouldn't do it.

"I couldn't anyway," he said apologetically. "I get all uptight, my throat seizes up. If there's nothing real there to play, something to hide behind, I just can't cope with it."

So, for the time being, I dropped my dreams of action features and placed my hopes in Roger and *The Idiot*. Anyway, I had other problems on my hands. Dinah was having a lot of trouble getting the American public to fall at her feet possibly because they suspected she only wanted to kick them in the teeth. The performance space she had booked had been closed down for health violations, and her latest beau had just walked out on her, taking with him her stash of Silly String. Dinah was beginning to suspect that the performing arts were not for her. She muttered things like "I'm sick of packaging myself for commercial audiences," and "The whole audience thing is degrading," moped around the apartment, screamed at people, and drank a lot. For a while it was difficult to tell if she was depressed or just rehearsing.

To top it all off, Dinah had taken a rabid dislike to Danny. Ms. Sharlip was used to being the center of attention; the usurpation of her audience was not something she greeted amiably.

"The guy sounds completely self-obsessed," she said. "I can't see what you get out of this friendship." (Yes, it's not like ours, Dinah, so sisterly, so supportive, so mutually giving.)

"He's not self-obsessed," I told her. "He's always bugging me to do something more with my life."

"Oh, great, so he's obnoxious, too," said Dinah.

Danny wasn't too keen on Dinah either. (It's hard to like someone who makes gagging noises when you call on the phone.) It was funny, you could not in the whole city of New York find two people less alike than Danny and Dinah. I was sure that both would eventually be stars. Danny, because of the one asset that he refused to exploit, and Dinah, because she had no asset that she would not exploit. Of course, Danny was sweet, serious, and extremely hard-working. Dinah was . . . not. So, don't ask me who I would bet my life savings on, because the answer would depress both of us.

When rehearsals for *The Idiot* finally got underway, Danny suggested I might like to see something challenging and invited me along. The show was everything I had expected: incomprehensible, filled to the gills with serious purpose, and so dull you wanted to die. Roger was no big surprise either: a short, balding man with a Napoleonic complex. He bossed Danny rather than directing him, and was a big believer in sarcasm as a means of communication.

But I did see something I had not expected. Watching Danny work his way through the part of Prince Myshkin, I realized that beautiful was not the only word you could use to describe him.

You would also have to add the word *talentless*.

Yep, Danny the Beautiful was also sadly Danny the Stiff. Not so spectacularly bad that he might one day be credited with a whole new style of acting, just . . . not good. I would love to say it was all Roger's fault, but I can't. Over the years, Danny and I have been through some pretty crummy productions, let me tell you, and in every one, Danny was beautiful, earnest, and boring. In real life, he's the most adorable thing you've ever seen. But when he steps out onstage, it's like the lights have dimmed. Time slows. I have noticed that audiences actually become resentful of his beauty; onstage, he becomes another good-looking hunk getting by on his looks, and people start pretending they'd rather be watching some ugly—but, you know, *real*—actor up there. Poor

Danny was determined to be an actor, and an actor was the one thing he couldn't be.

This only made me more determined to help Danny overcome his terror of commercial success, because he was my friend, and because I hoped to exploit that commercial success. But, as with all things exploitative, Dinah was way ahead of me.

"Hey, you know your friend, Danny?" This she asks one night as we're jockeying around the sink, looking to spit toothpaste.

"Yeah?"

"He's in a show, right?"

"Yeah." (Note my free-flowing, chatty style.)

"Well, I was thinking . . ."

"Uh."

"Maybe he could get me some work."

"I thought you had given up the performing business."

"So, it'll be my swan song."

I'm not even going to pretend that I struggled very much. It would be inflating my dignity, masking my failings, and you know what, *you* try and stop Ms. Sharlip from getting what she wants.

So, Dinah joined the cast of *The Idiot* in the part of a groveling peasant, a type that features large in these Russian epics. She quickly began sleeping with the stage manager and wound up with a few more "Hail, Prince Myshkin's" and "Holy Fathers" than the other peasants. This was naturally resented, but as Dinah pointed out, feelings of resentment probably helped the other actors' performances as peasants.

All in all, I was spending a lot of time on *The Idiot*, and I wasn't even part of the cast. I was sort of the show's unofficial gofer. Between calming Danny's anxiety that he would let Roger down, that he would let Dostoyevsky down (and me, I wanted to scream, and me! When you could be doing a soap that people actually *watch!* That casting agents actually *see!*), and coaching Dinah in her daily growing role—"More abasement, less hysteria."—it wasn't surprising that I didn't find a lot of time to focus on my own goals. Or even decide what those goals were.

Also, there was a lot of mediating to be done between Danny and Dinah. She pronounced him a no-talent; he pronounced her pushy, obnoxious, *and* a no-talent. She said it was hard for her to act like she worshiped Prince Myshkin. He said it was hard to avoid kicking her.

Meanwhile, I noticed a distinct chilliness in Roger's attitude to his star. Danny, of course, blamed himself.

"I haven't got it," he moaned after rehearsal. "I'm ruining the show."

Well, he wasn't, because you couldn't. The show stunk squarely on its own merits. Really, it was just your average, dismal, off-off-off Broadway production. No money, no recognition, tons of agita, and sex for those who know how to find it wherever they are. Critics were promised and never showed. Friends and family turned up, filled a few seats, and said insincere things in the lobby. I sold tickets at night and went to work groggy the next morning. Even so, I couldn't help but fantasize. Maybe the show would go somewhere. Maybe someone important would come and see it. And maybe that someone would notice little old yours truly. I could see it now, "You, yes, you, ticket girl. You're perfect—you're just what we need in the remake of the remake of *Godzilla*." I would play squashed person number four.

How did I start my meteoric career? Well, gentle reader, it's funny what seven little words can do. All it took was "Here's your change, have a nice day," and I was launched into the firmament of stars . . .

It didn't happen. Not for me, not for anybody.

Miraculously, by the end of the run, Dinah was still sleeping with the stage manager, and so she and I got to throw the cast party. (Something you might think Roger might spring for, but then, you never met Roger.)

So, it's a party. Fun, right? Laughs, right? Not with this crowd, baby. None of these people had the remotest chance of becoming famous—but they all wanted to act like it was happening tomorrow for them and you should get down on your knees and kiss their feet today. I was left wandering around my own apartment, with a lot of people looking at me like, "How did *you* get invited to this shindig?"

Dinah, busy exchanging tongue meat with her stage manager, was not a lot of help as a hostess, and so it was left to me to pass around the chips and dip, empty ashtrays, and find the bottle opener, not once, not twice, but twenty-three times. After a while, I was so short on sparkle and *je ne sais quoi* that the twenty-fourth time someone inquired as to its whereabouts, I snapped, "Use your fucking teeth."

Then, stricken with guilt, I spun around to see the person whose orthodontia I had just consigned to oblivion.

I was quite surprised at what I saw.

To wit, not a total asshole. (NotaTota, in shorthand.)

The NotaTota before me was slightly taller than I was, but he

---

THE AEROBICS OF *Celebrity* SPOTTING

THE SIDEWAYS LEAN
Useful for when you are sitting behind a celebrity at a movie and want a view of their profile to make sure it's really them. Keeping your bottom in place, bring your upper body to a thirty-degree angle, then return to original position.

had a very long neck, and a blinking, suspicious look that, given the circumstances, I thought showed good judgment. So I hastily laid my hands upon the wayward bottle opener and gestured that I wanted to atone by opening his bottle for him. Having established intimacy by this harmless but just slightly suggestive offer, I asked what his name was.

"Alvin." He drank. "Schremmel."

I struck a seductive pose. "And how do you come to be in my apartment, Alvin? Schremmel?"

Too much. Hit the boy with too much too soon. Alvin Schremmel half swallowed, half choked, and finally coughed up, "Lights."

Then he regained his composure and explained. "My brother did the lights."

"Oh, Kenny's your brother."

"Yeah."

"That's fantastic."

He said, "Yeah," but he was starting to look around for someone else to talk to. I don't know if this happens to you, but the minute someone I'm talking to looks like they're thinking there's someone better they could be talking to, I have this need to prove them wrong. Usually by babbling nonstop, and thereby proving just the opposite.

So, feeling dared, I said, "What did you think of the show?"

That got a reaction. A sizable one, complete with eye rolling, snorts, and something that sounded like a fart.

"Not much, huh."

"Not even not much."

I had to give him credit. Roger was standing just three feet away—minus Danny, I noticed—and Alvin Schremmel didn't even lower his voice.

"It was a little stiff."

"It was pretentious crap."

"Or pretentious crap. I can go either way. Are you in theater?" Are you someone? Someone disguised as a schlep? Incognito, so to speak, so these wanna-bes won't pester you?"

"No." He looked like he was about to say what he was into, then decided he would rather I embarrass myself by asking.

And I did. It's amazing what meeting one NotaTota in a roomful of Totas will do to you.

"Film," he said.

Big eye time. "Wow. What aspect?"

"All, really. I think of myself as a roving auteur." I had him hooked now, I could tell. It's not every girl you're going to try and impress by telling her you're a roving auteur. Only the really sad ones get that quality line.

Then he asked if I wanted to go to the Hungarian film festival next week. I said I would check my calendar. I could do with a NotaTota, but a roving auteur? Forget it.

Dinah and the stage manager were still giving each other the kiss of life, so I went in search of Danny. I found him in my room, sitting on my bed, staring at the television—which was only a little strange because it wasn't turned on.

There are times in life when you have to lie, and this was one of them. So, I took a deep breath and said, "I thought you were really good as Prince Myshkin."

He shook his head. "No, I wasn't. I wanted to be good. I worked really hard on the part, but it just wasn't coming."

"Maybe you weren't so well directed," I said gently.

"It's not Roger's fault. If anything, I let him down. He gave me this terrific opportunity, and I blew it."

I tried to persuade him otherwise, but there was no talking Danny out of his depression. He drank more than I'd ever seen him drink. Then he decided that he owed Roger a public apology for ruining his great theatrical venture. Weaving into the living room, he found Roger lip locked with the guy who had played Rogozhin. A scene ensued, one that frankly far surpassed *The Idiot* for drama and excitement. Danny announced he was packing his bags and leaving that night. Rogozhin promptly announced he was packing his bags and moving in. Whereupon, Dinah rushed up to me, and announced that the stage manager had asked her to move in with him, and that *she* would be leaving in the morning.

And that's how Danny and I ended up living together.

$\mathcal{C}$HAPTER FOUR

IN THE GRIP

Age 28-29: Win Tony. Move to the Dakota. Exchange witty banter with celebrities in the elevator.

$\mathcal{O}$**KAY, SO** I was not living in the Dakota, and the wittiest banter I exchanged with anyone was the newsstand guy whose kids' education was financed by my purchases. You want to know how my life was going? Give or take a major awards show, my average day went something like this:

24 HOURS IN THE LIFE OF A *Celebraholic*

7:30: Get up. Turn television on to the least revolting morning program. Wake-up process is complete when you no longer squint in the glare of the host's teeth.

7:45: Take shower. Review everything you learned about famous people the previous day. Wonder why you are not famous.

8:00: Get dressed. Compare each article of clothing to a better, nicer thing you could own, if only you were famous. *Or* wonder why so many famous people dress so badly when they have all that money.

Time will vary for this activity. Those suffering from the co-dependent form of the disease usually take very little time. Those suffering from the active form—like Dinah—will take hours. As a matter of fact, many of these people cannot hold down full-time jobs because getting dressed in the morning takes until lunchtime.

8:15: Knock on Danny's door, remind him of audition. Wonder

when he will become famous, so you can drop his name, for
God's sake, and live with him in his palatial mansion, highly val-
ued as the old friend who knew him when and who will tell him
those all-essential, truthful things none of those nasty, kiss-assy
hangers-on would dare say to his face.

8:30: Catch subway to work. *Do not get a seat.* Think how no
famous people take the subway. Remember interview with Uma
Thurman when she talked about riding the subway as an interesting real-life experience. Hate Uma Thurman for a little while.

9:10: Arrive at work. Greet Chet, the singing doorman who will
not greet you back, because with his earphones on, he cannot
hear you—or the occasional homicidal maniac.

9:15–10:00: Read newspaper at your desk. Begin with the gossip columns, proceed to the obituaries, and then on to the TV listings. Fridays and Wednesdays, read the movie reviews.

10:00–12:30: Try to make it to lunch. Everything you do, think
how you would not have to do it if you were famous.

12:30–1:30 (Okay, 2:00): Monday, read *People.* Tuesday, *The
Star.* Wednesday, *TV Guide.* Thursday, *The Enquirer.* Friday, *Entertainment Weekly.*

2:00–4:00: Avoid boss. Imagine what you will say to him when
you get your big break.

4:00–4:15: Wonder what Oprah is doing.

4:15–5:00: Estimate how fast your ass would be out of that
office if you got your big break. Allow for gloating time.

THINGS IN REAL LIFE YOU DO NOT HAVE TO DEAL WITH WHEN YOU ARE A *Celebrity*

Marriage. Celebrities don't worry about getting married. They know they're wanted. They do worry about divorce, which is much more expensive for them than it is for us. But that's why God invented the pre-nup.

5:01: Leave. Get on the subway. Go home.

6:00 to bedtime: These all-important evening hours can be spent in a number of activities, but they must include television. Most addicts will start to feel a little "off" if they miss *Entertainment Tonight*, although many supplement with *E! Gossip Show*. Hardcore addicts—like yours truly—watch both.

And that was it. That was how I spent day after day, week after week, year after year.

Now the sharp-eyed reader will have noticed one small but essential change in my lifestyle. I had a real job. (Well, "real" in the sense that it sucked five days a week instead of three days a week.) Hurrah, says the reader, you have made progress. No, sorry, it wasn't my fault. Getting real jobs, pulling yourself up by your bootstraps in a gesture that feels strangely like a wedgie—that's the work of family.

Around the time Danny and I moved in together, my mother got tired of my not having a real job. She started dropping little hints, saying things like, "Well, as long as you're happy . . ." when she asked how I was doing. (Well, no, I wasn't happy, but I knew I would be even less happy doing what my mother had in mind.) And you know how it is when people keep dropping these little suggestions. On your foot. After about the five thousandth suggestion and tenth broken toe, you give in. You call who they want you to call, you go where they want you to go, and despite all laws of desire, competency, and fair play, you get the job.

So where did I work? What glamorous, happening, *now* kind of job did I have? Well, I'll tell you. But just you. I wouldn't want word of this dream job to get around.

My real job was in publishing. ("I mean, you like reading," says my mother.) To be honest, it wasn't that bad. Through a friend of hers, she got me a job at a small yet humble imprint known as Otter Press, once a well-respected house, now an embarrassing backwater in the vast Lobel-Schraft Empire. I was an editorial assistant, which is a jumped-up title for secretary, thank you very much, and I'll say it, because I'm not going to pretend I get paid crap to do a glam job. Shit pay for shit work, that's my motto.

Soon after I started, we morphed from the small yet humble imprint known as Otter Press to something much, much better. That's when B. Arthur Bickerstaff blew into town. (And there are many people who could tell you just how much B. Arthur blows.) Overnight, Otter Press was transformed into Bickerstaff Books. B. Arthur was twenty-nine when he took over. He had been born with a lot of money, so the company decided he could handle the stuff and promptly gave him some more. Which he immediately spent. On an actor who turned out not to be a sex addict after all, on a rock star who decided not to go ahead with the divorce of the century, and, when all else had failed, on a cat who had gotten stuck down a well. A ghostwriter was hired for the cat, but walked

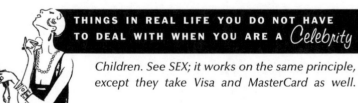

THINGS IN REAL LIFE YOU DO NOT HAVE TO DEAL WITH WHEN YOU ARE A *Celebrity*

Children. See SEX; it works on the same principle, except they take Visa and MasterCard as well.

out after the third meeting, owing not to artistic differences, but to allergies. By that time the story had died—the public having since moved on to the story of a beagle in perpetual heat.

B. Arthur wasn't just rich, he was really dumb. He knew every cliché in the book, but he could never remember them. "You the man" was a favorite, frequently and mysteriously abbreviated to "The man" and a finger point. He once spotted me reading *People*, and said, "Cho, yo! People!" (He pronounced it pee-pul.) His head bobbed. "Definitely, definitely. Gotta keep that finger on the pulse. Got to got to . . ." He started snapping his fingers. "Gotta have a pulse." He would move through the halls snapping away. "Gotta have a pulse. Gotta have a pulse."

B. Arthur didn't surf the net, he cruised it. Things did not have an impact—they were impactful (or impacted, as one wag put it). He sprinkled his incomplete sentences with French words (like *vacances* and *déjeuner*, as in *petite*). In fact, he was so dumb it was sometimes hard to believe he wasn't smart, and for a little while, the rumor went around that he was actually an idiot savant. After a while, someone claimed to have traced the rumor back to B. Arthur himself. That turned out not be to true, but neither was the rumor, and gloom descended upon the former Otter Press.

The reason that B. Arthur was generally assumed to have pulse was that senior management had none, and so to them he seemed wildly au courant. I mean, these were people who thought creative genius was a book where someone fucked or killed someone

THINGS IN REAL LIFE YOU DO NOT HAVE TO DEAL WITH WHEN YOU ARE A *Celebrity*

Commuting. Let's choose between the Lear Jet and the F Train.

in a way people have never been fucked or killed before. But alas, alack, their faith did not provide swift dividends. We waited impatiently for the cruel ax to fall—but the ax remained suspended. Having run out of all the money the company was going to let him play with, B. Arthur put the rest of his meager resources toward revamping the *Days* and *Nights* series that had been Otter's pride. These were, in a word, cheesy. But they were good-hearted, undemanding, and sold well enough to keep me in *People*. The *Days* series consisted of *Days of Danger*—which was our action series; *Days d'Amour*—our romance series; *Days of Doom*—horror; and so on. The *Nights* series was basically genteel porn, in which heroes and heroines scrambled out of their hoop skirts, armor, and nun's habits as fast as possible. We were also trying to develop a *Days of the Daimon* series, a sort of New Age/spirituality thing, but we couldn't find anyone who could stomach the stuff long enough to do the necessary market research.

As an assistant editor, I acted as liaison between the writers and Bickerstaff Books. I handed out assignment sheets, specifying whether our heroine should have green eyes and red hair or be a raven-haired vixen this time. If the soldiers of fortune should be saving the free world from renegade communists with their finger on the bomb ("Gotta have bomb," as B. Arthur would say), or terrorists ready to level the Eiffel Tower with a matchbook. Our writers were . . . writers: unhappy, underpaid people who let you know in no uncertain terms that they were shortchanging their talents to serve your crass, commercial needs, a message that you had to gently refute with a smile and the hint that better scribes than they could be found under a cardboard box in Penn Station.

Was I proud to work on a product with such a high dreck factor? Well, no, but it was a paycheck, and somebody had to protect the writers from B. Arthur. I had a good gig. People knew me, they

THINGS IN REAL LIFE YOU DO NOT HAVE TO DEAL WITH WHEN YOU ARE A *Celebrity*

Murder. When you are an average citizen, you worry about going to jail. When you are a celebrity, this is not a concern.

liked me. No one else wanted my job, so there was no competition. I ran the Dead Pool (name ten celebrities you think will croak in the next six months), the Divorce Pool (ten celebrity couples you think will croak in the next six months), the Closet Pool (ten people you think will switch sides in the next six months), and the Oscar Pool. Really, for a job my mother had come up with, it wasn't bad at all. It wasn't as nice as, say, having my own talk show, but it didn't completely blow.

Danny had also made inroads in his career—and every single one of them was a dead end. Since Roger's defection, his self-esteem was at an all-time low. Not only did he suffer the normal pangs of rejection, but he had become convinced that Roger had dumped him because he was just another Pretty Face.

Now, some of us might adhere to that old adage "Living well is the best revenge." And some of us might have thought that Living Well would necessitate a certain *kind* of success with a certain *level* of financial remuneration. A palatial home in Beverly Hills— that would hurt Roger. A spread in *Harper's Bazaar*, a dagger straight to his cheating heart. A megabuck movie deal would be the final insult, the victory that would bring him crawling back on his hands and knees, begging forgiveness.

That was *my* plan for revenge, but Danny had other ideas. Hoping to prove Roger wrong, he worked nonstop, dividing his time between classes, acting gigs, and waitering at Fido's, an elite restaurant those in the know pronounced "Fee-do's." He got cast in a hundred no-name productions that would never see the light of day. He was Ramallah the Gangsta with a heart of gold, he was a priest who saw a vision of the Virgin Mary on a cereal box, he was Officer Juanitra, the drag queen cop who looked *bad* in blue.

Needless to say, none of this was getting us any closer to Beverly Hills.

I tried to leave it alone. Danny's life was Danny's life. But every once in a while, something turned up that sparked a conversation about his career path. The conversations usually went something like this:

ME: Say, they're auditioning for a new part on *The Young and the Restless*. (That was me, the young and the restless— and unknown).

DANNY: The young and the what?

ME: It's a drama.

DANNY: What kind of drama?

ME: The kind they put on television where people can see it.

DANNY: Does it air before nine o'clock?

ME: A real star turn.

DANNY: Slam. (Well, not Danny, the door, when he got up and left the room, but you get the general idea.)

But without a doubt, the person who had the most success in the time since that fatal cast party was . . . you guessed it, Dinah. Didn't I tell you? Don't we all know that that's how the world works? Although Dinah had grown disillusioned with the performing arts—"Every asshole in this city wants to be a performer, and there are just too many assholes."—the flame of self-expression still burned brightly as ever. She still yearned to share herself with the world, and so she decided to take a more devious route to fame and fortune: art. The whole thing started when Dinah was making extra money modeling in the buff at the Art Students League. Someone had made the remark that she had a "disturbing form." That was all it took for Dinah to decide that if she could disturb one person, she could, with a little artistic license, strike panic in the public at large.

Now, having worked with Dinah on drama production sets, I was privy to some information that the art world didn't have. Dinah couldn't paint. She couldn't draw. She had less artistic dexterity in her whole body than most people have in their pinkie. But did that stop Dinah? By now you know better.

What did Dinah have to say when I pointed out the fact that she had trouble composing a reasonable stick figure? "Who's talking paint? I'm talking photography. Let the fucking camera do the work." And what, you might ask, did Ms. Sharlip photograph? Why, Ms. Sharlip, of course. Every part of her. She began with tits, moved on to ass, then full body shots and assorted apertures.

THINGS IN REAL LIFE YOU DO NOT HAVE TO DEAL WITH WHEN YOU ARE A *Celebrity*

Growing old. Celebrities do worry about this, but it means very different things to them. It means they will no longer get paid twelve million dollars per picture so that people can look at their hooties. For everybody else, it means spending your last days drooling among strangers while your beloved children look at their watches and wonder when you are going to die. Of course, celebrities are old when they are twenty-eight, and the rest of us have a little more time. But when you factor in quality of life, the difference isn't really that great.

And—call it a sign that the apocalypse is nigh—she was a success.

I mean, not major. But I was now going to quite a few gallery shows, and her stuff had started to appear in some of the more outré publications. Dinah's photography had the same qualities as all her other endeavors—crude, unappealing—but you couldn't look away. And it worked. Not that anyone was paying big money to see Dinah's mammaries, shot in bad light and at funny angles—but some people actually thought they might, and that was a huge step forward.

And of course, her photography career really took off when she started dating Lylo Wingate.

Now, for those of you who may have relegated the name Lyle (aka Lylo) Wingate to that dark corner of your mind where you store the names of Washington bimbos and people who appeared on *Hollywood Squares*, I will take a moment to refresh your memory. Lyle Wingate, Jr., was the son of—naturally—Lyle Wingate, Sr., a business magnate. And not just any business magnate. Lyle Wingate, Sr., was the big man in the world of bubble gum. If it rotted your teeth and got stuck in your hair, Wingate, Sr., was your man. One year, *Fortune Magazine* did a cover story on him: WHAT'S POPPING IN THE WORLD OF GUM? LYLE WINGATE MAY BE RIDING HIGH, BUT WILL HIS BUBBLE BURST? People get paychecks for work like that.

So if your father is big into bubbles, where do you go from there? You become a musician. And not just some white-bread, rich-boy musician, which some of us, unfairly, might have expected Lylo Wingate to be. Oh, no. You become def. You become phat. You get as close as you can to inner-city homeboy without actually having to be poor or un-white.

The story of how Dinah and Lylo met has been told many times before, but never in its entirety. So, here, for the first time in print,

THINGS IN REAL LIFE YOU DO NOT HAVE TO DEAL WITH WHEN YOU ARE A *Celebrity*

Taxes. I don't think we need dwell.

is the true and only slightly expurgated story of how these two crazy kids got together.

Dinah and Lylo met, appropriately enough, on television. One of our lesser talk show hosts, Lobo Wilson, ran out of genuine freaks and decided to do a show called "Art in America: Smut or Just Plain Bad?" And after everyone else turned him down, Dinah was invited to appear on the show, on the strength of some particularly candid shots she had done of her backside, called "The Kiss."

Lylo was the guest of honor. He was hot at the time (all right, lukewarm), off a song he had written called "Bitch Mommy from Westport," which had caught on with the radio stations of some of the more suspect academic institutions. So Dinah, Lylo, and a sculptor who worked in canine fecal matter went on the *Lobo Show*. I have the show on tape, and every once in a while, it's a hoot to get it out and watch as the snarling, toupeed "host" demands to know why America should pay for Dinah's "so-called" art.

"They don't," she said. "Nobody gives me a (bleep)ing dime."

"But you want us to," said Lobo.

"Sure," she said. "You want tampon companies to advertise on your show. So what? Everybody wants money from everybody else."

And at this point, Lylo chimed in: "This is like, America."

And Dinah said, "Yeah." And Lylo said, "Yeah," and the previously hostile audience cheered, because smut was one thing, but the right to get rich was something everybody could agree on. Perhaps sensing that he had lost his audience, Lobo switched to a commercial. But when they came back, he asked the sculptor if his art constituted a health code violation. The sculptor said, "I think this show constitutes a health code violation," and the audience, apparently proud of being labeled a biohazard, cheered.

After their yeahs of solidarity, Dinah and Lylo went out to celebrate and wound up wrapping tongues on a street corner somewhere. It was love, love, love, with only a slight hangover the next morning. End of story.

Well, if only. Dinah, you see, had found her dream man. He was rich, not ugly, and utterly without any socially redeeming content. That alone was enough to make him her dream man. The fact that he was number forty-seven on the college charts was, well, icing.

It's all very eerie—especially when you consider what happened to Lylo and Dinah later on.

Now, I would like to state for the record that I never liked Lylo Wingate. I tried. He was dating (well, fucking) my friend, and he was famous, so I was predisposed to look favorably upon him. Which just goes to show that intent has very little significance in this world of ours.

Dinah saw him only infrequently, and so she was not about to waste a whole date introducing us. But she had a show at her apartment, to which Lylo condescended to come, and at which Dinah condescended to introduce me.

Here is a transcript of our conversation—the sum total of all the words I have exchanged with Lylo Wingate in my lifetime.

ME: Hi, Lylo. It's nice to meet you.
LYLO: (Unintelligible)

That's it, folks. My one and only firsthand experience of the great Wingate. Later he told a crowd of hangers-on the fascinating story of how he became Lylo. According to Lylo, he went with Lyle until sophomore year in "college." (With Lylo, you put quote marks around college.) At one point, he got "seriously ripped" and made such a menace of himself (official reports indicate a certain amount of peeing out a dormitory window) that the cops arrived on the scene. Cornered, he was approached by a cop who asked his name.

"So I give it to him. And you know, I'm just getting it out the Lyl part when I fucking puke all *over* the man's shoes. So it's like Ly-*loooh*. You know, 'cause of the fucking barf."

Now Lylo—"cause-of-the-fucking barf"—Wingate would never have noticed Dinah had it not been for her minor success taking pictures of tits. And Dinah knew it. You might expect that this would diminish her passion for Lylo, but in fact it did just the opposite. "Shallow" was not a big drawback in Dinah's universe, and the fact that Lylo—number forty-seven on the college charts—Wingate would deign to slip her his Lincoln Log meant she was finally getting someplace. She was on the verge of becoming Someone.

It's a tragically common error for starry-eyed young women to make. A lucky, litigious few become trophy wives; most fade into

---

THINGS IN REAL LIFE YOU DO NOT HAVE TO DEAL WITH WHEN YOU ARE A *Celebrity*

Unemployment. Okay, a lot of celebrities go through lengthy periods of unemployment. You know what? Pay me a million dollars for two months' work, and I promise—I swear to God—I'll make it last the rest of my life. And we can swap. I'll give my fabulous job to any celebrity who wants it. And when they get fired right before they're ready to retire so the company doesn't have to pay out their benefits, well, they've got my shoulder to cry on.

oblivion and bad hair days. I like to think I would be immune to such poor judgment, but I can't honestly say that I've ever been tested.

Only once did I hint that Lylo's charms lay a little deep beneath the surface for casual detection. Dinah pretended an airy sophistication about the whole thing, summing up Lylo's attributes with one word: "Parties."

"Parties?"

"When he has a downtown type of gig, I'm his girl. I get into some good parties that way."

"So it's the connections?"

"Absolutely."

Well, it was better than hearing she loved the guy—or even liked him a whole lot—but I didn't believe her. All I had to see was the way she leapt to the radio every time "Bitch Mommy from Westport" was on the air to know Dinah wasn't thinking parties. She was on the crest, riding the wave. And the word *wipeout* never crossed her mind.

So, Danny was celibate and Dinah was in heat—where did that leave me? Somewhere in the middle.

Remember Alvin Schremmel?

The roving auteur?

That Alvin Schremmel.

Of course, you remember the inauspicious night that I met Alvin. Well, when everyone was done screaming, yelling, and crying, when all the bags were packed, threats were made, and doors were slammed, he and I somehow wound up in the kitchen doing things I don't usually do with people I met just two hours before and who are not, say, Ewan McGregor. All I will say is that we were both very drunk and very lonely.

And once you start a thing, it's sometimes hard to back away, unless one of you is actively repulsed, and I guess neither of us was. I know I said I would never sleep with a "roving auteur." But, hey, sometimes, nature calls—although what it says can't always be trusted.

Alvin was heavily into film. He was too short to act, didn't really want to direct, and couldn't seem to finish his screenplay. But he was a big critic, so we saw a lot of movies together. Alvin opted for the things with subtitles and obscure awards. I liked any-thing with anyone I might have heard of. And although Alvin com-plained nonstop about being dragged to commercial dreck, he always seemed happy afterward, because then he could talk about everything the filmmakers had done wrong that he, Alvin, would have done right. And if the movie starred a hunk du jour, well, I could count on Alvin buying me dinner and several rounds.

"I don't get it. What does J.J. Phipps have? Who does he have naked, compromising pictures of that he gets so much work?"

"I know what you mean."

"Moneywood must think people are . . . blind. Utterly moronic. Which they are, but . . ."

"Sure." Another good thing about Alvin: not a lot of energy need be expended. Batteries not required. A nod here, a "hmm" there, and he assumed you thought he was brilliant. You know, that you agreed with him. Actually, I didn't like it when he went on and on about people like J.J. Phipps. Alvin wasn't the worst looking guy by a long shot, but he had that geek pride thing where you can't buy any clothes after high school, and you can't pay more than fifteen bucks for a haircut, and if it doesn't say Salvation Army or surplus, well, it just ain't fashion. Guys like Alvin really shouldn't blame the J.J. Phippses of the world for raising the bar too high; they should feel guilty for dropping it into the toilet.

So why was I with Alvin Schremmel? Well, I liked to think I was one of those lone, bright spots in his life. It was a mitzvah kind of thing.

Finally, Alvin was not the only thing I had going in life. (Believe you me, a woman cannot live on Alvin Schremmel alone.) Maybe I wasn't flying regularly to the Coast to do story treatments. Maybe Meryl had better things to do than have Bloody Marys with me.

But I did know one famous person.

Sort of person.

I knew Norm.

Norm had four legs. Four legs and dewlaps. By now you know who I'm talking about, because they still show his commercials on TV. Norm the Wonder Dog, that adorable droopy basset hound that persuades you that, should you be unfortunate enough to have a beloved family member perish, that family member will have perished in vain unless you have Good Friend Life Insurance ("Just like Norm, we're man's best friend").

I'd like to say that I met Norm at some swanky do, but the fact is, he and his owner, Sal, lived in our building. Soon after we began cohabiting, Danny and I decided to move to Brooklyn, where the rents were at least close to humanly affordable. Sal and Norm lived upstairs in our brownstone.

Sal had had Norm for five years when the two of them were spotted by an agency talent scout outside a bakery. (Norm still cherishes his bakery products, but the agency tries to restrict his intake because of his weight.) At the time, Norm went by the name of Ulysses—James Joyce was Sal's favorite writer—but the agency renamed him Norm because they thought something more

THINGS IN REAL LIFE YOU DO NOT HAVE TO DEAL WITH WHEN YOU ARE A *Celebrity*

Getting up in the morning. Don't moan at me about five-thirty shoots. That's two months out of the year, and the rest of the time, the sun rises at three in the afternoon.

THINGS IN REAL LIFE YOU DO NOT HAVE TO DEAL WITH WHEN YOU ARE A *Celebrity*

Health care. Granted, celebrities have a lot of health problems. Not the normal ones, but they are prone to illnesses we are not. Like drug addiction. And leaking breast implants. But I bet you the studio doesn't enroll them in some byzantine HMO.

down market would appeal to a wider audience. Norm was a hit from the get-go. He started with shoes, went on to cars, did a little dog chow, before getting hired by Good Friend, and the rest, as they say, is stardust. Now a celebrity for three years, Norm remained unchanged. He loved Sal, he loved his bakery products, and as long as he had both in large quantities, he was a gentleman and a professional. True, he sagged. True, he drooped. He was in a state that means death to most acting careers. But to most of us, excess bags and baggage only made Norm more lovable.

We were all very nice to Norm, because you never knew when he might be able to do something for you.

So, that was it. My life. Bickerstaff Books, Danny, Dinah, Alvin, and a few thousand celebrities. Here I was, nearing the thirty line; I knew nobody famous and I was nobody famous. I ate nowhere interesting, and my address was one my own mother had difficulty remembering. I rode the subway everywhere, and my usual destinations were work and home. Was I bereft? Depressed? Unfulfilled? Let's put it this way . . .

If I was, I didn't know it.

I went for very a long time without recognizing my celebraholism or its malign impact on my life. In fact, up until the very second I got hit in the kisser with the proverbial pile of shit, I was in deep, deep denial about my condition.

CHAPTER FIVE

HITTING BOTTOM

*O*F YOU are a celebraholic, one of the red-letter days in your life will be the day you hit bottom. The moment comes at different times for different people, and with varying degrees of severity. For some, revelation can come during a routine viewing of *Entertainment Tonight*. Others require something more humiliating as the final proof that they are no longer in charge of their lives and that their addiction is. Honest to God, until my butt hit the cement, I had no idea how low I had sunk. Even as I stood on the precipice of the awful truth, I remained blinded by the spotlights. There I was, happily going about my business, watching six hours of television a day, buying seven to ten magazines a week, avidly discussing the problems of people I had never met.

I just thought I was your average American citizen.

And yet . . . there were signs. Signs that, even if I did not recognize I had a problem, people around me did.

Fact!

Friends of celebraholics do not mount interventions. They just stop talking to you.

An early warning came while Danny and I were eating breakfast. I was reading a story in the *Enquirer* about a new young actress when a thought occurred to me. Holding up the paper, I asked Danny, "Do you think she's gay?"

Danny didn't look up. "I don't know."

"I think she might be."

"Then she might be."

"She's really into animals."

"Uh-huh."

"And she's always talking about this friend she has, how she's her mentor, how much she owes her. They seem a little intensely bonded to me."

"You know what? I gotta go."

Another sign? Danny wasn't telling me about the celebrities who came into Fido's anymore. One night I asked him who came in that night, and he said no one, and then the next day, I read about Jack Nicholson having dinner there.

I just figured he didn't sit at Danny's table.

Danny wasn't the only one who was less chatty. All of a sudden, Dinah was giving me the silent treatment. Now, the way I saw it, the one good thing that might have come out of her tawdry little liaison with Lylo was . . . well, some really good dirt. But I knew Dinah was not a sharer. I could even understand why she wouldn't want to dish about Lylo's famous friends. But then out of the blue, she didn't want to dish about *anybody*. I would make some harmless remark, like, "Hey, I think So-and-So is stepping out on his wife," and she would get all frosty with me, like I had insulted her best friend.

"I just don't think you should say things like that about people you don't know," she said.

I didn't think anything of it at the time.

The conversations got shorter.

"Hey, Danny, did you hear that what's his name is going into rehab?"

"I really gotta run."

"For painkillers. Isn't that a neat euphemism for heroin? Painkillers."

"Yeah, see you, 'bye."

Slam.

"What I can't believe is they got photos of the guy. His hands are all over her, and he's claiming entrapment."

"Yeah," said Dinah. Was that a yawn I heard?

"You think his wife will stand by him?"

"Well, I fucking wouldn't, that's for sure. Look, I gotta go."

Click.

"Ma, did you hear he's suing the newspapers?"

"Who is?"

"The one they found in the hotel room with the blonde."

"Is this someone I know?"

"No."

"Someone you know?"

"No."

Click.

"Hey, Alvin, what do you think about . . ."

"Oh, not this shit again."

Click.

The pace of modern life. I understood. Danny, Dinah, Alvin, my mother . . . well, they were busy people. I was busy people, too. That's why we lived in New York, we were all very busy people. I didn't need to be on the phone all the time. I didn't need to chat. I had my own things going. Michael Jackson and Madonna were having babies. Hugh Grant was caught parking.

Okay, so I didn't notice I was on the brink of destruction. Maybe I should have. But there was a lot going on in my life.

THE SHIT HITS THE FAN

It was a day much like any other day. If you had told me when I got up that morning that by the end of the day my life would be set irrevocably on a new and thorny path, I would have snapped on *Regis* with a wry chuckle and said you were fooling yourself.

I think it was a Thursday. (It was toward the end of the week, but *People* hadn't come out yet, so Thursday seems accurate.) I got up. I went to work. On the subway, I read the *Daily News*. Over breakfast, I skimmed the *Post* and *Newsday*. Then I sent some e-mail passing on the rumor that a testosterone-heavy male rock star was in fact a woman.

At ten-thirty, I met with an author, Hank Laufler. Pudgy, bespectacled Hank wrote the breathless, bosom-heavy prose of *Days d'Amour*. Normally, he was old reliable, but lately he had run into problems. He had just started a new book, a medieval epic he should have been able to write with his eyes shut. But the first three chapters he had sent us had hinted at a new direction in his work—one Bickerstaff Books didn't care for—and it was up to me to set him straight.

I liked Hank. He was one of our sweeter, goofier authors, and I wanted to be as gentle as I could with him. When he had been sat down and given a cup of herbal tea, I said, "So, Hank, we got your first three chapters."

Hank gripped his portfolio protectively on his lap.

"And I just have a few questions."

A spasmodic nod.

"This first scene . . ."

"In the garden."

"Right. It's very nice . . ."

"I like it, too." He leaned forward enthusiastically. "I worked very hard on the description of the roses. I feel they foreshadow Camelia's spiritual awakening."

"Spiritual awakening?"

"It comes in the later chapters."

"Ah. Well, I think we may need to cut back on the roses. Thirty pages is a lot of foreshadowing."

Hank frowned. "Oh."

"Also, the scene with the duchess . . ."

He was leaning forward again. "Yes?"

"Maybe not the time for a lengthy discussion on the architecture of monasteries."

"I felt it was integral to the character."

"But by chapter three, Camelia is supposed to meet Raymond at the king's tourney."

He gnawed his lip. "I thought I would delay their meeting a bit. Build some tension."

"But if they haven't met, there is no tension. There is no tension, because nothing is happening."

"I think there's a lot happening."

"Hank, we have a hundred-fifty pages here, and all Camelia has done is smelled roses and kibbitzed about monasteries. In chapter four, she's supposed to realize that she doesn't hate Raymond but feels a deep bodily response to him, Saxon barbarian though he is."

"All right," said Hank. But he looked miserable.

Writers are, as a rule, delicate blossoms. But one has to be firm with them. Otherwise, no money gets made.

I said, "There's another small problem."

"What?"

"Your description of Camelia." Hank's eyes darted off to the side. "My notes call for her to be a ravishing brunette, with a cascade of hair resembling a perfect dark malt. Voluptuous yet slim, with eyes the color of cornflowers, and a haunting, full mouth."

"I made her brown-haired and blue-eyed," said Hank

I picked up a page and read aloud: " 'Not a conventional

beauty possessed of the banal prettiness that was the standard of the times, Camelia had the power to bewitch men. Her fleshiness made her far more enticing than the paltry slender wraiths that crowded the court. An adorable double chin peeked out from her collar. Her blue eyes—which were almost gray in certain light— were witty and intelligent, her mouth exquisite not for its shape but for the gentle wisdom that fell from its lips.' "

Hank's own adorable double chin rose from its collar. "Reubenesque was much in vogue in the past."

"It's 1100, Hank. Reuben isn't born."

"I think she sounds like a beauty."

I think she sounds like your mother, I thought. "Hank, the point is not what you think sounds like a beauty, but what the formula calls for. We pay you to write the formula." I handed over the pages. "Please deliver."

He took them, mumbling unhappily, "She was blonde and green-eyed last time. Next time it'll be red with brown eyes—I just wanted to do something different."

"Well, don't," I told him.

And there was one other surprise that day. Around two-thirty, Alvin called to see if he could come over that night.

"I know we didn't make plans," he said, "but my toilet backed up and overflowed last night."

So romantic, a girl could die. But as it happened Danny was away for the week, auditioning for a repertory company in New Jersey. So I told Alvin sure, come on over, we'll watch a little TV, eat a little Chinese food. Alvin said he would be by around seven.

I made one last phone call to set up an appointment with a new writer who was about to start on our *Days of Dust* Western series, and called it a day.

It was a warm, pleasant evening. On the way home, I splurged on a European tabloid that carried a particularly tasty story about one of the Monaco girls. Tomorrow was Friday; *People* would be on the newsstands. All was right with the world.

It was cruel, my sense of well-being.

Outside my building, I ran into Sal and Norm. If anything could brighten my already chipper mood, it was the sight of Sal sitting on the stoop, reading the paper while Norm dozed beside him. They say dogs grow to look like their owners, but I would wager that Sal had a belly and bags under his eyes long before he got Norm.

Stopping by to say hello, I remarked on Norm's peaceful—some might say inert—state.

"He had a long day's work," said Sal, patting his meal ticket affectionately on the rump.

"And did he have a good day's shoot?"

Sal shifted uncomfortably. "Actually, not so much. They were a little displeased with him."

"How so?" I looked at the snoozing megastar. Lumpen, baggy, sagging in all the right places—how could he fail to please?

"They're concerned about his weight." In his sleep, Norm snorted indignantly. And wetly. "They think he's hitting the Danish a little hard."

I looked, but it was hard to assess Norm's flab in his current sprawl—how much was Norm and how much was gravity—but he looked all right to me, and I said so.

THE AEROBICS OF *Celebrity* SPOTTING

THE BATHROOM DASH
Useful when a celebrity is in the same room, but on the other side of it. Simply hurry as fast as you can in the direction of the celebrity. If noticed, exclaim loudly, "God, I gotta take a wicked whiz!"

"Yeah, me, too. But the camera adds ten pounds, and the agency is 'concerned.'" Sal made a face. "Also, we have a little problem with his . . . thing. His things, maybe I should say."

"His ears?"

"Nah, his . . . you know . . ." Sal made a juggling gesture with one hand.

"The things that make little Norms."

"Yeah. They kept winding up in the shot." Sal shrugged. "And they're not so aesthetic, if you know what I mean."

I peeked. "They look fairly magnificent to me. A fitting testament to Norm's virility."

"A little too much of a testament, maybe. America doesn't want to see Norm's hoo-hahs. Those commercials air during family hours."

"Couldn't they . . . airbrush them out?"

"Yeah, that's what they suggested. Only in a more permanent sense." Sal shifted uncomfortably again—and who could blame him, given the topic under discussion. "But I couldn't do that to him."

"Of course you couldn't." Norm's ear twitched. "The idea. Would they suggest such a thing to George Clooney?"

"They said I should think of it like breast reduction surgery."

"You shouldn't think of it at all."

"No, no. You're right." He reached down and gave Norm a friendly scritch-scratch on the back. "Hell, what could they do to me?"

"Nothing. And if they try—we'll protest."

"Thanks."

"The public shall speak." And I went up the stairs, envisioning crowds chanting "Keep Norm's nuts! Basset balls best! Hands off Norm!"

I was still thinking about Norm's privates predicament when

Alvin arrived, twenty minutes early. Alvin was often early, because (a) he didn't have anything else to do, and (b) he was an inconsiderate person. But I was in such a sunny mood, I didn't mind. I gave him a kiss, handed him the remote, and told him to make himself comfortable.

I even let him order squid, that's how benevolent I was feeling. Boy, was I dumb.

Everything was going fine, up until the minute we turned on the television. There wasn't a lot on, so we tuned in to that show where they collect the most outrageous moments from the week's talk shows. You know, the weirdest moms, the most sexually active teenagers, the ugliest breakups. Not exactly my cup of tea, but if those people aren't exactly celebrities, they want to be celebrities and faux celebrities were better than nothing.

During a clip from *Florinda!*, Alvin started to get restless.

ALVIN: God, these people are fucking morons.

ME: If you were dating my mother behind my back, which one of us do you think you would choose?

ALVIN: I can't believe these pathetic drones. (Let me tell you something. Alvin knew a thing or two about pathetic drones. I can admit this now.)

ME: If I were pregnant, and there was something wrong, and it was me or the baby, would you kill me?

ALVIN: What?

ME: You'd kill me, right?

ALVIN: Can we turn this off?

ME: Would you tell me if you were a cross-dresser?

It was around this time that Alvin decided he had to go home. Something felt wrong, he couldn't say what. I was used to this sort of thing. A lot went suddenly wrong with Alvin Schremmel, a man for whom very little had gone noticeably right most of his life. (His dearest wish—in *life*—was to change his name to Charles Wallace. Charles Wallace Schremmel. After the genius kid in *A Wrinkle in Time*. All right? Does pretentious even begin to cover it?)

At the time, I thought nothing about it, except maybe relief that I wouldn't have to watch another *Star Trek* rerun. But as the door shut behind a hastily departing Alvin, I had the faintest whiff of déjà vu.

I gotta go . . .

Slam . . .

Click . . .

Was I missing something here?

If so, I couldn't think what it was. So, I quit brooding, forgot about Alvin, and went back to polish off the mu shu pork. For the rest of the evening, I channel-surfed, blissfully unaware that my life was about to take a drastic turn.

The phone rang sometime around eleven. I remember, because I was watching the news. There had been a crime of passion on the *Benny and Rubeno Show*. Bongo, their prize elephant, had stomped on Rubeno's head in a fit of jealousy when Rubeno had stroked the trunk of a rival elephant. I was really engrossed in the story, so I let the machine pick up, and forgot all about it until the commercial break, when I got up to go to the bathroom and saw that I had a message.

It was from Alvin.

Here are the highlights:

He was breaking up with me.

He was breaking up with me because I didn't have a life.

I lived through other people's lives.

The lives I lived through were pathetic and worthless. I was a parasite who fed off other parasites.

He was too good, his life too fine, to be joined with such an empty existence.

So, good-bye.

Oh, and good luck. Because I really needed it.

I stood there, stunned. Then, thinking I must have heard wrong, I pressed REWIND, then PLAY, and listened to the message again.

I hadn't heard wrong.

The questions began pounding in my head. What was Alvin thinking? What the hell did he mean? Was he serious? Was he drunk? Why didn't he have the guts to tell me face-to-face? *How could he break up with me on an answering machine?*

I tried to call him back, but the gutless little fuck didn't have the nerve to pick up the phone. After that it took about five minutes for full-blown rage to kick in. (Roughly the amount of time it takes to pour rum and Coke into the same glass.) Screw Alvin Schremmel. Was I really going to let Alvin—known heretofore as Alvin the Snob, Alvin the Prick, and Who-the-Motherfuck-Does-He-Think-He-Is Alvin—put a value on my life?

Of course not. I would think nothing more about Alvin Schremmel. I would consign his dumb theories of social development to my mental disposal unit. I had a life. I had a lot of life.

But just to be sure, I did a quick inventory.

Friends: Yes. (But none that seemed to be speaking to me at the moment.)

Sex Life: Yes. (Until half an hour ago.)

Job: Yes. (Rotten and underpaid, but a job.)

A Larger Purpose in Life: . . . Yes.

Yes. Absolutely yes.

And . . . what was this larger purpose?

To be famous or the friend of famous people.

Maybe Alvin had a point.

No, no. Alvin did *not* have point. Alvin, I reminded myself, was a prick. A prickless prick. Prickless pricks do not have points.

I took my place on the couch, and in a symbolic act of defiance, I changed the channel, turned up the volume.

A pregnant actress had sold her house in Miami to buy a smaller one in the Hamptons.

A rock star was back in rehab, after being apprehended by the police doing 120 on the freeway.

The parents of a child star were locked in a nasty custody battle (over the child's residuals, not the child himself).

I felt a whole lot better.

For about five minutes.

Maybe it was the rum and minimal Cokes, but as I watched, these strange thoughts kept coming into my head . . .

Why do I care? Who are these people? What impact could their lives possibly have on mine?

Frankly, that's when I got frightened. My mind was not behaving normally. Pink rabbits and men in white coats seemed destined to put in an appearance any minute. Between the rum and the romantic trauma, I was beginning to feel distinctly unstable and in need of support.

So, what did I do? I called Dinah at the Dead Dog, where she was working that night.

I came straight to the point. "Alvin dumped me."

"Alvin?" Dinah had to shout to be heard above the crowd. It's quite the rowdy little tea party down at the Dead Dog.

"Alvin Schremmel." (I've been seeing him for four years now?) "The guy I met at the *Idiot* cast party?"

"Oh, yeah. That guy." (Not a clue here, ladies and gentlemen, not a clue.) "Well, good fucking riddance. He was a little prick."

"Alvin's not really the point."

"How could he be? Little prick."

"Do you think I have a life?"

A long pause. "Define life."

"Well, do you think I pay too much attention to celebrities?"

"Hey, asshole, no pissing on the pool table—Sorry, what?"

"Alvin broke up with me because he says I have no life except for celebrities."

Another pause.

"Do you think he's right?" Save me, Dinah. Say no. Say that Alvin is a little prick. Say I have a life.

"You know what?" Dinah finally spoke. "This is too weird a conversation for the phone. Come to my place tomorrow. We'll figure it out."

Hanging up, I thought this was an alarming amount of vagueness from a woman not known for her tact.

I went back to the rum and Coke.

I channel-surfed and waited for oblivion.

As anyone knows, television can make you feel better because you see a lot of lives worse than yours. On the other hand, it can also make you feel worse because you see a lot of people who think they have all the answers to your problems. For example, on one of the late-night talk shows, they had a woman on who talked about women's low self-esteem, and how it's related to rejection, and how you must, must, must separate your self-image and feelings of failure from the opinions of those around you.

I tried to separate my feelings of failure from Alvin, but I couldn't. His voice on the answering machine haunted me. As I thought and drank, and thought and drank, Alvin's voice began to evolve into another, grander voice. It grew deeper, sounded more intelligent. And it kept saying over and over . . .

You don't have a life.

You live through the lives of others.

Don't depend on others to do things just so you have something to watch.

It was when the voice began to boom a little that I realized I was hearing the Voice of Destiny (voice-over courtesy of James Earl Jones).

Alvin, you don't have to listen to. But when Destiny and James Earl Jones tell you something, it's wise to pay attention.

Sometime around two in the morning, I turned off the television. I went to bed, resolved to change my life (i.e. get one). Okay, so Alvin was a jerk, but even a jerk can be right sometimes, and much as I hated to think so, this might be one of those times.

It was time to admit it: I was addicted to celebrity.

I tried saying it out loud. "I am addicted to celebrity."

It made my throat itch.

"I am addicted to celebrity and I need help," I told the ceiling. Then I tuned the radio to the all-night gossip show and fell asleep.

I woke up the next morning with a crashing headache and a desperate need to be out of the house. Dinah had said I could come over at two. By twelve o'clock, I was on the road. I had vague notions of stopping by Alvin's and planting an ax in his skull, but they generally don't give Academy Awards to ax murderers, so I set the idea aside.

Dinah still lives in Manhattan. How does she afford it without a regular salary? The old-fashioned way: she has weak, gullible roommates. Yours truly was just the first. Currently, she was sharing with some dancer who was always on tour. As I walked through the door and saw what Dinah had done to his apartment in his absence, I hoped for his sake that he was never coming back. Sheets hung from the ceiling, nailed into poles she had running from wall to wall. Candle wax and body paint were all over the floor. The kitchen windows had been painted over for a makeshift darkroom. (Dinah never ate, so she didn't find this the problem that most of us would).

When I got there, she was prowling around the living room, examining various pieces of "art" she had spread out across the room. Big, glossy body parts everywhere you looked. "I'm applying for a show," she told me, chewing on a thumbnail. "I'm trying to decide which pieces I should submit."

I don't know if you've ever been in this situation—where you have to offer an opinion about something about which there can be no opinion. I mean, what do you say? Your nipples look pinker in that shot than the other? Your backside is exceptionally rosy here? It's impossible.

"What do you think of this one?" She stood next to a large, blooming shot.

"Great. Very powerful."

"I call it 'Anus.' Too technical?"

"Maybe a tad. Try something more in the Romantic tradition."

"Rosebud."

"That could be anything. Nipple. Mouth. Clitoris."

"Blowhole."

"Butthole."

"I like that. 'Butthole.' It's got that techno-industrial thing happening."

"Dinah?"

"Yup?"

"Do you honestly think someone is going to want to hang a picture of your anus in their living room?"

"Sure, why not? They're all assholes anyway. Assholes buy buttholes."

Dinah prowled a while longer, then folded herself into a pretzel of nervous energy and said, "So, how do you want to kill him?"

"Who?"

"The little prick who dumped you."

"I don't."

"Then what are we talking about?" Poor Dinah. Deprived of bloodshed. You could almost feel sorry for her.

"That question I asked you . . ." I didn't feel up to repeating it.

"What question?"

"About life. Having one. If you think I do."

That was a little elliptical for Ms. Sharlip. She blinked and said, "Start again."

I repeated the question in somewhat more sequential order and wondered why she hadn't offered me anything to drink. What was the point of having friends who worked as bartenders if they didn't know when to offer you a fucking drink?

Dinah said, "You don't think you have a life."

"No, Alvin thinks I don't have a life."

"Well, who cares what Alvin thinks? I thought we were done with Alvin."

"We are . . ."

"So . . ."

"This is not about men who don't love and the women who love them. This is about lives. Having real ones."

"Oh, a real life."

"Yeah." I nodded.

"You don't."

"You're saying that. That's what you're saying."

"Absolutely."

"It's not . . . you're not suggesting that that's the question I'm asking you. You know, like, 'You think you don't have one.' And you're going to tell me that I do."

"No, I'm saying that you don't."

"Have a real life."

"Yeah. Why? Did you think you did?"

"I don't know."

"I mean, you watch all that TV."

"Everybody watches TV." Not too defensive here, not defensive at all.

"Yeah. But you talk about pretend people like they're real."

"So?"

"You get *TV Guide* delivered."

"You know what the circulation of *TV Guide* is? You know how many people read that magazine?"

"Do you underline?"

"I don't know what you're talking about." It's sad, where denial can lead you.

"The shows you watch. Do you underline?"

Well, I did. I folded corners and cross-referenced with reviews. But Dinah didn't need to know that. She was making her point.

"I mean, it's totally okay . . ."

Hopeful, I looked up. Was Dinah regretting how hard she had been on me?

"A lot of people in America don't have lives."

From Ms. Sharlip, this was kindness.

Just then, the phone rang. Dinah answered. I wondered who it could be. But when her voice melted into something that sounded halfway between a gargle and a coo, I knew.

Lylo.

"Yeah . . . oh, yeah . . . mm-hmm . . . yeah, yeah, yeah . . . oh, yeah." Maybe it was something about not having a life, but I was having a hard time imagining the other half of this conversation.

"Right . . . okay . . . yeah. Yeah, okay. Yeah, see you." She hung up, and said to me, her oldest friend, her friend in desperate need, "Go. Lylo's coming."

"You could have exterminators in." That's what I wanted to say. But I didn't. Lylo wasn't coming over to my house. He wasn't calling me and engaging me in scintillating conversation. He wasn't taking me to parties and introducing me to people.

Let's face it, I didn't even have pictures of my nipples lying around.

So I went home. The lifeless banished by the lively. I don't know, maybe it was my sudden exile into the nonexistential, but it felt like a long way from Dinah's house to mine. As I sat on the train, I kept watching my fellow passengers and wondering what they knew that I didn't. Had they discovered some vein of excitement in their daily lives that somehow eluded me? Or were their lives just as boring and drab as mine, only they didn't know any better?

One woman looked like she had a life. She was flipping through a magazine and she was thin. Thin people always look like they have lives. It's something about their actual body shape, the way it makes them look like they spend all their time running from one fabulous event to the next, constantly pursued by throngs of admirers. Next to her was a woman with her child. The kid kept putting her feet up on the seat, and the mother kept slapping them down and telling the kid, "Stop it. Stop—I said stop it." Was that a life? Had that woman thought at some point that having a kid would give her a life? Was she disappointed now that she knew it was just as boring and frustrating as everything else?

There were a few teenage girls yakking it up in the corner— they didn't expect to have a life yet, and even if they did, they had no idea what one was—so they didn't count. Next to them was an old man reading a newspaper; you had to figure he had had his life already and was on his way out.

None of these people looked outstandingly exciting. I doubt more than a hundred people knew they existed. I could not imagine what they did all day that would be any more interesting than what I did. But none of them looked like the failure I felt like.

I did notice one thing: none of them paid the slightest bit of attention to anyone else. I, on the other hand, was watching everyone.

Was that it? The watching? Was that the story of my life (or non-life)? I looked around the train again and realized that the vision I had had in college—of the world divided between people with names and faces and people with no names and no faces—had come to pass.

And somehow, somewhere along the way, I had wound up without a name and a face. And without a life.

CHAPTER SIX

THAT FIRST STEP

$\mathcal{I}$T WAS just as well that Danny came home the next day. Because while celebraholism is not yet big business, alcoholism is, but you gotta be Liz Taylor to afford Betty Ford.

Since my pep talk with Dinah, I hadn't moved from the couch. I was gorging on TV and tabloids, adding to my regular reading the kind of publication that links celebrities not to other celebrities, but to three-headed dachshunds from Mars.

But when Danny lugged his bags through the door, I snapped off the television, shoved the more offensive rags under the couch, and shrieked, "How *are* you? How did the audition go?" Rescue me. Tell me you got a fantastic part. Tell me you have a life. That I have a life because you do.

But Danny disappeared into the kitchen. "They went in a different direction."

Back to blahness and depression. Back to the television and . . .

No, no, fight it, fight it.

"Yeah, how so?"

"Well . . . black."

I nodded. "I guess, for August Wilson."

Danny emerged with a soda. "I told them I could do it."

"Sure."

"A good actor would never be a distraction because of how he looks."

"I'm sorry, Danny."

Danny tried to smile, then peered at me. "You look awful." He put a hand on my forehead. "Are you okay?"

"Just dandy, except I have no life."

"Beg pardon?"

"Danny?"

"Yeah?" He was looking really worried now.

"You never liked Alvin, did you?"

"Well . . ."

"You can be honest."

"We never had much in common . . ." said the prince of the frog. "You know, except you."

"Well, now you have nothing."

"You broke up with him?"

It would have been easy to say yes. Yes, I ended it because I realized how much more fabulous I was than he and I couldn't stand him a second longer. It would have been easy to maintain dignity, but I never had before, so I didn't see why I should start now.

"He broke up with me."

"Why?"

"He said I was an existential vacuum."

"That's good or bad?"

"I think bad. Danny?"

"Yeah?"

"Do you think I have a life?" I looked hard into his beautiful eyes. Danny, for once, act. Please act.

He said carefully, "Do you think you have a life?" As always, he

Hollywood Marriage—
WHEN YOU KNOW IT AIN'T GOING TO LAST

When they get each other's name tattooed on their bodies.

chose the wrong part. I want the cheerleading pal out of a Rodgers and Hammerstein musical. He gives me Oprah.

"What do I know? I'm a parasite in an existential vacuum."

"You are not."

"No, I am."

Danny shrugged. "Okay, so you are."

"I am?"

"If you say so. I'm not going to argue with you."

He wasn't? Why wasn't he? Since my talk with Dinah, I had been sort of counting on Danny to argue with me about this. And now he wouldn't argue. Why?

Because Alvin is right. You're a parasite in an existential vacuum.

I am not.

You are. Alvin thinks so, Dinah thinks so . . .

Alvin is a jerk and Dinah is . . . Dinah.

So why isn't Danny arguing?

Because . . . because . . .

Because I was a parasite, an existential vacuum. Because I was addicted to celebrities.

"Danny?"

"Yeah?"

"I am addicted to celebrities. And it's time I did something about it." Danny gave me a gentle, understanding look. The kind you give to people when they've got one leg over the window ledge. "I'm going to give them up."

Hollywood Marriage—
WHEN YOU KNOW IT AIN'T GOING TO LAST

When one half of the sketch says, "This is the person I was destined to be with."

He patted my arm. "I think you're overreacting. You're you. There's nothing wrong with being you."

I lifted one finger. "I am never going to be famous."

Danny nodded. "Okay."

"I don't have any talent, and I'm not shallow, pretty, or ambitious enough to get by without it."

"Fine."

"Not being famous and watching people who are famous is unhealthy." Danny nodded in agreement. "Ergo, I should stop."

"That makes a certain amount of sense," Danny admitted.

"Will you help me?"

"I will absolutely help you," said Danny.

As anyone in recovery will tell you, often what divides the successfully recovered from the failures is support. Now, unlike those socially recognized illnesses, celebraholism does not have a group support network. (Nor are there specific drugs a doctor might prescribe to make withdrawal easier, and this is something I would like to look into. Not everyone who attempts to overcome celebraholism is going to have my willpower.)

So, I was going to have to fall back on friends and family. Or, in my case, friends. Or, let's face it, Danny. There was no way I was going to rely on Dinah for emotional backup. As she would tell a drowning man, Dinah doesn't do hand-holding.

Once I had convinced Danny that I was serious, he was behind me a hundred percent. With his help, I worked out a detailed withdrawal program. Certain substances and behaviors were easy to identify as symptomatic, and were banned. I winced as *People* and E! were put on the list, but I squared my shoulders, grit my teeth, and thought of the finer things in life. Like . . . like . . . well, those finer things.

"No more TV entertainment shows," said Danny.

"Right."

"No cheesy rags."

"Uh-huh."

"No tell-all bios. No Oscars."

I hesitated. "The Oscars are a cultural event. The Oscars don't count." He looked at me. "Even you watch the Oscars, Danny."

"I'm not six deep into tabloids, and I own shirts that do not have people's faces on them."

Sometime around midnight we finished the list and stuck it on the television. (I voted for the refrigerator, but Danny said we had to fight the problem on its own turf.)

"I'm going to do this, Danny. Don't worry."

"Okay."

"You watch."

"I will."

Sunday night, I went on a farewell binge. I finished up every magazine and newspaper in the house. I watched E! until my eyeballs fell out and thumbed through all the best bits in my celebrity biographies. The binge concluded with a ceremonial burning of *TV Guide* in the toilet. On Monday morning, I woke up ready to start a new, healthy, celebrity-free life.

From now on, I would be the center of my own universe. I would look to no one but myself for diversion. I would follow only the activities of people with whom I was on a first-name, speaking basis.

I was free. Free of the shackles of celebraholism.

That morning, I marched straight into the bowels of the New York transit system, armed only with an improving novel. *The House of the Dead* (by Fyodor Dostoyevsky, as I'm sure you know). I didn't even glance over to see the puzzled expression on poor

Mr. Papagalou's face when a woman who guaranteed him a buck fifty every morning didn't buy so much as a single *Post.* Truth be told, I didn't trust myself within three feet of newsprint. I knew me. I would start by reaching for the *Wall Street Journal* and somehow end up with the *National Enquirer* in my hand.

I was all right on the platform. Feeling strong, resolved, and only slightly bug-eyed from last night's televisual excesses, I took out my copy of *The House of the Dead,* and turned to page one.

"Our prison stood at the edge of the fortress, right next to the ramparts. You would sometimes take a look at God's world . . ."

Hollywood Marriage—
WHEN YOU KNOW IT AIN'T GOING TO LAST

After the adoption of the first orphan.

Before I could be further improved, the train arrived. Tucking Fyodor under my arm, I got on. Then, as the doors slid shut, every one of my fellow passengers opened their newspapers. In an instant, I was engulfed in a sea of headlines.

There was a story, I could tell from the thickness and height of the type. The Big Story—whatever it was—was all around me. Should I look? How could I not look?

I opened *The House of the Dead.*

"Our prison stood at the edge of the fortress, right next to the ramparts. You would sometimes take a look at God's world . . ."

Just then, a woman turned to reach for the pole, and I got a glimpse—accidentally, I swear to God—of the *Daily News* cover. There was a photograph, a picture of someone. Someone I thought I recognized . . .

"Our prison stood at the edge of the fortress, right next to the ramparts. You would sometimes take a look at God's world . . ."

I should look, I decided. I should just look, so I can know, and stop thinking about it. Just look at the picture, don't read the headline. Once you have read the headline, you have ingested information. You have been contaminated. A photograph of a single person is not necessarily a story. Just one look, and that's all.

"Our prison stood at the edge of the fortress, right next to the ramparts. You would sometimes take a look at God's world . . ."

I looked. Only to find that the woman with the *Daily News* had moved away from me. The front page of the *New York Times* loomed. There was no picture that even vaguely resembled what I thought I had seen. Just gray men in gray suits—just right for the Gray Lady. Rats.

I couldn't look now. Looking now would be seeking out the story that I wasn't supposed to care about. I was weak, so weak. I couldn't be trusted at all. I buried my head in Fyodor and wondered why no one had ever discussed the importance of a great opening line with him.

"Our prison stood at the edge of the fortress, right next to the ramparts. You would sometimes take a look at God's world through the cracks of the fence: surely there must be something to be seen?"

The woman with the *Daily News* had taken a seat. As the train pulled into the next stop, a seat opposite her opened up, and I thought, I could take that seat. I could take that seat, and in the process of sitting down, I would just naturally look in her direction, toward that big, bold headline, in big, bold typeface. I couldn't help but see it. And that's not looking. That's seeing. Seeing is different. You can see all kinds of things without looking for them.

An old man flopped into the seat.

It was back to Fyodor.

". . . surely there must be something to be seen?—and all you could see would be a corner of the sky and the high earthen ramparts, overgrown with weeds, and on the ramparts the sentries pacing up and down, day and night; and then you would think that whole years would go by, and you would still come to look through the cracks in the fence . . ."

Oh, God, I couldn't do this. I couldn't. I was in agony. Everywhere around me, the world was screaming. Today was happening, and I was missing it.

". . . whole years would go by, and you would still come to look through the cracks in the fence and would still see the same ramparts, the same sentries and the same little corner of the sky . . ."

When I say I barely made it to the lobby of my workplace, I'm leaving out the gorier details for the sake of my more sensitive readers.

Next—breakfast. Even that was a problem, because who eats breakfast without reading? I couldn't possibly go back to the ramparts and the sentries, and those fucking, fucking weeds, so I read my yogurt carton instead. It was fascinating. And only marginally more fascinating was the heat warning on my cup of coffee.

People say when they give up smoking that their sense of taste is vastly improved. Blind people are known to have extremely acute hearing. Deprivation has its rewards, I suppose, in making you more sensitive in other ways. But in my case, this was a crashing downside. Never had my neighbor's radio sounded so loud. Never had newspapers rustled so enticingly. Never had the words of coworkers—their banal greetings, their first complaints of the day—sounded so alive with the potential for gossip.

Somehow, I don't remember how (it's probably like childbirth, you forget the worst of the pain), I made it through the Monday morning meeting. My coworkers were half distraction, half depressant. Distraction, because they were living, breathing human beings, who might at any moment say something about living, breathing human beings a lot more interesting than they were. Depressant because, since they didn't, they seemed like the most godawful people I had ever met.

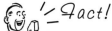

Fact!

```
The first disadvantage of a celebrity-free
life will become immediately apparent in the
early days of withdrawal.
```

Boredom.

Head-banging, throat-squeezing, mind-numbing nuclear boredom. Never have the words "How flat, stale and unprofitable/ seem to me all the uses of this world" rung so true. I couldn't figure it out: what were you supposed to do with your mind for sixteen hours a day if you couldn't think about famous people?

At lunchtime, not trusting myself to act normally in the presence of the casual lunch date, I called Danny. Anything rather than stare at the wall, imagining scandalous headlines. It was getting to the point where I was imagining some pretty far-out things, like the ghost of Lucille Ball molesting Minnie Mouse.

"How are you?" he asked.

I said through clenched teeth, "This is hard, Danny."

"I know."

"It's really, really hard."

"I know, I know."

He knew. What did he know? The man was in a restaurant, sur-rounded by celebrities, and all he cared about was whether they wanted the soup or salad frisée as a starter.

After Danny, I called, in this order, Dinah, my mother, the psy-chic hotline, Sportsphone, a stock hotline, the weather, and the talking clock—three times. I spent my lunch hour listening to canned voices, and thought, How is this a more authentic experi-ence than the *National Enquirer*?

By two o'clock, I had passed into that phase immediately rec-ognizable to all caffeine addicts: I was shaky, extremely tired, and irritable. All in all, it wasn't the ideal time to make the acquain-tance of Ivan Feiffer, the new writer for *Days of Dust*, our Western series. B. Arthur had signed him up, and he was coming into the office to get the basic instruction on *Dust*, and its heroes—Sheriff John, his sidekick Trooper, and a horse named Dog—from yours truly. I put my head down on the desk and prayed that he might be late. Or forgetful. Or hit by a bus.

At two-thirty on the dot, Ivan Feiffer was buzzed in.

After the introductions, which went congenially enough, con-sidering my state of mind, I went over the story basics with him, everything he needed to know about Sheriff John, the man who kept the law in the little town of Smokeyville; the loyal if slightly dim Trooper; Nancy, the still beautiful woman whose hard demeanor hid

Hollywood Marriage—
WHEN YOU KNOW IT AIN'T GOING TO LAST

When one of them brings Mom or Sis to the Oscars.

a well of sorrow; and, of course, Sheriff John's trusty steed, Dog. Not to mention Red Wing, the wise Kiowa able to speak with the spirits of the land, a thing that came in handy from time to time.

When I was done, Ivan Feiffer laid his hands decisively on his legs and said, "Well, I can't tell you how excited I am about *Days of Dust.*"

Hollywood Marriage—
WHEN YOU KNOW IT AIN'T GOING TO LAST

When the male half starts showing up at bars where young ladies remove their bras—or where young men put them on.

I managed a smile. "That's great." This Ivan Feiffer was a perky fellow, a little shorter than he might have been, but all in all, not too shabby for someone who meant to live off the salary we paid him. Surprisingly, he was somewhere around my age; usually by the time we got our hands on writers, they had all the zip and pizzazz of your average slug.

"I have some really great ideas about what we can do with the stories, plotwise."

Another smile. "No, you don't."

Thinking I was imposing false modesty on him, he smiled broadly. "No, I do."

"No," I said, smiling just as broadly, "you don't. You don't have ideas. You have structure. You don't have inspiration, you have rules." I gave him a file. "The rules are all in there. How many men Sheriff John kills, when he kills them, and how he feels about it. You'll also find Trooper's mistakes, numbers one, two, and three, as well as Trooper's big moment when he comes through in the clinch and redeems himself."

He frowned for a moment, then said, "The color of Dog's mane?"

"In there."

"The kind of headdress Red Wing wears?"

"In there."

"The size of Dog's shlong?"

"He doesn't have one. Miss Nancy has no nipples, and Trooper's got no nuts. Only Sheriff John, and his are of a more metaphorical nature."

Ivan nodded over the file once. "Okay."

It was time for him to leave, but, being a writer, he wasn't getting it. I was just about to ask if he needed directions to the front desk, when he said brightly, "So, tell me about Bickerstaff Books."

My window of sanity was fast disappearing. Crossing my legs, I said, "What do you want to know?"

"Oh, I don't know. The history of the company, what kind of books you publish, novels, stuff like that."

Oh, doo-doo. In fact, mega doo-doo. If my senses had not been so whacked out from withdrawal, I would have spotted it a mile away: Ivan was a novelist. An unpublished novelist. An unpublished novelist in New York. I glanced heavenward and thought, God, God, how could You—on my first day of celebrity abstinence—send me an unpublished novelist?

Unpublished novelists are bottom-dwellers, the dregs of the creative food chain. You can smell the desperation on them. Some fix you with cheesy smiles and bright eyes. Others try the deadpan pseudo–serial-killer air of ennui. But you can still smell it on them: the sheer, panting, pathetic desperation.

Ivan was the bright-eyed, desperate smile type of guy. He was trying to be nonchalant, but I could see it—that sweaty-palmed, wet-eyed dreamer was there, all right, absolutely certain that I was the answer to his prayers.

He blurted it out: "I've written a novel."

"Don't worry, it'll stay between us."

"Maybe you wouldn't mind taking a look at it?"

"I would mind."

"Ah, come on. Give me break."

"Right leg or left?" I got up and opened the door.

But he stayed in his chair. He was a persistent little unpublished creep, I gave him that. No doubt he was told to be, by some book called *How to Get Published!* Bought by unpublished suckers who—surprise, surprise—stay that way.

"Hey, come on, I know you like novels." He pointed to *The House of the Dead*, which was lying on my desk.

"Do you like Dostoyevsky?" I asked him.

"Love him." Oh, ick—that breathless reverence they get when they're talking about dead published authors. Live published authors, by the way, never get this reverence. Live published authors all suck, in the humble opinion of live unpublished authors.

I picked up *The House of the Dead* and handed it to him.

"It's yours. See you in two weeks."

As Ivan Feiffer left the office, I was torn between two powerful and conflicting emotions: one, that he had wasted fifty-three minutes of my time on earth, and two, that fifty-three minutes wasn't nearly enough. Because the fact was, with Ivan gone, I had the whole rest of the day to get through, and I wasn't sure how I was going to make it.

But, just at the moment I was vaguely regretting the lack of exitable windows at Bickerstaff Books, the phone rang.

It was Danny, in a state of breathless excitement. "You will never believe what I am about to tell you."

Oh, God, was I saved? Was Ivan Feiffer merely a trial to test my will? To see if I was worthy of having a friend in the next billion-dollar action extravaganza? I am worthy, Lord, I am!

When the female half develops a passion for one
of the following:
  a. Buddhism
  b. Scientology
  c. Designer drugs

"What, Danny? What?"

Danny inhaled solemnly, then announced, "They're doing *Cyrano* at the La Salle."

So much for signs. So much for passing tests and trials and Ivan Feiffers, and getting a goddamn thing in return.

"The La Salle? What is this, Cyrano in a G-string?"

"They've changed management," said Danny. "The auditions are next fucking week; you've got to help me."

"Who's directing?" Someone, I prayed, a real someone, not some schmuck . . .

"Magalda Bernadin."

Schmuck city.

Danny said breathlessly, "I have to find out which translation they're doing."

You see—translation. With Danny, it's always translation. Nobody needs to translate soaps. Nobody needs to translate Schwarzenegger.

"Will you help me?" he asked.

"Of course, I'll help you."

"God, I'm nervous already. You think I can do it?"

"Christian? Standing on your beautiful head."

"Not Christian. Cyrano."

"Oh," I said. "Of course." And sunk slowly under the desk in despair.

So, as my first day of recovery drew to a close, did I celebrate? Did I wing my way to an expensive restaurant and quaff bubbly beverages? Did I hand myself over to a masseuse and let him pound away the pain and strife?

Not exactly.

This was the extent of my thank-you to myself: I went to the makeup store with Danny and waited while he bought putty for his nose. The owner of the store said to me, "Such a gorgeous face. Why does he cover it up all the time?"

"Why do people walk on hot coals?" I replied.

We went home. I collapsed on the couch and tried to avoid the sight of the television, which Danny had thoughtfully covered with a sheet to diminish temptation. Danny also thoughtfully made me dinner, brought me liquids with alcohol in them, and— not quite as thoughtfully—talked nonstop about *Cyrano.*

"I'm going to do the dueling speech," he announced.

Only the most complex, laugh-driven speech in the whole thing. The one where you need impeccable timing, undeniable charisma, and the courage to be restrained when you're dying to overdo it. Oh yeah, and talent. You need that, too.

"Really? I was thinking maybe the balcony speech. It's so romantic."

"No, he's speaking as Christian. I don't want to even remotely remind them of Christian. They'll never think of me for Cyrano

Hollywood Marriage—

WHEN YOU KNOW IT AIN'T GOING TO LAST

Bad combos: Male star and winner of any major pageant. Female star and any lesser crew member (i.e., grip, cameraman, assistant director).

Hollywood Marriage—
WHEN YOU KNOW IT AIN'T GOING TO LAST

When she's twelve and he's seventy-two.

---

otherwise." He frowned. "You think I bought enough putty?"

"Five pounds? Enough putty."

As he put away the dishes, Danny said, "You know I once met Magalda Bernadin?"

And never washed your hand again, I thought. "That's great. Maybe she'll remember you."

"I doubt it. I met her with Roger. He's sort of a friend of hers." He smiled sheepishly.

"Oh, Danny . . ." Why could this boy break hearts in person and never on stage?

"Dumb, right?"

I patted his hand. "Understandable. But dumb. He was a jerk."

"Head knows that. Rest of me . . . not so sure."

"That's called rejection. Why don't you return some of those phone calls from all of those eligible bachelors who keep phoning?"

He shrugged. "Why don't I? Hey"—he reached out and tapped me on the hand—"how was your first day of Cold Turkey?"

(First? I have to go through this again?)

"It really wasn't too bad." Ignore, please, the shaking hands, the foam-flecked lips. "Not bad at all."

"That's great. I bet you beat this thing."

Danny went to his room to immerse himself in *Cyrano* and thoughts of unrequited love. I sat on the couch and tried to figure out if I had a life yet. Was this a proper existence? Dealing with

Hollywood Marriage—

WHEN YOU KNOW IT AIN'T GOING TO LAST

When their friends start telling the tabloids, "They're incredibly devoted parents."

people like Ivan Feiffer? Listening to Danny and his impossible dreams of theatrical triumph, to Dinah and her fantasies of world domination through anal exposure?

What about sharing an address with a famous basset hound? How much did that count for on the existential significance scale?

Probably not much.

Admitting that you have a problem is the first step on the road to recovery. And that's just swell. But it's also a fact that every step after that first one feels like shit.

But surely, I thought, once purged of its former frivolous obsessions, my life would begin to take shape. Without the distractions of celebrity, I would be able to focus on developing my skills and talents (which were what, exactly?). I would find the direction that had so long eluded me. I would be a good friend. An industrious employee. I would vote. I would have broad views. I would do things for my fellow man.

I would have a life.

But was it worth it?

Yes, I told myself.

Are you sure?

Of course I'm sure. Why go through all this pain and hell and suffering if it's not worth it?

Fuck the pain and hell and suffering.

No. Pain and hell and suffering make you a better and finer person.

Bullshit. Turn on the television.

No.

Turn it on . . .

No.

TURN IT ON!

And then it happened. The Sign. Like the locusts upon Egypt, like boils upon the ass of Job, there was a Sign.

The TV came on *all by itself.*

It's not actually that miraculous. What had happened was I had shifted and leaned slightly on the remote, which had fallen under the cushions on the couch. And so the TV came on. And even through the sheet—which was really pretty threadbare—I could see what the morning's headlines had been all about.

Fuzzy Winterspoon was getting married.

Now some of you, for whatever bizarre reason, may not recall the life and times of Fuzzy Winterspoon, or why her engagement would be covered in the news.

It's very simple.

Fuzzy Winterspoon had lived her whole life in the news. Her birth (illegitimate, if we use that word anymore) daughter of BZZZ guitarist Wes Fumbly and model Mara Whipple, her baptism in the Catholic faith of her mother and then the adopted faith (Buddhism) of her father, her entry into a trendy kindergarten, her first drug rehab, her acceptance into Brown, and how she was absolutely forced to drop out in order to take advantage of the fabulous opportunity offered to her by a world-famous director.

The media turned out in full force for the gorgeous, gorgeous film premiere, reported endlessly on her rapturous love affair with wholesome boy wonder Chris MacIntyre, their breakup when Chris was found in the arms of hunk Peterson Wonderson, Fuzzy's subsequent fall off the wagon, triumphant recovery, and so on and fucking so on.

And now Fuzzy was getting married. Little Fuzzy, happy at last.

I could have turned off the TV, I admit it. But the damage was already done. Two seconds of exposure, and I was panting for details. My fingers were itching for the touch of slippery paper, my ears tingling for the jaunty monotone of the TV announcer's voice. Details, I needed details. I just managed to catch the groom's name: J.J. Phipps, hunk du jour/serious actor manqué. But where had he asked her? How had he asked her? Was she thrilled or just so, so happy? All around me, in the air, factoids were calling to me: "Listen, listen . . ." Tantalizing factoids were slipping away, becoming yesterday's news to everyone but me. ("You didn't know they were engaged? Christ, *everyone* knew that.") Have to know,

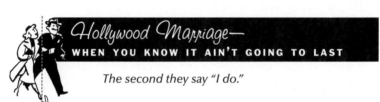

Hollywood Marriage—
WHEN YOU KNOW IT AIN'T GOING TO LAST

The second they say "I do."

have to know, have to know . . . the words pounded away at me.

I tried to pull myself back from the brink. I tried reasoning with myself: Why was it important to know? What in my life would be lesser if I failed to know the details of Fuzzy Winterspoon's life?

Answer: everything.

No. No. I can fight this, I thought as I frantically flipped channels, looking for details. I can beat it. I can. Just one more detail, and I'll turn it off. One little fact, a rumor, a quote, an opinion from a source close to the couple . . . and I'll turn it off.

I swear.

CHAPTER SEVEN

BREAKTHROUGHS AND CRACK-UPS

*A*T ONE-FIFTEEN in the morning, Danny caught me red-handed.

He had gotten up to go to the bathroom when he heard the telltale sound of canned voice-over and rushed into the living room, to find the TV warm and me with the remote in my hand.

Oh, the recriminations.

The finger-pointing.

The babbled excuses.

Heads were hung, hands were wrung, and at least a tear or two was shed. At one point, I offered to chop off the offending hand, but Danny, instantly grossed out, said that wouldn't be necessary.

"I'm weak," I whispered.

"I know." He patted my face and gave me a Kleenex. "You know what you need?"

I sniffed. "What?"

"A twelve-step program."

No, what I needed was one of those spas, the ones located in peaceful tropical climates, where they massage and spoon-feed you twenty-four hours a day until you are limp, toxin-free, and have a really good tan.

But I couldn't afford that, so I was stuck with Danny and the twelve steps—whatever they might be. Obviously, there were no steps for celebraholics (also no spas in tropical resorts), so Danny had to sort of make it up. But that was okay, because before Roger, Danny had been involved with an alcoholic, and he knew this step stuff like the back of his hand.

"Do you admit that you are powerless over celebrity addiction?"

I nodded.

"That your life has become unmanageable?"

"I don't have a life to manage, Danny, that's the whole point."

Danny said I needed to take a moral inventory of myself. I did. Then he said I had to ask my higher power for help.

I shook my head. "Even I know that God has better things to do than cure me of celebrity addiction." Like save penguins or something.

"It doesn't have to be God as in father, son, and holy ghost. It's however you envision your higher power." I must have started looking panicked, because he said, "Look. What you need is more contact with real, everyday people. For now, let them be your higher power."

"Okay." Danny didn't know it, but he had just basically become my higher power.

A key part of the process, according to Danny, was the making of amends. This meant you had to go to all the people you had hurt in the past because of your addiction, and tell them that you were sorry you had caused them pain.

I balked here, I admit it. For starters, I wasn't entirely sure what I was apologizing for. Even if I accepted that nonstop celebrity observation was not a Good Thing, I couldn't really see how it affected anyone else. So I told Danny that it was a little hard to believe that people suffer from secondhand celebraholism, but Danny disagreed. There was absolutely such a thing as secondhand celebraholism. It was called boredom.

Another thing I had to consider, according to Danny, was the fact that I personally had lowered the level of public discourse in America. Apparently, it was my fault that we as a nation talked more about breast implants than the national deficit. If I didn't buy the magazines with Fuzzy Winterspoon on the cover but instead bought the *Wall Street Journal*, the world would be a much better place. Babies would not starve, the rain forests would be more or less intact, and we would have switched to solar power long ago. Through my addiction, I, all by myself, had decreased the IQ of every man, woman, and child in America by at least ten points.

"Amends," I said, yawning. "Got it."

At four-thirty in the morning, I still wanted to go to a spa, but since I was no richer at four-thirty than I had been at one-fifteen, Danny turned the shower on full blast until the bathroom steamed up and I could at least imagine I was in a sauna.

And that maybe Cher and Susan Sarandon were there, too, and we were all trying to figure out what to do with our evening.

THE MAKING OF AMENDS

You know how in movies people are always fessing up to past transgressions and are greeted with tears and open arms by friends and family—who say they don't care about the past, they just love them so, so much?

That didn't happen to me.

I called and made a lunch date with Dinah. Lunch was not a particularly good time for her, since it occurred just around the time she was waking up, but in my case, she was willing to make an exception.

"I'm a celebraholic," I told her.

"What?" Having gotten out of bed about fifteen minutes ago, she was still a little slow on the old uptake.

"I'm addicted to celebrities."

Dinah shook her head.

"Remember how you said I should stop talking about people I

don't know, people we only know *about*? I have to start talking about something other than celebrities."

"Who the fuck else would we talk about? Everybody else is fucking boring."

"This is that real life thing," I reminded her.

"Oh, that," said Dinah.

There was a long pause.

"So," I said, trying it out. "How are you?"

Dinah made a face. " '*I'm fine. How are you?*' This is pathetic. Do I have to go along with this?"

"It would help me if you did."

Dinah moved restlessly. I couldn't tell which was the greater burden—not talking about famous people or helping someone.

"How's Lylo?" I asked.

She frowned. "I don't want to talk about Lylo."

"Why not?"

"Because he's an asshole."

Was this . . . pain I saw on Dinah's face? "What did he do?"

"Nothing. He didn't do anything."

"Did you have a fight?" This was feeling not bad. I felt a little bit like Oprah. *"That must have been very painful for you." "Caller, you say what?"*

"No . . . I don't know. It's not important. Just for some reason, he's not calling me."

"Have you called him?"

"Yes."

"How many times?"

"Forty-three." She looked defiant. "He has my Blondie album; I need it back."

"Dinah, you cannot be hung up on this guy."

"Why not?"

"Because he's barely a human being."

"So? I don't need a human being."

Now to most people, you would say something like, "But you deserve a human being." But it wasn't just that I wasn't sure that Dinah did; I was beginning to see Lylo's hold over Dinah. Minor celebrity though he might be, major dickwad that he certainly was, he was her only tenuous link to the Nirvana of the Rich and Famous.

And for the first time in my life, I felt sorry for Dinah Sharlip. I reached out to pat her hand, but she snatched it away and said, "Oh, for Christ's sake."

Before we left, I made my amends and apologized for all the times I had bored her with my celebraholism.

"That wasn't so bad," she said. "Now you're a fucking yawn-fest."

Next I saw my mother.

"I want to apologize," I told her.

"For what?"

"For paying too much attention to celebrities."

"What are you apologizing to me for?"

"Well, because, it must have caused you some kind of pain." Where were the tears? The Big Hugs? Didn't anyone watch movies of the week anymore?

"It caused me a few boring evenings, but that's okay. It happens."

"Well, I make amends for the boring evenings."

My mother looked at me and shook her head. "Make amends to yourself. You're the one who got shortchanged on the deal."

So, okay, I had made amends. Presumably, everyone was feeling a lot better now—everyone except me. Valiantly (I think) I tried to stay focused on the program. But recovery was not getting easier. Waking up first thing in the morning to the real world, delivered courtesy of NPR, was not a happy experience.

You want to know the true enemy of the recovering celebraholic? Distribution. It is not an easy thing in this world to avoid *People* magazine. That first week of my recovery, every single goddamn magazine put the news of Fuzzy Winterspoon's upcoming nuptials on the cover. Everywhere I went, there was the newly engaged Fuzzy, the future Mrs. J.J. Phipps, her silver and turquoise engagement ring prominently displayed. The ring had been specially carved by an obscure branch of the Sioux, just for Fuzzy. This branch of the Sioux loved J.J. ever since he played a half-white, half-Sioux renegade in *Tribal Passion*.

I covered my eyes when I walked past newsstands. I took a different route to work, read status reports at lunchtime, and helped Danny rehearse *Cyrano* at night. I listened, I made suggestions, I encouraged. I said a lot of things like "It's starting to work," and "I'm feeling it," and "You've got that moment down." It was amazing: Danny was the actor, and I always wound up putting on the performance.

"I think it started to click that last time," I told him.

"I felt it clicking," he said, and started over.

I tried, people. I really, really tried.

Just as smokers will find that they must give up certain habits because those habits recall too strongly the pleasures of cigarettes, I, too, had to give up long cherished haunts and pastimes. I had to avoid particular neighborhoods because they were conducive to celebrity spotting. Conversely, other places were a painful reminder of how low I had fallen. The train was the worst. No place in the world reminds you of your suck status like the F train. Every day, twice a day, I had to sit there, staring off into space, with nothing whatsoever to distract me.

If cold turkey was supposed to hurt, then this really hurt. Celebrities might be just a cheap and shallow distraction, but the world was a dull, gray place without them.

Two weeks later, I learned one of the most important things about recovery.

Fact!

In order to recover, you must have the courage to face backslides.

In the beginning, it was no big thing. Minor stuff. A magazine here, an Internet trawl there. And no matter how hard I fought it, I always seemed to be around when people started talking about celebrities. I mean, I don't want to rag on them, or call them unsupportive, but certain people were no help at all. One coworker in particular, a woman named Felice, read all the magazines I used to read—only she got them delivered at work. For hours, they would lie there, provocatively sprawled on the floor of her office. And if I walked a little slower as I passed by, well, I ask you, is that my fault or Felice's?

I tried to hide my lapses from Danny—not an easy thing. As the audition drew near, he was taking off more and more time from Fido's to prepare his monologue. Talking to him on the phone was my one defense against cravings. (Dinah now refused to speak to me, I was so boring, and one can only take so much of the talking clock.)

One afternoon I called Danny one too many times.

What happened was this: the mailroom had just brought Felice a batch of tabloids. One of them had a picture of a former child star on the cover—a child star that I had always had theories about, if you know what I mean. The temptation was unbearable. Five times I made excuses to walk by Felice's office (Xerox machine, coffeemaker, two potty breaks, and an "Oops, forgot where I was going"). Didn't work. As hard as I tried, I could not make out that

THE AEROBICS OF *Celebrity* SPOTTING

THE BENDS

When a celebrity is sitting behind you. Bend all the way over the waist, as if you are retrieving something from the floor. As you come up, affect light-headedness and end the movement in a Sudden Swivel (see page 15).

headline. By the fifth time, Felice was giving me some strange looks, like did I want something, because if I didn't, fuck off.

I was trying very hard not to walk past Felice's office for the sixth time when I called Danny at home.

"How's the monologue going?" I asked brightly. Too brightly.

"I hate it," said Danny. "I don't want to talk about it."

"Oh. What did the restaurant say when you called in sick?" Please, Danny, talk to me. I don't want to walk by Felice's office again. She's noticing, and she thinks I'm a sick woman.

"Oh, they were pissed off, but screw them."

And then I heard it. A faint, faint hum . . .

"Danny? Do you have the TV on?"

"What? Oh, yeah. It's nothing."

"But you have it on." He did have it on; I could hear it.

Danny sighed. "A friend of mine has a cottage cheese commercial; I promised him I'd try and catch it."

"What channel is it on now?"

"Um . . . seven."

I glanced at the clock. "Oprah. Oprah's on."

"I'm not even watching, to tell you the truth."

"Just tell me what she's talking about, and I won't ask another thing."

"Something about the Grammys, totally dull . . ."

"A special?" I whimpered. "A preview?"

"Maybe . . ."

"Does she have guests? Are they nominees?"

"I don't know any of them."

"When their names come up under their faces, tell me who they are."

"No."

"Please, Danny."

"No. I'm turning it off."

"Please, Danny, I can't take it . . ."

"It's off. Forget it. Forget it happened. So," he said, changing the subject, "what do you want to do this evening?"

"I want to watch television," I said through gritted teeth.

"There's a great nature program on, about goats in the Andes . . ."

"I want to watch *Entertainment Tonight.*"

"They have really interesting mating habits."

"I don't care," I snapped. "I don't care about the mating habits of goats. I care about the mating habits of famous people. I care how they mate, where they mate, how many times, and with whom. I care about what they eat. I care about the clothes they wear. I care about what pets they have, what toothpaste they favor, what cars they drive, and the two months out of the year they call work. That's what I care about Danny, and I am *dying*, do you hear me?"

Oh, yes, Danny heard me. Danny heard me. Felice heard me. Joanne heard me, and Louis down the hall heard me. People in a meeting heard me, and they came out to see who was screaming like a madwoman, and should they call the police. Even B. Arthur, who never heard anything in his life, heard me. He was staring at me, puzzled: like, how could I be so uncool?

If I had had anywhere to go but home that evening, I would have gone. But one of the drawbacks of having No Life—I was starting to think of No Life as an actual illness—was that you have a limited repertoire of friends to turn to when you don't want to face certain other friends. Dinah was back on with a vengeance with Lylo, my mother had a class to teach, and so, chagrined, shamefaced, I schlepped home to face a very pissed-off higher power.

Danny was reading when I came in. He looked like a man who was definitely feeling in the mood for amends.

"Sorry about this afternoon."

He turned a page of Uta Hagen's *Respect for Acting*. "That's okay."

That wasn't one of those "That's okay's" that means it's okay. This one meant "Keep going."

"You've been incredibly supportive, and I took out my frustration on you, and that's not fair."

"Mm-hmm." Another page got turned.

"I'm really, really sorry."

Maybe it was the second "really." Danny looked up, and smiled. "I was in a crappy mood because of the audition." Relieved, I sank into a chair.

Danny asked, "So, is this really hard? Giving it up?"

I nodded.

"Why don't you stop trying? Or just cut back a little?"

"No, it's something I should do." Why, I wasn't sure, but I knew if I said anything else, Danny would argue with me, and I was too tired to be argued with.

"Maybe you should try therapy," he said. "It might help to talk it out with someone who isn't in the entertainment field."

I made a listless noise of agreement, and Danny and I parted friends. But what neither of us knew was that in the end, therapy turned out to be the single most significant turning point in my whole recovery.

Admitting that you have a problem is the first step. Admitting that
it is beyond your power to cure yourself and it's time to call in the
expensive experts—that's the second step. It used to be tremen-
dously unfashionable for celebrities to seek outside help for their
addictions and ailments. But now, thanks to Betty Ford, it's a different story. Recovery is a great way to revive a flagging career. It
not only gets you on the cover of *People*, it's a really good excuse
for having allowed your career to fall into the toilet. "I was so
whacked out, I had lost control of my life," laments So-and-So.
(And you're supposed to think, Oh, that explains why he did *Free
Willy 7: Willy Rises*.)

Which is why, after my initial reluctance, I started to like the idea
of outside intervention. In some ways, this was the most celebrity-
like thing I had ever done. Maybe I couldn't take up residence in
Smithers, but at the very least I could find a caring professional who
would pat my hand and tell me it was all my mother's fault. If I
couldn't talk about celebrities, at least I could talk about myself.

But I was brought up short when I realized the dismal lack of
expertise on my particular ailment. I asked around—saying I had
"this friend" who needed help—but no one knew of any therapists
who specialized in curing celebrity addiction. Then I realized I
would simply have to turn to a run-of-the mill shrink, like every
other fucking neurotic in New York.

A word of advice: when looking for a therapist, don't respond
to flyers you find in the street. I mean, think of what you find on
the street, even since the advent of the pooper scooper, and I think
you'll see my point. I wish I had.

I found Doris Byrd in a handful of flyers left in our lobby, along
with the Chinese restaurant menus and nail salon coupons. You
couldn't miss her flyer—it was a piece of bright orange paper with
the message:

DORIS BYRD

THERAPIST

"I don't just save lives—I repair them!"

It was the words *sliding pay scale* that caught my eye. I called the number, got a very officious-sounding answering machine, and left a message. Two days later, Doris called me back. She said she had an opening in her client base and was able to schedule an interview.

"An interview?" Jesus, you had to be qualified to have a nervous breakdown in this town.

"To assess our compatibility," she said briskly. "I will attempt to ascertain the nature of your neurosis—or psychosis, or personality disorder," she said, graciously allowing I might be a lot sicker than I thought. "Then I will make a judgment as to whether I can help you or not."

"I'm a celebraholic," I told her. "That's my problem."

"I think it's my job to diagnose," she said, and hung up.

Okay, downside number one was definitely the bossy cow routine. On the other hand, you want a therapist to maintain a certain hold on things, and Danny confirmed that a strong hand was probably what I needed.

Downside number two turned out to be that Doris the Life Saver was on the top floor of a fifth-floor walk-up. When Doris opened the door, two cats came scrambling out with an air of desperate escape. But she scooped them up and took all three of us into the apartment. The cats were placed on the floor, where they wandered around my legs, meowing something that sounded suspiciously like "Jesus Christ, another sick fuck."

Doris the Life Saver said nothing to me for the first three quarters of an hour. While I babbled madly about myself, she maintained a maddening stone face that gave me no idea what she was thinking. (Either "Ka-ching! A real sicko!" Or *"Bor-ing."*)

Finally, I said that there was no point in my coming back if she didn't talk.

"We can talk about why that's important to me, but you have to do it in the meantime. I mean, you don't have to say much, but part of the reason I'm here is that I need to start interacting with real people. You're contributing to my dysfunction," I added lamely.

So the next session, Doris the Life Saver said something. She fixed me with an intense look and asked me: "Do you have any idea how much paper is wasted to produce these magazines you read?"

"Um, no, I don't."

"How many trees are slaughtered?"

"No."

"How many ecosystems are destroyed?"

"Gosh, let me think . . ."

Doris ranted and raved for a good twenty minutes—something that I had thought was my prerogative. Pretty quickly, it became clear what I had on my hands: a genuine, bona fide quack. And not just any quack, but a quack with a political agenda. Doris the Life Saver was, in fact, Doris the Socialist Shrink, Doris the Hack Quack, a one-woman rainbow coalition, switching hue from red to green in the blink of a dialectic.

"You have no sense of yourself as Your Self," she told me.

"I see."

"You feel that you only exist through barter."

"Well, and universal acclaim."

"You're another sad victim of the capitalist system."

"Me and the former Soviet Union," I said brightly.

"A cog with delusions of grandeur."

"Ah."

At our next session, she said, "Look at how much you consume. Celebrity is just a cheap oil to aid consumption of product."

"Well, I don't want to buy, I want to sell."

"Why?"

"Why?" I looked at her, incredulous.

"Any asshole can sell themselves," she said dismissively.

"And any asshole can sit on the shelf way past their freshness date."

As I handed her my check, I told Doris that I required something more therapeutic than outright abuse.

At our next session, she tried to be supportive. "I'm sure you're incredibly talented at something. You just have to find what it is."

"I'm not."

"Everyone is, at something."

"Well, I'm not."

It was a short session.

Finally, the bright and happy day of Danny's *Cyrano* audition arrived. I say bright and happy because it meant I no longer had to watch Danny stalk around the house with five pounds of putty on his nose, brandishing a radio antenna. All that was left for me to do was accompany Danny to the La Salle and hold his hand until it was all over.

I would be happy to describe our destination as the once proud La Salle Theater, but that would be a lie. Located in that no-man's-land beyond Eighth Avenue that certain people will insist represents the True Theater (because that's the only place they've ever worked), the La Salle was a dental office in the fifties, a pet food warehouse in the sixties, and a strip joint in the seventies. In 1992, it was bought by the Lowenthal Brothers. The boys' mother was a former hoofer, and on her deathbed, they had promised her they would buy a Broadway theater so that her ghost would have somewhere to visit. It was said by some that Mother Lowenthal haunted the premises, and this was a good thing, because, well, somebody had to.

You know how they talk about the magical atmosphere of a theater? Well, the La Salle retained a strong aura of its pet warehouse days. The substandard wiring and suspicious stains on the floors were, in my opinion, glamour overkill.

Danny and I climbed up the firetrap stairs to the audition room. But just before we went in, Danny reached for the doorknob, then stepped back.

He said, "I'm scared."

"Don't be."

"I swear I'm going to piss myself."

"Well, piss with panache."

He smiled. He also looked like he was going to throw up.

"You'll be amazing," I said. "Got your nose?"

Danny held up a plastic baggy with a lump of putty.

"Then let's go."

And through the door we went. Through the door and smack-dab into a row of nervous actresses seated in a line of folding chairs that stretched the length of a long corridor. Danny and I took the last two folding chairs. I looked down the line, and wondered why so many Roxannes and no other Cyranoes. Then again, maybe fortune was finally smiling upon Danny.

The door at the end of the hall swung open. Twenty-four hopeful heads swung with it. A solitary head emerged. Black. Bald. A smile that was halfway between sympathetic and sadistic. I saw the clipboard and knew we were in the presence of power.

He cast a glance down the line, lingering, I thought, on Danny. "Everybody here for the Magalda Bernadin *Cyrano*?"

Lots of nods.

Another slight smile. "Anybody reading for Christian?"

One no. A loud no. From guess who.

The gentleman with the clipboard sauntered down our way.

He gave Danny a number and said, "No Christian, huh?"

Danny said, "No," but I said, "Yes," earning an elbow from Danny and a big smile from the Man in Charge.

Mr. Clipboard called for number thirty-one. I glanced at the card in Danny's hand. He was number forty. Lots of time to get nervous and tentative. I nudged him gently, asked if he wanted to get up and stretch his legs.

"No, I'm fine," he said with a dangerous hint of the deadly monotone that can be his trademark as an actor.

While Danny ran his lines and played with his nose, I sat and worried. I wasn't a hundred percent on Danny's monologue, but I had hopes that in the heat of performance, he would suddenly take off and deliver it with passion born out of nerves and anxiety. Such miracles, I understand, happen every day in the theater.

The minutes trudged by. I flipped through the pages of *Variety*, made mental notes of all the auditions Danny should be going on instead of wasting his time with this one. Then the man in charge called for number forty. I gave Danny a hard pinch for good luck and mobility, and with something approximating coordination, he made his way down the hall, through the door, and hopefully to fame and fortune.

I waited and tried to think positively. Maybe Danny would get the part. (And maybe Andrew Lloyd Weber would become a lingerie model.) Maybe the novelty of a truly beautiful Cyrano would attract massive media attention. (And maybe Santa Claus and the Easter Bunny would get married and adopt the Tooth Fairy.)

All these happy musings came to a short, sharp stop when Danny came back a way too fast few minutes later, followed by a dispiriting call for number forty-one. Walking straight past me, he started down the stairs. I clattered down after him and chased him out onto the street.

Panting, I said, "Just give me a one to ten."

"Two."

"You're exaggerating."

"You're right. Minus two."

"Why? What happened?"

He was on the corner now, jumping up and down, frantically trying to hail a cab. I was about to remind him that we couldn't afford cabs, but I didn't have to worry. No cabbie in their right mind was about to pick up Danny, lobbing himself into the air like a pogo stick, his putty nose swinging more and more dangerously with every leap.

"Did you forget your lines?" Thinking of course he didn't.

"Of course I forgot my lines."

"But then you remembered them, right?"

"Right."

"And then?"

"And then I sucked. Why won't these fucking cabs stop for me?"

Stepping off the curb, I raised my hand. A cab screeched to a halt. "It's something about the putty," I told Danny.

As we careened down the West Side Highway, I said, "Sucked in what way?"

"As in big time."

"Did Magalda Bernadin say that?"

"I don't need Magalda Bernadin to tell me I sucked." He ripped off his nose. "I can't believe I did this to myself . . ."

I decided it was time to look on the bright side. "I think the guy with the clipboard liked you."

"Who cares?"

"Well, you don't know. He might have a lot of influence. He looked to me like one of those people who really runs the show, in a behind-the-scenes kind of way."

"Magalda Bernadin runs her own shows, believe me."

"I bet you get a callback."

"I bet I die in poverty."

Now, this was not like Danny. Such crass commercial anxiety was much more my line of thinking. I wondered what was bringing this on. Was Danny, at thirty, experiencing a midlife crisis? He'd always sworn that age meant nothing to him, that he would actually be happy when he got older, because then he wouldn't be typecast as the pretty-boy lover. But maybe Danny was finally figuring it out that if you hadn't played Romeo, no one knew your name when it was time to cast Lear.

Danny brooded, staring out the window at New Jersey—a sight not destined to raise the spirits. "Maybe I should get out of New York . . ."

"Don't be silly."

"They have theater outside of New York," he said stubbornly. "*Real* theater. Not . . . helicopters and dropping chandeliers."

I tried to suppress mounting panic. The threat was twofold: one, Danny had even less of a chance of being discovered treading the footlights in say, Duluth, and two, no matter how dedicated a friend and leech I might be, I certainly wasn't living out the rest of my life in some hick town for the sake of Art.

"You're just depressed," I said.

"I'm not 'just' depressed. I'm seriously depressed."

We rolled homeward, Danny mulling his future in the sticks, me plotting like mad to get him to stay. I paid for the cab—a little guilt never hurt in negotiations—and assured him he would feel better about things in the morning. As Danny stomped up the stairs, Norm emerged from his apartment, ready for his afternoon stroll. Danny glared, but Norm ignored him, preferring to snuffle at some dead thing in the street. Stars never notice the little people.

The minute we got into the apartment, Danny fell facedown on the couch, moaning softly into the lint-raddled fabric. Between my withdrawal and his auditions, that couch was getting a lot of wear and tear.

I was just about to say something caustic about auditioning for *Camille* when the phone rang.

"See," I said, pointing at the phone. "I bet that's Magalda Bernadin, right now."

"Saying thank you very much for sucking. You made our decision very simple." Danny threw Uta Hagen across the room. One could understand—it wasn't like she'd done him a lot of good.

But it wasn't Magalda Bernadin. It was Dinah.

"Jesus, where the fuck have you been?" she demanded in the style coached at all the very best finishing schools. "Is your TV on?"

"Of course it isn't."

"Well, put it on."

"What is this, a test?" She knew I was supposed to be off the stuff.

"No, it is not a fucking test. Turn it on."

I found the remote and did so. "What channel am I looking for?"

"Oh, any channel. It's everywhere . . ."

"What's everywhere?"

"You'll know when you find it."

I flipped from channel to channel. Commercial, commercial, commercial . . . and then a sight too mind-boggling to comprehend.

I must have gasped, because Dinah said, "You've found it, haven't you?"

There was Dinah, on my phone *and* on my television screen. There was an enormous crowd of press surrounding her. I tried to make out her surroundings, and when the camera swerved suddenly to the left, I saw the words *17th Precinct.*

I whispered, "Dinah, what have you done?"

CHAPTER EIGHT

FAME AT LAST

*I*T **WASN'T** me!" Dinah shrieked. "I wasn't driving."

I motioned for Danny to turn the volume up, and a voice came blaring into my living room.

". . . twenty-eight-year-old rap sensation Lylo Wingate was arrested late last night on charges of drunk driving and vehicular manslaughter, stemming from the death of eighty-seven-year-old Buster Rosen. The beloved owner of Rosen's Deli had been on his way to the fish markets when he was allegedly struck by the rap star's car at a Lower East Side crosswalk."

"Oh, Jesus, Dinah . . ."

"What are they saying?"

"Shh, let me listen . . ."

There are times when *surreal* is an inadequate word. This was one of them. For half an hour, the three of us stayed glued to the television. We watched Lylo Wingate being escorted in handcuffs from his East Side town house.

We watched Lylo's parents rushing past reporters.

We watched Lylo's revoltingly appropriate SUV being towed by a police truck.

We watched as an attorney for the Wingate family assured us that it was all just a terrible mistake. (Like somehow Mr. Rosen's flattened person was some kind of ghastly misinterpretation.)

An on-site reporter on the Lower East Side informed us, "Witnesses tell us that just prior to the incident Mr. Wingate had been drinking heavily in this club, The Crack."

Switch to shot inside the club. A six-foot twelve-year-old with a shaved head blinked nervously at the reporter's microphone. A caption identified her: "Melissa, Bartender at The Crack."

"Well, yeah, he was definitely drinking," said the twelve-year-old.

"Did he have a lot to drink?" the reporter asked.

"I don't know," she said doubtfully. "Like, seven, nine shots?"

"Was that my name?" Dinah asked. "Are they talking about me?"

"No."

"I thought they were talking about me."

"They're not talking about you, Dinah."

I expected that to annoy her, but she said, "Well, that's probably good."

"Why is that good?"

"I said probably good."

Lylo's presence might have gone undetected were it not for the delicate sleeping habits of one Mrs. Rowena Mallard. Mrs. Mallard had apparently been roused by the sound of Lylo's CD player booming forth his latest single, "Bleep You, You're Bleep." She went to her window just in time to see Mr. Rosen struck down, and she did see an SUV pull away.

She did not see who was driving it, but she had just enough time to write down the license plate number.

Finally, Buster Rosen's widow, Lila, was interviewed at the deli. "He was a wonderful man. He didn't deserve anything like this to happen to him." She was surrounded by about twenty Romanian

Celebraholic ORGASM MOMENTS—
THE GOOD, THE BAD, AND THE UGLY

The entire O.J. trial, from the White Bronco Chase to Dominick Dunne's open mouth at the verdict.

guys, all of whom were crying and using their aprons as handkerchiefs.

"The rap star was driving with a suspended license, stemming from an earlier incident a year ago . . ."

At that point, Danny got up and said, "I can't watch any more of this." Over his shoulder, he called, "Your boyfriend's a dickhead, Dinah."

"At least I've got one, asshole," she screamed—into my ear, thank you very much.

"Look," she said. "We've got to talk."

"Well, I would say so, Dinah."

"I can't tell you anything over the phone. Can you meet me for lunch tomorrow?"

I thought for a moment. "I have therapy tomorrow."

"Oh, well, excuse me if I thought my potential incarceration might mean more to you than your irreparably damaged psyche."

"I'll postpone," I said.

"Okay. And also, don't call me at home, 'cause I won't pick up. Lylo says we need to stay out of sight and off the phone."

"Fine."

"And also, I need a favor."

"Whatever. Just tell me that Lylo was driving . . ."

"*Not over the phone,*" she hissed, and hung up.

The moment Dinah's voice had faded in my bruised and battered ear, the words "Duluth" and "real theater" flashed through my consciousness, and I went to find Danny. I knocked on his door but heard no invitation to come in.

"Danny?" I knocked again. "Danny?"

Then came the muffled response: "I think I'd like to be alone, thanks."

"Are you okay?"

"Sure."

Fact!

Sometimes you just have to quietly withdraw from the room and let the star sob until the scene fades out.

So I did.

You know how it is with old friends. As much as you know they're going to hell in a handbasket, you're still a little surprised when the collect call comes from Hades. Even when I woke up the next morning, I wasn't fully aware that Dinah had, finally, Really and Truly Fucked Up.

The first clue came from Danny, who tossed me the newspaper with a snarled "Prince Charming made the front page." And he had—in every paper. As far as the tabs were concerned, Lylo *was* the morning news. "RAP HIT AND RUN!" howled one. "BUBBLE BOY BLOWS IT!" screamed another, taking a slightly different editorial stance. He even made it on to page eight of the metro section of the classier broadsheets.

As I read the papers on the subway to work, I decided one thing: This was not a thing that could have happened to just anyone. It happened to Lylo because he is a living, breathing example of why stupid white people should not have all the money that they have. If Lylo had been your average stupid drunk needing to get home from the Lower East Side at four in the morning, he would have had to hail a cab, poor Mr. Rosen would still be alive, and that would have been the end of that.

When I got to work, I had three e-mails about Lylo. Already,

already, there were jokes, the same tasteless haw-haws that crop up like fungus after any tragedy.

Did you hear about the new Lylo Wingate action doll? Assault and battery not included.

What's the new special at Rosen's Delicatessen? Buster on flatbread.

But I really started to get a sense of just how weird this whole thing would get when I went to a meeting and found everyone talking about Lylo's little hit-and-run, which some people were calling "the accident" and others "the murder." At our staff meeting, Felice said she was really, really sorry, but Lylo should be locked up for good right away, without any kind of trial or anything, because this was the sort of thing where his daddy's money was just so likely to get him off. A woman from marketing pointed out the constitutional drawbacks of such a scheme, and the debate began.

Meanwhile, I sat completely still and realized that I was on the verge of a celebraholic fantasy of almost erotic proportions.

Picture it: You're in a room full of people, all heatedly discussing the story of the moment—and you are close friends with one of the parties involved. You know more about it than anyone there, and if you choose to speak, you enter a state that is, well . . . tantalizingly close to actual celebrityhood.

It's all right, take a little break, put a cold cloth on your forehead, or do whatever you have to do.

Celebraholic **ORGASM MOMENTS— THE GOOD, THE BAD, AND THE UGLY**

Kim Basinger's rambling rant in the weird one-armed dress at the Oscars.

For a moment, I fantasized. I envisioned myself describing the details of Dinah's frantic call. Repeating the precise words (all five of them) I had exchanged with Lylo Wingate. Correcting the errors I heard. (Felice was under the impression that Lylo's father was in plastics. It was enough to make the lip curl with scorn.) I could have had everyone in that room at my feet.

All I had to do was open my mouth.

And yet . . . I pulled myself back from the brink. Because for the first time in my life, this was really happening. To someone I knew. At the very least, Dinah was a witness. Which made me the friend of a witness. And while I wasn't sure what that meant, I did know I couldn't go shooting my mouth off.

> JUDGE: Didn't you tell Felice Brenner that you thought the defendant was a big fat asshole?
> ME: Well, yes, your honor.
> JUDGE: Bailiff, take Mr. Wingate to the electric chair.

I didn't really want Lylo getting 4,000 volts because he was a big fat asshole. (I mean, imagine where this kind of social policy might lead us.) And no matter how I looked at it, there was no way to say anything without mentioning Dinah.

> ME: Well, it was a dark street, it was hard to see the old man.

Celebraholic ORGASM MOMENTS—
THE GOOD, THE BAD, AND THE UGLY

Liz marries Larry Fortensky.

FELICE: How do you know?

ME: My friend told me.

FELICE: And how does she know?

ME: Oops.

But then Marcia Wagstaff from production said, "I heard on the radio they're not sure that the Wingate kid was driving the car."

As this news was greeted by a prolonged series of "ooohs," I felt a distinct chill down my spine.

"Who else would be driving it?" I asked.

"Some people say it might be that chick he was with."

It took me a moment to recover. Then I snapped, "Some people, as in Lylo's lawyers?"

"And others," said Marcia stubbornly.

"Why would some rich brat hand over the car keys to someone else?"

"Because he was drunk," said Marcia triumphantly. "Because he knew he was in no condition to drive."

Ook.

At that point, Felice rattled her papers impatiently and suggested we get started because she couldn't afford to be wasting this kind of time. We ran through the business of the day in about five minutes flat, and as we filed out, Marcia shot me a nasty look and said, "I just hope they get *whoever* killed that poor old man."

I managed to keep it together until I was back in my office and

Celebraholic ORGASM MOMENTS—
THE GOOD, THE BAD, AND THE UGLY

Cher wears her first Bob Mackie to the Oscars.

then proceeded to collapse in a state of total crack-up anxiety. *"Some say it might be that chick." "I hope they get whoever killed that poor old man."* It was starting. The spin was starting. Dinah, my poor helpless Dinah, was in the clutches of public opinion. The drama-hungry masses already had their eye on her as the possible driver—something that was not going to escape the attention of Lylo's lawyers.

The public likes a plot twist, and Dinah would be that plot twist, unless she got her act together pronto. I hoped to God she was doing something to protect herself. But if she wasn't, then I had a few suggestions. Squeal before you are dealt, that was my motto.

Thank God we were having lunch. I would demand to know the full truth, and then we could decide what Dinah should do next. Thank God, I thought, she has friends like me to confide in.

"I can't tell you anything."

That's the first thing Dinah told me, five seconds after she sidled into the diner, scooting out through the crowds, looking . . . well, exactly like someone who wants to be noticed.

She sat down, fingers poised on dark glasses, swiveling left and right to catch unsuspecting peepers.

"Calm down," I said.

"Everyone's looking at me."

"Because they think you are insane."

Celebraholic **ORGASM MOMENTS—**
THE GOOD, THE BAD, AND THE UGLY

Pee Wee Herman is caught playing with himself in a porn theater.

"They're all reading newspapers."

"People do that at lunchtime." Dinah rarely ate lunch, so how would she know?

"They're reading about the unidentified companion and thinking 'Isn't that her over there?' "

The waiter appeared and asked if we wanted coffee. I said, "She'll have coffee—*decaf.* I'll have regular."

"Don't say my name," Dinah whispered when he had gone. "I don't want anyone hearing my name."

"You're Thumper from now on."

"And I mean it. I can't tell you anything. I mean, that guy right over there could be from the *Enquirer.*"

"Look, you don't have to talk . . ." I took a pen out of my bag and placed a paper napkin between us.

Dinah shook her head. "Nothing on paper, for fuck's sake."

"It's not paper, it's a napkin. I'll throw it away, I promise."

Shielding the napkin with my hand, I wrote. *"TV what % tru?"*

Dinah shrugged. Then she grabbed the napkin and scribbled furiously. The waiter brought our coffee, and she was still writing. Finally, when he had left, she turned it around for me to see.

"Have no idea and will not answer. Everyone say different things, so how fuck do I know?"

I wrote, *"U in car?"*

Dinah gave a minuscule nod.

"L in car?"

Dinah grabbed the pen out off my hand and scrawled, *"DON'T SAY HIS NAME!"*

I wrote back, *"DID NOT SAY NAME! Was BLANK in CAR?"* (I wanted to write Big Fat Asshole, but the napkin wasn't big enough.)

Dinah's head moved forward, then off to the sides, threatened to do a 360, but approximated something like a nod.

"Who was dri—"

Dinah ripped the napkin off the table, shredded it, and sank the remains in her coffee.

I stared at her for a very long moment. I stuck by my theory that a spoiled brat like Lylo would never hand his car keys over to someone else. On the other hand, Dinah was a not unforceful personality. If she thought Lylo was too blotto to drive—which obviously he had been—would she have taken over the wheel?

I said in a low voice, "How much do you like this guy?"

"More than I should."

"Considering . . ."

"Considering that he's an asshole." A chair scraped as someone got up from a nearby table, and Dinah jumped.

"Take it easy."

"I'm feeling really paranoid." She inhaled sharply. "I need a favor."

"Anything . . ."

"I have to stay with you."

. . . but that.

"What do you mean?" Would I be harboring a fugitive? How exciting. Punishable by law, but exciting.

"Your place. I have to live there for a little while." She covered her mouth with her hand and mumbled, "The press is going to pounce any minute."

"But we don't have any room." I said stupidly. "I mean, there's Danny's room and mine and . . ." (You know, because occupancy is supposed to count for something. It's a common mistake. The Indians made it with the Pilgrims, and so on.)

She started rocking back and forth. "Oh, God, I can't handle this."

"Calm down." I pushed a glass of water toward her.

"This is not happening. Oh, God."

People were beginning to stare.

"You're just . . ."

"I'm freaking out."

"You're freaking out, that's all. Breathe."

"I can't breathe."

"No, you can. You just . . . inhale. Like this." I showed her.

Fixing her eyes on me, Dinah imitated my rhythm until her breathing slowed to normal. Then she took a sip of water and whispered, "The thing is, my roommate's still out of town. Having the place empty is giving me the creeps."

"I understand." And I did. Dinah knew her celebrity history. Cut off from Lylo, about to be hounded by the press, Dinah was deep into what I call Marilyn Monroe syndrome. It was just like Bridget Dowl in *The Dead Kitten*. Fuzzy Winterspoon in *A Little Knowledge*. Right now, Dinah saw herself as the Woman Who Knew Too Much—who inevitably became the Woman Who Had a Fatal Accident.

I paid the check, and we got out of there. Once on the street I said, "You need a lawyer."

"I'm not charged with anything."

"Yes, and we want it to stay that way."

"I don't have money for a lawyer."

I almost screamed, "Lylo has money for ten lawyers," before I remembered her paranoia about names. "Yes, but someone else does."

But Dinah already had her sunglasses on and was ready to make her escape. "I'll bring my stuff over tomorrow," she said.

 *Celebraholic* **ORGASM MOMENTS—**
THE GOOD, THE BAD, AND THE UGLY

The Monicagate transcripts are released on the Web.

"Fine." Danny will kill me, but fine. Anything for you, Dinah, you're a joy to be around.

And then she was gone. And I hadn't warned her about her potential as a fall gal.

And I had agreed to let her stay in my house.

And I was fucking late for my therapy appointment.

I rushed downtown. What with everything that was going on, I was actually very impatient to talk with Doris. I needed to put things in perspective. Was I doing the right thing? The moral thing? What if Dinah really had been at the wheel? Did her involvement not bother me because she was my friend—or was there another reason? Murderers have a certain cachet in our society. We like to watch them, and a lot of them like to be watched. Think about the Claus von Bulow case. Look at Jack the Ripper—over a century and still going strong.

Could it be? Was murder merely a symptom of celebraholism?

I knew something was wrong the minute I walked into Doris's apartment. As I sat down, I noticed that she was looking distinctly sheepish. She even shooed the cats away from my legs.

Sitting down, she said, "I have something to tell you."

"Okay."

"It's something upsetting."

"All right."

She waited. "Are you prepared?"

Celebraholic **ORGASM MOMENTS—**
THE GOOD, THE BAD, AND THE UGLY

Diana's wedding; Diana's divorce; Diana's funeral.

"I'm prepared, Doris. I'm sitting down and everything."

"I'm not a psychotherapist."

"I guessed that."

"I'm not even a social worker."

I nodded.

Doris the Hack Quack said, "God, you're going to be seriously pissed at me."

She looked pathetic. I said, "I won't."

"The thing is . . . actually, I'm more of an artist."

"Great."

"An actress . . ."

"Not great. Oh, Doris . . ."

"I'm sorry," she wailed. Sniffing, she reached for the box of Kleenex. "It's just that I feel intimidated, performing in front of crowds, so I got this idea that I could perform for individuals in a comfortable setting—you know, a place I felt safe—by doing this. I used to play a homeless woman."

"Doris, I feel betrayed."

"I know," she said miserably. "I know. Look, I'm going to make it up to you."

"You're going to let me sue you for a million dollars?"

Her eyes bulged as if I had punched her in the stomach. And for a moment, I wanted to, but then she looked so desolate, it was hard not to feel sorry for her.

She went to her desk and got out an envelope. "Here, this is your money. In cash."

I opened the envelope, and, yes, I counted.

"If it means anything," Doris said, "I can totally understand how you feel about being famous."

"Understand? You're way more desperate than I am."

"Do you want drugs?"

"From you? No."

"I'm supposed to prescribe drugs if treatment looks unsuccessful."

"Well, I'd say this was pretty unsuccessful."

"Look, let me at least give you this." She got a book down from the shelf. "This book completely changed my life."

I glanced at the cover. *Entitled! Ten Steps to Successful Self-Expression.*

"It's all about externalizing your needs and desires," explained Doris.

"Is that legal?"

"I really think you should read it."

I looked at the author photo of Dwayne Lophat. "I know him."

"Oh, he's everywhere. He's widely respected."

"He's widely exposed." I had a look at the number of residences Dwayne listed under his author bio. "And well compensated for his loss of privacy."

"He's a genius," said Doris reverently. "Take the book. Really. I want you to have it. It's my way of saying I'm sorry."

"It's a very meaningful gesture, Doris."

"Really?"

"No."

Exhausted, I made my dismal journey home and tried to assess. If asked to sum up my life in one word, would it be . . .

    a. Bad
    b. Rotten
    c. Worse

My friend was a possible felon, my shrink a definite fake, and my roommate a future taxpayer in Duluth. Which made me . . . ? A frustrated, failing-in-recovery celebraholic going downhill fast.

And once I told Danny the good news about our new roomie, I would probably be a frustrated, failing-in-recovery celebraholic in traction.

Or, if my luck held, Danny would just be so pissed off he would pack his bags and leave for Duluth there and then.

So, all in all, I was in a state of deep, deep depression when I got home. If life was going to suck this much, there didn't seem much point in having one. Throwing myself onto the couch, I picked up the remote and was about to take that great leap off the wagon when it happened . . .

Another sign.

No magic TV this time. This time it was the phone. I was in such a rotten mood, I almost didn't pick up when it rang. But something, some higher power, prodded me, and I picked up just before the machine went on.

A nice, deep voice asked if Danny was home.

Bored, thinking it was another of Danny's suitors, I said, "He's home if you're Magalda Bernadin."

"Well, I work for Ms. Bernadin."

It's funny how the heart can beat faster for two completely different reasons: joy and sheer panic. On one side of the major aorta: Success, hurrah! On the other side: Off-Broadway, piss, sucky, boo.

"Are you calling about a job?"

"In a way," he said amiably. My heart leapt. "But not the one he

Celebraholic **ORGASM MOMENTS—**
THE GOOD, THE BAD, AND THE UGLY

Farrah Fawcett's meltdown on Letterman.

wanted." And sank. "Listen, I think your friend is very special. He has a really rare quality." (Yeah, gorgeous and cheap.) "But we're not interested in him for Cyrano. Not because he isn't talented, it's just . . . he's a guy."

"And Cyrano is what, a marsupial?"

"He's a woman. In this production. We're doing a lesbian interpretation where Cyrano is in love with Roxanne, but because she's a woman, she has to use Christian as a beard. Sorry, I guess he misread the ad."

"I guess so." The story of Danny's life.

"We are interested in him for the part of Christian. But I got the impression he wasn't keen on the idea."

"Danny's a very good actor," I said. "He can give out all kinds of impressions."

"Does that mean he might be interested in auditioning again?"

"You betcha." Danny in an off-Broadway lesbian interpretation of *Cyrano* may not have been Danny in *Lethal Weapon V*, but it was a hell of a lot better than Danny in Duluth.

The caller, whose name was Julian Foster, gave me the who, what, where, and when of the audition. Then, after a pause, he asked, "Is Danny there?" I said no, but I would be only too happy to pass on messages.

"Tell me, does he ever answer the phone on his own?"

"Not too often," I said.

"Is someone in particular calling him these days?"

Celebraholic **ORGASM MOMENTS—**
THE GOOD, THE BAD, AND THE UGLY

Julia Roberts marries Lyle Lovett.

"Lots of people with sore dialing fingers."

"Shy?"

"Headshy."

"If I called back sometime, you think you'd let him answer?"

"I'm just Danny's business advisor."

"So you never interfere with his love life?"

"Absolutely not," I said silkily, and we hung up.

Euphoria! Danny was loved! Danny was saved! Danny would do Christian in New York, forget he had ever heard of Duluth, and we would all live happily ever after.

Unless . . .

Unless . . . Danny refused to audition for Christian, refused to call Julian back, and felt even more strongly about the charms of Duluth after finding Dinah in situ.

I was having a vision of Danny ramming a toothbrush up Dinah's nose when I decided these were desperate times, requiring desperate measures, and did what I had been wanting to do since I walked through the door.

I turned on the television.

So, there.

Guess what the big story was?

Following yet another story on the perils of breast implants (accompanied by all those highly necessary visuals) the newscaster announced that they had just received word that Lylo Wingate had been spotted leaving his lawyer's offices. A tired-looking Asian-American woman in a trench coat appeared on screen.

The newscaster coughed importantly. "Jessica, what can you tell us?"

The woman's eyebrows shot up, like her preferred answer would be, "That you're a ding dong," but she got herself together and told us that Lylo Wingate had been seen leaving the offices of Pierce, Goldblum, and Smith just *minutes* ago. "We spoke to him there."

Cut to a scene of frantic reporters leaping around Lylo, who halted in mid-stumble to avoid collision with a microphone.

"Lylo! Lylo! Did you . . ."

"Lylo, are you . . . ?"

"Lylo!" We saw Jessica shoot forward. "Lylo, did you know Buster Rosen? Did you know what kind of man he was?"

Cornered by Jessica, Lylo looked confused. Dark glasses can hide a lot, but stupidity shines through every time.

"What?"

"How do you feel, knowing you may be responsible for the death of such a wonderful man as Buster Rosen?"

"Uh . . . who?"

And I'm sure Lylo would have said more, but at that moment, the forces of Pierce, Goldblum, and Smith grabbed their gabby client and hustled him off to the nearest cab.

Jessica turned solemnly back to Dan. "So, you see Dan, this terrible tragedy has become even more senseless."

Dan shook his head. "He didn't even know."

"That's right, Dan. We asked what he felt about Buster Rosen, and all Lylo Wingate had to say was 'Uh . . . who.' "

Well, what can I say? I was completely disgusted. What kind of world did we live in where someone like Lylo Wingate could go from low-level pseudo celeb to huge star just by running someone over?

And once Lylo became a huge—albeit loathed—star, it was only a matter of time before Dinah became a huge star, too.

I brooded. There was something about this whole situation with Dinah that disturbed me. Something elusive, something I could not put a name to . . .

Okay, so I could put a name to it.

It was envy.

Ugly, sticky envy.

And before you accuse me of going off the deep end, let me explain.

Everything interesting was happening to someone else.

As usual.

Danny was desired. Dinah was about to hit the big time in celebrity killer circles. And not a fucking thing was happening for me.

For a moment, I seethed, imagining the headlines, the magazine covers, the book deals, the *Barbara Walters* interview.

Oh, I could just see it now.

> <u>BARBARA:</u> And did you feel terrible? When you learned what had happened to Buster Rosen?
>
> <u>DINAH:</u> Oh, yes, very much so.
>
> <u>BARBARA:</u> It must have been very hard, your boyfriend is driving, you're in the car . . .
>
> <u>DINAH:</u> (Wipes away a tear) I don't like to think about it.
>
> <u>BARBARA:</u> But still, you have had strong support from your friends. Can you tell us something about them?
>
> <u>DINAH:</u> Friends? What friends?

Facing misery so soon after euphoria is hard—the drop in altitude can leave you feeling queasy. Willing myself to look away from the television, I rummaged around in my bag for one of the mags I had bought that morning. And as I did, I found the book

Celebraholic **ORGASM MOMENTS—**
THE GOOD, THE BAD, AND THE UGLY

Michael Jackson is charged with molesting small children; he marries Lisa Marie Presley shortly thereafter.

Doris had so thoughtfully given me at the end of our session, *Entitled! Ten Steps to Successful Self-Expression.*

I held the loathsome thing between two fingers, trying not to breathe in. I hadn't dared dump it before I was a safe distance away from Doris's apartment, so somehow it found its way home with me. Maybe it was desperation, maybe curiosity, maybe that nameless impulse that got Pandora into a world of trouble, but I actually cracked the cover of the wretched book.

We'll use the term "book" lightly. This thing was a compilation of lists, interspersed with a few meditations with the relative depth of a fortune cookie. In fact, the one stand-out feature of this book was that it contained the first self-test I have ever successfully resisted taking. There was nothing, absolutely nothing, to help the recovering celebraholic—or anyone else, for that matter.

I turned the thing over and sneered at its creator. Dwayne Lophat, owner of multiple dwellings and stacks of cars. A bottom-dweller, feeding off the neuroses of others. You fraud, I thought. You self-satisfied fraud. You rich, multiple-dwelling–owning, Lexus-leasing fraud . . .

Hold on. Wait a minute.

I flipped to the author's credits again. The good doctor had written several of these pearls—nay, strands—of wisdom, which was why the good doctor was such a wealthy man.

Perhaps I was looking at this the wrong way. Maybe Dwayne Lophat had spoken the truth.

 *Celebraholic* **ORGASM MOMENTS— THE GOOD, THE BAD, AND THE UGLY**

Woody Allen announces to the world: "The heart wants what it wants."

I had another look at *Entitled! Ten Steps to Successful Self-Expression.*

Dwayne wasn't completely stupid. After four bestsellers, the man had some clue as to what the people want. He had lists. A lot of them. Quick zippy little road maps to your own personal Nirvana. There was an Entitled Diet (Did I eat lots of high-fiber foods and drink eight glasses of water a day? And spend hours on the toilet? Thank you, no.). The Entitled Exercise Program (Twenty minutes of yoga every day.). The Entitled Mantra ("I am Myself.").

And of course, the Three Principles of Entitlement:

"Principle Number One: You are the center of your own universe.

"Principle Number Two: Every act must move you forward in a material or spiritual sense.

"Principle Number Three: You can make no one else happy if you yourself are not happy. Therefore, your chief goal in life is to make yourself happy."

I threw the book across the room. This was exactly the kind of reasoning that made people like me disappointed when we were not megastars worshipped by millions. (If you don't worship yourself, Dwayne would argue, how can you expect others to worship you?)

Well, Dwayne, people should not have to be megastars.

They should be allowed to be . . .

Schlubs, losers, nonentities.

 *Celebraholic* **ORGASM MOMENTS—**
THE GOOD, THE BAD, AND THE UGLY

Frank Gifford gropes a stewardess, as his wife, Kathie Lee, is accused of running sweatshops.

No, no, that was Dwayne-speak.

They should be allowed to be . . .

Not stars.

Supporting cast.

Bit Players.

Great Bit Players.

Hmm . . .

If someone named Dwayne Lophat, whose medical degree was written on a sanitary napkin, could help millions of people, so could I. And so I would. With my very own self-help book. A book geared to people like myself. People who needed the help I had needed, help adjusting to the fact that they will never ever be famous.

That they are, in fact, Bit Players.

No, no, *Great* Bit Players.

And just what was a Great Bit Player?

What could we do, we people who could not be famous but for whom real life would always lack a certain undefinable something? What would reconcile us to our own obscurity yet allow us to enjoy comfortable proximity to the rich and secure? As I thought and pondered, pondered and thought, a vision came to my head. A sort of mystical, existential vision, the sort that probably came to Dwayne Lophat right before he cashed that million-dollar advance.

I saw a scene from *All About Eve*. It came in hazy at first, but

Celebraholic **ORGASM MOMENTS—**
THE GOOD, THE BAD, AND THE UGLY

Meg dumps Dennis; does Russell (not necessarily in that order).

my Higher Power adjusted the contrast, and soon the whole thing was coming in clear as day. An early scene. Bette Davis was sitting in her dressing room, saying witty, acidic sorts of things, and brushing her hair in a way that hinted she needed a serious drink.

But Bette Davis wasn't the only one in the vision.

Somewhere in the background, picking up discarded costumes, rolling her eyes, running Margo's bath, keeping it all together was . . .

Thelma Ritter.

An intake of breath at the ecstasy of the vision. Thelma Ritter—the original Great Bit Player. And then there was Eve Arden in *Mildred Pierce*. Toto in *The Wizard of Oz* . . .

The Great Bit Player. The Professionally Marginal, the Gloriously Overlooked. The person who always knew what was going on even when the heroine was completely clueless. The person who listened endlessly to the star's troubles—then let her have it square between the eyes when she needed to hear the truth about that rotten, lousy, no-good cad. The person you always noticed, even though they stood in the background, behind the principles. The person who didn't talk as much as some of the others but who had all the best lines.

And so the Great Bit Player was born.

Doris the Hack Quack was right. Dwayne had made me feel much better.

*C*HAPTER NINE

THE PERILS AND PAINS OF ARTISTIC INTEGRITY
(NOT MINE)

*N*ow, **you** might think that I woke up the next morning and said, "Boy, that was a dumb idea."

But you'd be wrong.

Despite the enormity of the undertaking, despite the fact that becoming a Great Bit Player would require more drive, will, and energy than I had ever even thought of possessing in my lifetime, I knew I had to forge ahead.

I had to forge ahead for all those people who were convinced their lives were shit because they weren't celebrities.

Also, I had to forge ahead for Danny and Dinah. Both of whom desperately needed taking in hand if they were to avoid winding up in, respectively, Duluth and jail.

It is the primary directive of the Great Bit Player to save the star. Great Bit Players clean up messes, and since there was quite enough mess around, it was time to get busy.

But how to start?

I lay in bed and brooded.

And with the bright clear vision of the newly enlightened, I saw the truth.

By avoiding the instruments of celebrity news, I had deprived myself of an invaluable resource. If I was going to help Dinah and Danny, I needed all the information I could get.

So—go forth and seek enlightenment.

In a state of trembling anticipation, I went out and withdrew thirty dollars from my bank account. Then I proceeded to the newsstand. And at this newsstand, I purchased . . .

Nine glossies.

Five supers (supermarket tabloids).

Four dailies.

A *TV Guide* and two packs of gum.

Then I went home and . . .

WARNING: THE FOLLOWING CONTAINS HIGHLY EXPLICIT AND PROVOCA-
TIVE CONTENT AND SHOULD NOT BE READ BY THOSE IN THE EARLY STAGES OF
RECOVERY, AS IT COULD LEAD TO RELAPSE.

What can I say?

What words can possibly describe the feeling?

For a long time, I just sat, holding my newly acquired stash in
my arms. The weight of them, all those pages, all those stories, all
those pictures, there in my arms, waiting to be opened and plun-
dered. I leaned down and inhaled the bitter scent of newsprint,
the heady stench of perfume samples, and nearly blacked out.

Where to begin, where to begin? A slim, yet impudent super?
The fat, sleek glossies? For a second, I lingered over the dailies,
up-to-the-minute, the very latest news, but somehow, somehow,
after all these weeks of deprivation, not enough, not nearly
enough. I needed substance, perspective, the bigger picture.

I reached for the fattest glossy and pulled it from the pile. Oh,
the floppy heft of an unopened magazine, the delicate flicker of
the pages. I let my fingers close on the sharp corner of the cover,
then hesitated. Was this wise? There was every chance that I was at
risk for overdose. Suffering the debilitating effects of cold turkey,
could I handle full-tilt glossy?

There was only one way to find out.

Flinging the first page aside, I was assaulted, transported, cata-
pulted into the cheapest glimpse of heaven the world has ever
known. So much color. The sight of it, the bold, bright headlines,
the vicious call-outs, the shocking photos, amazing true stories,
confidential tales, quotes of the week, the bubble heads (contest!

movies! tunes!) a blast of image and type, those tinted boxes where they hide the juiciest morsels, tidbits you have to suck like marrow from the bone.

And those faces, all those dear, dear, beloved faces. The past, present, and future famous. They were still there; they'd never left. The actors, the directors, the fabulously rich, the fashion designers, and the royals. The stray member of the literati, the soap stars looking for exposure, the old guard, the up-and-coming. They flew by in candid shots, posed shots, couples, singles, pairs, friends who might be lovers, "lovers" who might be friends. In a matter of a hundred pages, I could find out who was marrying, divorcing, homemaking, having babies, snow-boarding, going red, back to blonde, working, fucking, in rehab, out of rehab, and should be in rehab.

There it was, every bit of them, their worst dates, their greatest dresses, their ugliest hair, their bad behavior and good works, fabulous marriages and even better affairs.

Even now, I can't tell you how much time passed. All I can tell you is that slowly I became aware of a sensation of deep well-being. A profound sense of peace. A feeling that all was right with the world, and, even more important, all was right with me.

But! I had to remember that I had a mission. Gone were the days of mindless consumption. This was *research*. I had to find out what, exactly, was going on in the Lylo Wingate case. I reached for the nearest daily, stopped when I got to the first mention of Lylo, then just kept going.

GREAT BIT PLAYERS *Hollywood* HALL OF FAME

Birdie Coonan (Thelma Ritter) in All About Eve

This is what I learned:

Lylo was making a big splash in the letters section of the tabs. Not only did he get a lot of news coverage, he was now getting op-ed space and letters. One sincere citizen had this to say:

If the recent death of Buster Rosen proves anything, it is that our let-it-all-hang-out, no-consequences society has raised (if that's the word I want!) a bunch of thugs who have no respect whatsoever for human life.
                                                                    P. Hewitt. Far Rockaway

It's funny how these things go. It's the nature of celebrity—certain people, certain events strike a chord. They don't just happen; they take on some whacked-out universal significance. Who they are, what they did, illustrates people's darkest fears, their brightest dreams . . . their most cherished prejudices.

And that's what happened with Lylo. With two monosyllables, Lylo had propelled himself into national notoriety. It was the "Uh . . . who?" heard round the world. Those two words made it clear that Lylo was one of those people who only acknowledged the existence of, say, thirty other people on the planet. Buster Rosen had not been one of those thirty people. Millions of people realized that they too were unknown to Lylo Wingate, and therefore, in his eyes, of no consequence. Therefore, judging by what had happened to Mr. Rosen, they too could be run down like a dog.

And if Lylo didn't know who Buster Rosen was, the media made damn sure that everyone else did.

In life, Buster Rosen was a perfectly nice man, but in death, a star was born. So, who was Buster Rosen, you ask, other than the beneficiary of a slow news week? Well, Buster Rosen owned a delicatessen on the Lower East Side. You may have heard of it, Rosen's Delicatessen, a plucky survivor of gentrification, defying all nutritional wisdom to serve overstuffed sandwiches with schmaltz on the table and a decent pickle on your plate. Fine. Only it didn't stop there. Buster Rosen, it turns out, also took an interest in community affairs. He donated sandwiches to a local shelter, he let the teachers and the cop on the beat eat for free. And he had a scholarship fund, paid for with corned beef and chopped liver, to send city kids to summer camp. That's right, Dinah and Lylo had not killed just any eighty-seven-year-old man; they had killed a saint.

This was not lost on our local political luminaries, who were lining up to bravely stifle the tears over the loss of this good simple man who, even in his eighties, continued to work behind the counter. Pols were fighting tooth and nail to see who could come up with the earliest trial date—the most popular one being "yesterday."

It wasn't lost on the TV pundits either, who repeated, "A quiet man, a working man—a man who gave so much of himself to the city he loved so well." Quickly switch to pictures of Lylo looking rich and stupid. The message was clear: karmically speaking, this was a bad deal for New York.

All you had to do was tune in and you could find someone, somewhere, eulogizing Buster Rosen. Segments based on what I call the Plink Plink Theory. They always start with a slow fade to a shot of the individual accompanied by a few *plink plink* piano notes to evoke sorrow. Anything the person ever did in his or her life is a triumphant achievement or a hard-won victory or a heart-breaking setback. There are a lot of interviews with tearful friends and family members. "He was the most . . ." "The finest . . ." "A great . . ." "A wonderful . . ." The script always includes the line "Many people don't realize how difficult it is to . . ." (be extremely rich, have plastic surgery, put on deodorant).

There was another thing I learned that morning.

Dinah was no longer the "companion."

Now she was Fatal Attraction, Girl on Killer Joy Ride, and Date of Death.

Sometimes, she was even Dinah Sharlip. Which wasn't good. The press was on to her now, sniffing, eager, and anxious. Because there were, as every paper and news report reminded me, still questions about who had been at the wheel on the night Buster Rosen was killed.

Having finished my research, I tenderly set aside the last of the glossies. Then, taking a cue from Danny's twelve steps, I made a list of my goals as a Great Bit Player. (This is something you will need to do when you reach this step, so pay attention.)

My list read as follows:

1. Keep Dinah out of jail.
2. Help Danny become famous.
3. Write a bestselling book.
4. Get a life.

Any doubt I might have had about the need to become a Great Bit Player disappeared with Dinah's arrival. She showed up that night with more luggage than was lost on the *Titanic*. Danny was working the dinner shift at Fido's, so I hid her stuff in my room (it would have been easier to pack the room in her bags) until we broke the happy news.

GREAT BIT PLAYERS *Hollywood* HALL OF FAME

Ida Corwin (Eve Arden) in Mildred Pierce

Dinah had a look around the place and heaved a nostalgic sigh. "Jesus, I can't believe you live in such a dump."

The soul of graciousness, that was our Dinah.

"The only good thing is I don't think the press will clue in to where I am. They know who I am now."

She said it casually, but I heard the tremor in her voice.

Determined to begin her salvation, I sat down and said, "I know you don't want to tell me what happened . . ."

"That's right."

"Because of the trial."

"Mm-hmm . . ."

"Okay, but just say yes or no."

"No."

"No, you didn't do it."

"No."

"You did do it."

"No."

"You're not going to tell me either way."

"Yes."

And she turned on the television and refused to speak to me for the rest of the evening.

Dinah's silence left me to think one of three things: She was having paranoid visions of Kennedys crawling into her bedroom and forcing a thousand pills down her throat. Or . . .

She wasn't guilty, but she was planning to say that she was,

GREAT BIT PLAYERS *Hollywood* HALL OF FAME

Asta in The Thin Man

because she loved (pause here for gagging sound) Lylo, and thought this would bind him to her forever. Or . . .

Or . . .

The truth was something I didn't want to hear.

This was my least favorite of the three theories.

Dinah was asleep in my room when Danny came home, but he awoke the next morning to find her at his breakfast table. I would call his reaction mixed: he was torn between jumping out a window and throttling her. I figured as long as he remained torn between murder and self-destruction, she could stay.

Over cornflakes, I gave him the news that Magalda Bernadin wanted him to audition for the part of Christian. His reaction to this news was a little more . . . vehement. Even for Magalda Bernadin, he refused to even think of playing Christian. Wouldn't call Julian back, wouldn't even discuss the matter.

I admit it, I was bewildered. I wondered if he had gone completely off the deep end. Maybe he was turning into Garbo—only without the success, riches, and fame.

As politely as I could, with as much respect for artistic integrity as I could muster, I argued. Danny argued back. For fifteen minutes, artistic integrity did battle with rank greed and ambition. At which point, Dinah looked up and gave Danny a long and thoughtful stare.

"You know, Danny, you're a major wuss."

Danny said, "Sorry?" It's funny. Outside of a Steve McQueen movie, I wouldn't have thought a spoon could look like a murder weapon.

"Well, like this audition for . . ." Her hand swung dismissively in the air.

"Christian," I said helpfully, moving a fair distance from the spoon.

"Right. Why don't you go for it?"

"It's a pretty-boy part," said Danny.

"And you're not pretty."

"It's just not much of a dramatic challenge."

"Uh-huh. You know what I think? I think you set these ridiculous artistic standards for yourself, so you never have to deal with actually coming through for the audience. You don't quite come across as Peer Gump—"

"Gynt."

"Oh, *yeah.*" Dinah crossed her eyes. "And then you just say, well, I tried something really hard and failed, and that's a lot better than failing at some lousy soap."

"Dinah, is there a reason we don't see more of you?"

"Come to think of it, you do the exact same thing in your personal life. Is there any more banana?"

That afternoon, I added a fifth goal to my Great Bit Player Game Plan.

5. Get Danny and Dinah to live in close proximity for at least a month without one killing the other.

Dinah might have won the first round, but Danny quickly figured out that one way to drive Dinah crazy was to say nasty things about Lylo. Home and hearth now had an ambience similar to that of Beirut.

But then, no one had much good to say about Lylo. A grand jury had dispatched him for trial with record speed. The hate mail to the papers was showing no sign of letting up. Even the writers at Bickerstaff had removed their heads from the customary spot—set snugly between their butt cheeks—and taken notice

For example, one bright, sunny morning, Hank Laufler arrived, clutching his newest submissions. The first words out of his mouth were: "Wasn't that awful what that Wingate kid said?"

I wanted to say, What do you expect? Everything he says is awful. Hank said, "I mean, you'd think with the money and everything, he'd have lawyers who could help him, polish him up a little. He must be a rotten human being."

"Some people are unpolishable, Hank," I said. "Can I have the manuscript?" He handed it to me. "This is more or less what we wanted?" I asked hopefully.

Hank's left eye began to blink independently of his right one. "Well . . ."

Well, Hank? I ask for reassurance? I ask for a hassle-free day, and you give me "Well"?

"Do you want to talk it through, Hank?"

"I thought, maybe . . . see what you think."

"Sure, Hank. Give me your ideas." The man was sick, you had to be gentle. Hear him through, then tell him it stinks. In the nicest way possible, of course.

"I thought we could . . . well . . . not have her get married."

"Not have Camelia marry Raymond?"

"Right."

"Have Camelia marry Eldred." Straws, I was clutching at straws.

"No." Hank, too, was being gentle. I appreciated that. "Have her marry no one."

"No one."

He took my echo for agreement. "That's right. Have her free. Independent. Needing no man for fulfillment."

"Hank, even Gloria Steinem gets laid."

He looked hurt. "Camelia's not Gloria Steinem."

No, of course she isn't. She's your mother. Your virgin mother who shall remain pure and deliver the Infant Hank into this evil old world in a way that does not interfere with her hymen.

"Hank."

"Yes?" Big hopeful eyes.

"Here's what people want . . ."

"Yes?"

"Fantasy. Your job . . ."

"Yes?"

"Is to fulfill it. Don't try and improve on it. Don't try and make people better than they are. Just . . . do like the man said, and give the people what they want."

"People want nicotine," he whispered. "People want cancer."

"I know, Hank, but this is a cheap romance. It has no carcinogens. Hank, you know what you should do?"

"What?"

"Write a different book."

Hurting people, as Sade once said, is never easy. Gathering up his spurned manuscript, muttering bitterly of rewrites and compromises, Hank focused on the only villain he could afford. As he left, he said, "I hope they give that Wingate kid a million years."

Readers, take note: Never, ever become a tabloid headline.

GREAT BIT PLAYERS *Hollywood* **HALL OF FAME**

Jeff (Bill Murray) in Tootsie

When you are a tabloid headline, you become the reason people like Hank Laufler have rotten lives. You become the reason the subway is late, the cause of the boss's obnoxious behavior, and the force of nature that put dog doo in a pedestrian's way. B. Arthur doesn't like Hank Laufler's book—whose fault is it? Lylo Wingate's.

And to make the day even more fun, I had a meeting with Ivan Feiffer that afternoon to go over the chapters he had submitted. They weren't all that bad. In fact, they were pretty good. (B. Arthur had written "Slam dunk!" in the margins.) And I knew it was going to bug the hell out of me to give Ivan the good news.

I was just on my way to shock the system back to life with caffeine when the phone rang. To my shock—and yes, horror—it was Doris. You remember Doris. My "therapist."

After the hellos, how are yous, was I still addicted's, she said, "You know, I've been thinking, I'd love to see you again."

"I don't think so, Doris."

"I think we could really be friends. You know, you were my most successful client."

"You apologized and gave my money back. That's success?"

"Oh, not in terms of treatment. God, no." She laughed. "In terms of the role. You really got into the role with me."

"You deceived me and ripped me off."

"Nobody came for as many sessions as you did."

"Thanks, Doris. That helps."

"You'd still be coming if I hadn't decided to be honest. That's why I figure you owe me."

"I thought we were talking about being friends."

"Oh, sure," she said. "But the thing is, I really need that dynamic in my life. I have this need to perpetuate my illusion on another human being. You know, to be seen the way I want to be seen."

"I think you need somebody fresh for this venture, Doris."

"Well, I thought so, too, at first, but nobody else has answered the ad. I was thinking we could have coffee."

"We could not."

"I have some interesting new insights into your condition."

"What about your condition, Doris?"

"The way you go through life, it really puts you in the power of a lot of people."

"The way you go through life, Doris, should put you in the power of a straight jacket."

Wouldn't you know it—no sooner had the word *straitjacket* left my mouth than our future Updike sailed into my office. Plopping himself into a chair, a lot snappier than he had any right to be since I despised him, he gave me a jaunty little wave. Bidding a swift good-bye to Stephen King—"Ciao, Steve, see you at Beeba's"—I hung up.

"So," he said, pointing to his chapters, "what did you think?"

Trying to inject a more formal tone into the proceedings, I said, "B. Arthur had no substantial problems with your submission."

"That's what you call him? B. Arthur?"

Poop. "Mr. Bickerstaff had no substantial problems with your submission."

"That's hilarious. B. Arthur." He smiled. Like we were friends or something. "So, what's next?"

"The next five chapters," I said brightly.

"All the way through Trooper's tragic misfire at Bald Rock?"

"You got it."

He leaned his chin into the palm of his hand. "Do you eat lunch?"

"Not with novelists."

"That's a shame. I was going to pitch the idea that Trooper's tragic misfire should kill A Horse Named Dog instead of Miss Hetty."

"Really? I thought you were going to pitch your novel."

"That's during coffee. What do you say?"

"I say no."

Now he leaned all the way in; he actually put his elbows on my desk. All pretense had been dropped. His eyes were wide, pleading. A sheen of perspiration shone on his upper lip. I swear there were tears in his eyes. First novelists, I thought, should all be taken out and shot. I don't know why they all pitch to me. I have no power. B. Arthur has all the power. In the same way that the brain mass of animals is in inverse proportion to their bulk, so is brain mass in inverse proportion to allotment of power.

"Just read the first chapter."

I made a face like I was thinking about it.

"Does it have a dog in it?

"No."

"Then I won't read it." This is an amazingly effective ploy. First-time novelists are so used to arbitrary scorn and rejection that they will believe any excuse you give them. Occasionally, people have said, yes, they do have a dog in their novel, in which case I tell them I never read anything with dogs in it, owing to an unfortunate incident in my youth.

"What if I put a dog in it?" he asked.

"Honestly—don't bother." I stood up, a sign which even the most feeble-minded could have interpreted as a cue to go.

Ivan rose from his chair. "Any kind of dog you particularly prefer?" he asked humbly.

"It changes from day to day," I said. "Good-bye, Ivan."

"Can we still have lunch?"

"We were never having lunch. Make sure Miss Hetty dies poignantly." And that was that, out the door, good-bye Ivan Feiffer. Except that the little goon called me that afternoon.

After announcing himself, he said brightly, "Hey, about my novel?" He waited for me to say Yeah? I didn't say Yeah. "I put a dog in it."

"Oh."

"Right on page four. Then again on page fifty-three."

"Doesn't sound like significant character development to me."

"So, will you read it?"

"No. I'm off dogs now."

A pause. A long pause. "Ah."

"Sorry. Lizards do it for me now."

"Lizards."

"Yep."

"The story's set in Chicago."

"Well, there you go."

"But I'll see what I can do."

"Don't compromise your artistic integrity."

"No, no."

"I couldn't stand that. I hate books with no artistic integrity."

"No, absolutely. Just, you know, a lizard somewhere."

"If you feel strongly."

GREAT BIT PLAYERS *Hollywood* **HALL OF FAME**

Belle Watling in Gone with the Wind

"I do. I think a lizard might be just what it needed," he said, and hung up the phone.

Maybe it's not a nice thing to say. Maybe you'll think less of me as a person. But tormenting Ivan Feiffer was the most pleasant, soul-satisfying thing that had happened to me in a long time. They say people should suffer for their art, and I've never been one to argue with popular opinion.

But my good mood didn't last. On the way home that night, I started thinking about Danny, who despite Dinah kicking his artistic integrity in the goolies was still refusing to audition for Christian. I bugged him to call Julian every chance I got, and this made him unhappy. He was also unhappy about Dinah being in residence. And most of all, he was unhappy with himself for not fielding calls from your more remote Russian directors, begging him to play Chekhov in the buff.

Somehow, some way, I thought, we had to find the metaphorical stool in Schwab's, and set Danny's butt squarely upon it.

I walked through the door to find Danny home and on the phone. As I flipped on the news, I heard him say, "No, I'm sorry. I'm really not interested. No, thank you for asking, but no."

Then, "Yeah, I have your number, but . . . really, I'm not going to change my mind." Danny hung up.

"Who was?" I gave him the innocent-as-the-driven-snow smile.

It didn't work. Danny snapped, "Just what did you tell that guy from the audition?"

"Guy from the audition?"

"Julian what's-his-face."

Oh, you mean the good-looking, charming guy with theater connections? God forbid we hear from him.

"I think I said you might be interested in a second audition. Yes, you're right, it's a shooting offense."

"Just stay out of it," said Danny.

But I was not in the mood to stay out of it. I'm a Great Bit Player now, Danny, we don't stay out of things!

"Even if you don't want the part, it couldn't hurt to perform for Magalda Bernadin again."

"I *am* interested in the second audition," he said fiercely. "I'm doing the fucking second audition."

"Oh. Fab." I reviewed the mental tape a moment. "So what was all the 'no, sorry, not interested' jazz?"

"The guy asked me out."

"The *fiend*."

"I'm serious."

"He doesn't strike me as the type who's about to fling you on the casting couch, Danny."

"That's not the *point*," he said. "The point is . . . It's . . ." From the television, the newscaster said, "And today's events in the Lylo Wingate murder investigation . . ." Danny screamed, "Oh, for fuck's sake, turn it off. I can't stand to hear any more."

Hastily, I shut it off. "Danny, what's wrong? Is it Dinah?"

He sank into a chair. "No. Yes, but no."

"Do you need her out of here? I'll get her out if it'll make you feel better." The guy seemed on the verge of a nervous breakdown. Dinah could wait. Nervous breakdowns had Dinahs, not the other way round.

"No, that's not really it. I don't know, I should be happy with this audition—even if it's a part I don't want—but . . ."

"But what?"

"Who cares? It won't lead to anything; it's just going to be another show nobody sees and nobody cares about, and when it's over, I'll be right back where I started."

I couldn't believe what I was hearing. I had always hoped it would get to Danny one day. The indignity of regular employment, the galling reality of anonymity. But it never had. I had watched and waited for a sign that he was growing disillusioned. But no. Through all the downs and lows, he had been frustratingly resilient, the James Bond of optimism.

And now, finally, he was broken.

And I felt rotten.

"You'll feel better after the audition," I said lamely.

He shrugged. "Maybe."

"I'm sorry about Julian."

"No, it's okay. I overreacted."

"I just thought maybe it was time to move on from Roger."

"Of course it is. It's time to move on from Roger. It's time to move on from acting. It's probably time to move on from New York . . ."

"Danny, if you do that, I might wind up living with Dinah permanently. You wouldn't want such a thing for me, would you?"

"I guess not."

I glanced around the apartment. It was strangely tranquil. "Where is our unwanted guest, anyway?"

"Oh . . . she's out. I saw her before she left. She said something about a meeting with Lylo."

I was instantly suspicious. With the trial about to start, Lylo's timing was . . . smelly. "What does he want?"

"Who knows?" Sighing, Danny went to the bookshelf and took *Cyrano* down. "God, I hate this character."

GREAT BIT PLAYERS *Hollywood* **HALL OF FAME**

 George Downes (Rupert Everett) in My Best Friend's Wedding

"Danny, he's a pretty boy with a hard-on."

"Not exactly me these days," said Danny, and disappeared into his room.

So I, like a mother, waited up for Dinah. The news that she was seeing Lylo had me really worried. What did he want all of a sudden? What was the big rush? Why did Lylo—"We must not meet"—Wingate suddenly want to meet, for Christ's sake?

Dinah rolled in at two in the morning. One look at her and I knew something was wrong. She was twitching the wrong way. Scratching parts of herself she usually left alone. Her eyes were rolling sarcastically, but they looked . . . what? Red? Damp? Tearful?

Getting up from the couch, I whispered, "Danny said you went to meet Lylo."

"Yeah, I met with Lylo." She sat down, pulled at a loose thread on her sock.

I gave her a drink because she looked like she needed it, then gave one to myself because I, too, needed it. Then I said, "Well?"

She took off a shoe and threw it across the room. "I shouldn't be talking to you about this."

"You're not," I said. "Not really."

"Yeah, but I was thinking about it."

Never in my life have I given such a sincere rendition of I Won't Tell Anybody, I Swear. My hand was on my heart, my eyes didn't blink, my voice broke in all the right places. I almost reached out and took Dinah's hand and pressed it warmly.

After a few swallows of bourbon, Dinah said in a small, small voice, "I've been called as a witness."

"Well, you were expecting that, right?"

"I guess. But there's a little problem."

"With the case."

She nodded.

"With the . . . evidence?"

She nodded again.

"They have evidence that might convict Lylo?"

A shake of the head.

"They have evidence that might convict you?" Oh, God, Dinah, don't do this. The public wants Lylo Wingate. They don't want to burn you, some little nobody; they want to fry someone they have really and truly hated for all of three weeks.

"Dinah, please tell me who was driving that night."

Panicked, she glanced around the apartment, like bugs would start springing out of the sofa. "I can't say anything, I can't."

"Does Lylo want you to say you did it?"

"I can't."

"Don't do it, Dinah. Don't say you did it if you didn't. And I know you didn't."

"How do you *know* that?"

"Because . . . because . . ." Because I know Lylo did do it, because he's a prick, and maybe bad things happen to good people, but pricky people ought to do pricky things. Don't destroy my illusions here, Dinah.

"Because I do. I know you, and I know you didn't run that guy over."

She shook her head. "Wasn't like I gave him a whole lotta help once he was down."

"Well, no. But we're talking about who was at the wheel."

She nodded.

"And we know who was at the wheel, right?"

She was quiet a while, then said, "Well, I know." She got up. "I'm going to bed. This conversation never happened."

"Dinah, let me come with you. To the trial."

She turned around and looked at me. "Why? What can you do?"

It was a good question.

Unfortunately, I had no answer.

$\mathcal{C}$HAPTER TEN

MORE SURPRISES (AND THEN SOME)

$\mathcal{A}$ **WEEK LATER,** Danny read for Christian. Two days after that, Julian called to say he had the part. Danny thanked him politely, jotted down the rehearsal times, said thank you again, and hung up.

If there was a subtext along the lines of "Thank you, thou dusky-eyed god, you have only to speak and I shall be thine," I missed it entirely.

Nonetheless, I broke out the champagne, did the obligatory jig, and said palpably stupid things like "Magalda Bernadin, I can't believe you're going to be working with Magalda fucking Bernadin."

"Yup," said Danny, and drank.

"You must be so amazingly excited," said I, in what's known in the theater as a prompt.

" 'Cited as can be," said Danny, and drank some more.

Then after he had drunk quite a bit more, he said, "Come on, it's a crappy little off-off-Broadway show. It'll be forgotten in a week."

But what Danny didn't know was that the Magalda Bernadin *Cyrano* was going to be his launchpad to international megastardom. To that house in Beverly Hills. To script approval and butt doubles. Even to Ibsen for the Deaf in Central Park, if he so desired.

Because the Great Bit Player was set to go into action.

While Danny labored away at the laborious Christian, I set my mind to parlaying this crappy little off-off-Broadway show into a three-picture action serial.

The key thing, it seemed to me, was to get Danny seen. Beautiful as he was, charming as he was, the fact remained that over one billion people were ignorant of his existence.

This was a problem.

Now, we didn't have to reach every one of those one billion people right away, but making contact with the fifty or so who could introduce him to a good half of the world's population was essential.

Which brought us to problem number two. How to get the attention of those fifty or so when every single other loser on the planet was also trying to get their attention. At first glance, the odds looked insurmountable.

But we had two factors on our side—three, if you counted my desperation. The first was that Danny was nice to look at. The second was that Julian liked to look at him, and if my instincts were correct, Julian was a man with connections.

I waited until rehearsals started, gave it a week or so for Julian to become really and truly smitten, and then called him from my office.

After some idle chitchat about Danny's fabulous looks and adorable disposition, I said I certainly hoped we would see Julian around the apartment some time.

"Hmm," was what Julian said.

Then I came to the point. "You know, Julian, the reason I called is because Danny needs some help."

"Hmm." Julian, I was learning, had the ability to say things like *hmm* in a way that conveyed many emotions. This *hmm*, for those of you listening at home, meant *Yes, he certainly does.* What I was looking for was a *hmm* that indicated *Sign me up on the dotted line, I'm ready, willing, and able to do whatever it takes.*

"He needs help getting noticed."

"Hmm." Translation: To me, this means doo-doo.

"So that he can get more work."

"Hmm." Translation: See above.

"He's getting desperate, Julian."

"He's an actor. All actors are desperate."

"Well, if this actor gets much more desperate, he's threatening to go to Duluth."

"Yeah, well, bully for Duluth."

For a moment, I was stumped. The Duluth threat had been my trump card. But clearly we were no longer talking to the same love-mad fool who had so delicately inquired about Danny's professional and personal availability. And it didn't take a genius to figure out what had put the chill on Julian's ardor: Danny was playing hard to get. Too hard.

"You know, Julian," I said, "Danny was very badly hurt by someone he loved not too long ago."

"Was he?" He was trying to be brusque, but I could tell, the interest was there. It's those big brown eyes. They hook them every time.

"As a result, he can be somewhat standoffish."

"Not a problem for me," said Julian the Liar.

"Come on, Julian."

"I don't know what you're asking me."

"Help me catapult Danny to megastardom."

I paused. Perhaps a tad too strong. This Bit Player stuff was tricky.

Julian sighed. "Can I ask why you think I'm ready to help you?"

"You're not helping me; you're helping Danny."

There was a longish silence. Then Julian said, "Look, I have been trying to help Danny. I took him out to lunch, I threw out all these ideas, told him the kind of auditions he should be going on—he didn't want to hear it."

"I know. His nose got all wrinkly, and his eyes clouded over, and before you knew it, you were talking about the weather. I've been there, and I sympathize. But believe me, he's much more receptive now."

"That's a lie, but I'll think it over," he said gently, and hung up.

With things started (stalled, yes, but at least started, people!) on the Danny Fame Front and the Free Dinah Front, I focused my newly energized attentions on Great Bit Player Point Number Three:

3. Write a bestselling book.

Now, it's perfectly reasonable to ask why. Why, having met failure in so many artistic endeavors, I should be so confident in my abilities to pull this one off.

One simple reason: concept.

This would be what's called a concept book. The concept book has several advantages over the novel, which I will outline here for further instruction:

1. You don't actually have to write it. As I understand it, you sell the concept on a few choice examples and a catchy title, collect your check, and the researchers take it from there.

2. There are many great concept books in literature. *The Prince* by Machiavelli is one. *The Communist Manifesto, Siddartha* . . . Philosophy or self-help? You be the judge.

3. People buy concepts. They don't buy novels. A novel is about ideas. An idea is not a concept and so is not marketable.

At least that's what I thought at first. But once I was settled on the couch, pen and pad in hand, I found it curiously difficult to get started. I have to admit, I began to understand that writing is . . . hard. That writers actually have some definable talent when it comes to putting words together that other people don't have. I always thought it was a big scam.

As I wrestled with the opening chapter (okay, first page), I came to two conclusions:

1. The *Days* writers might actually deserve a raise.
2. I needed help.

There was only one problem: I was completely lacking in friends with any discernible writing talent. It's a sad statement about the publishing industry today, but I, an employee at Bicker-staff Books, couldn't think of a single soul able to string words together in a clear, attractive sentence. The project was way too commercial for Hank Laufler, who, at any rate, had his own problems, and none of the other *Days* authors lived in New York. Well, one of them did, but I was fucked if I was going to entrust my future fame and success to First Novelist at Large Ivan Feiffer.

Or so I told myself for a week or so. Then I buckled.

I can't explain it about novelists, but they make me itch. They pretend not to want to be famous, when anybody knows they would kill to be recognized. There was Ivan Feiffer in my office, and in spite of the fact that he was bright, talented, and more than a little on the cute side, there was just something about him that made me squirm.

But I have to give him credit. He listened to my proposal for collaboration—I left out all the relevant details, in case he got the idea of writing the thing himself—and said, "Well, I'm flattered."

"So that's a yes."

"That's an I'm interested in hearing more about the project. But I think we should meet outside the office . . . avoid any impropriety." Said with a straight face, I give the man credit.

I said, "Lunch."

"Dinner."

"What kind of dinner?"

"The kind you eat after six."

"Would it involve shellfish?"

He hesitated. "Do you want it to?" He had learned, I guess, after the business with dogs and lizards, that I could be quixotic. That's okay. With writers, you want to keep them nervous.

"I might be more inclined to partake if you sprung for half a dozen oysters."

"I thought you needed my help."

"I thought you wanted to have dinner with me." (Oh, come on, Ivan. I might need help, but you have a first novel you desperately want me to read. It's no contest.)

He thought about it, then said, "For every oyster, you read one chapter of my book."

"Are you out of your mind?"

"One oyster, one chapter." We were in serious negotiations now. Screw the money, now Ivan's novel was involved.

"One word." I was almost liking him. It's so cute when the powerless try to bargain.

"A paragraph."

"A syllable."

"A page. Come on—six oysters, six pages, that's more than fair."

"Done."

He smiled. "I know you're going to love it."

THE AEROBICS OF *Celebrity* **SPOTTING**

THE SIDESTEP
When someone is standing between you and the celebrity. Move left foot left, bring right foot alongside it. Repeat.

"I won't love it, Ivan."

"You will. It's great. Well, the first three chapters are great. Then there's this little lull until you get to chapter seven, but then it really takes off . . ."

"Ivan, your faith in yourself is touching. But I already know, without reading a word, that your book is rotten."

"You haven't read it."

"I don't have to read it to know it's rotten. It's a first novel."

"So?"

"All first novels are rotten—it's common knowledge."

"No, it's all second novels that are rotten."

"No, just by then, everyone's on to you."

He stared at me. "There are *many* great first novels."

"Name them."

"*Tender Is the Night*, F. Scott Fitzgerald."

"Yawn."

"*The Sun Also Rises,* by Hemingway."

"Snore."

He thought hard. *"The Pickwick Papers."*

"Not as good as the later stuff."

After that, he got quiet for a little while, then said in a small voice that he would meet me at the Oyster Bar at seven o'clock.

"Gone with the Wind."

This is the first thing Ivan said when I met him that evening. I, of course, arrived at a discreet eight minutes after seven.

"What about it?" I sat down.

"It's a great first novel."

"It's an *only* novel, Ivan. Like *To Kill a Mockingbird.* Only novels don't count."

He looked deflated for an instant, then said gamely: "I'll think of something."

Futile optimism—the hallmark of a first novelist.

I thought it was a good idea to find out something about Ivan's background: where he grew up, what schools he went to, history of plagiarism, things like that. He was a Chicagoan by birth, New Yorker by choice, and a writer, he admitted, for lack of any other talent.

"It's the only thing I've ever been able to do," he said, putting a fairly butch amount of horseradish on his oysters. "I mean, if I were better looking or better at standardized tests . . . who knows?"

"Who knows?" I said brightly and thought, Another reason for abolishing standardized tests: they give the world more novelists.

Ivan watched carefully as I consumed the sixth oyster. Then he pulled an envelope out of his bag. "Six pages," he said. I took the envelope—a bargain was a bargain, and six oysters were six oysters. But when I started to take the pages out of the envelope, he said, "Don't read it now."

"Why not?"

"You won't be able to concentrate."

Which, of course, had been the whole point, but when Ivan offered a second round of oysters, I put the envelope in my bag. I would read it at home—on an extended visit to the potty.

"Is this your first first novel?" I asked.

"Nuh-uh." Ivan swallowed an oyster. "Third."

I smiled. "Industrious."

"Unlucky." He smiled. "My first first novel was a historical family saga, set in Basel in the sixteenth century."

"Fascinating."

"It was eight hundred and twenty-three pages long."

"And no one took it? Amazing."

"Well, as one agent said to me, there's noncommercial and then there's unsellable. So, my next book I made very commercial.

A Harrier jet blew up on page one, a woman stripped naked with a poodle on page ten. The first thing I told the reader about the hero was that many women thought he was better looking than Leonardo DiCaprio."

"What went wrong with that one?"

"In chapter five, I revealed that the hero was a post-op transsexual."

"Worked yourself into a niche market there."

"I got bored," he said apologetically.

"So"—I braced myself—"what's this one?"

"A boy comes of age in Chicago."

My head fell on the table. Tactless, I know, but I couldn't help it. Six whole pages of coming of age in Chicago. Not even the oysters made it worth it.

"Let me guess—he wants to be a writer."

"That's right."

"And he comes to New York."

"Uh-huh."

"Gets turned down by women in all sorts of sweet, self-deprecating scenarios."

"Yep."

I moaned.

"Look, I figure, they don't want anything I write anyway, so why shouldn't I write what I want to?"

"That's a beautiful and self-defeating statement." I drank, then suggested, "Why don't you make him the post-op transsexual?"

Ivan smiled. "My mom would get upset."

"I thought that's why people became writers, to upset their mothers."

"Not me," said Ivan Feiffer. "I like my mother."

"So, he could like her a whole, whole lot. In that sort of twisted way."

172 • EMMI FREDERICKS

"Should we . . . get down to business? What's the project you need help on?"

"I don't need help."

"No, of course, I meant . . . polish. Editing. Streamlining." Ivan at least had learned the first and cardinal rule of freelance writing: kiss ass, kiss ass, and then, when your lips are numb, kiss some more ass.

I outlined the whole scheme—leaving out certain key details—and its prospects for success (considerable), time expended (reasonable), and profit sharing (equitable at ninety-ten).

Ivan listened, then said nothing for a while. A long while.

Then he said, "Wow."

"Good, huh?" For a moment I really was nervous he might steal it, but I was the celebraholic, I was the one who was symptomatic. Writers don't know from real life—Ivan Feiffer could never be raw enough to report firsthand the agonies of celebraholism.

He made a noise like *umph*, then signaled the waiter for another drink.

"Two," he called in a shaky voice.

After finishing the first beer, he said he had a few questions. I said to fire away. Question one: Was this satire? I assured him it was not. Was it purely for the money? No, but money was not wholly separate from the considerations. Had I gotten the idea from someone else? Certainly not.

Did I really think this was a problem? In other words, was I actually *serious*?

"Of course I am."

Ivan blinked. "But . . ."

"What?"

"Well, don't you feel ashamed?"

"No."

"No guilt whatsoever?"

"No."

"You don't wake up at two o'clock in the morning, your conscience throbbing like a stubbed toe?"

Well, at this point, I rose from the table and announced that I was leaving. I shouldn't have been surprised by Ivan's reaction, but I was. Actually, I was a lot more than surprised. I was seriously pissed off, and I told him as much before stalking out of the Oyster Bar.

I had walked about a block when I became aware of a seriously puffing Ivan Feiffer behind me. "Wait," he panted. "Slow down . . ."

"Why?"

"I'm sorry."

"You're sorry because I have your lousy novel—"

"No . . ."

"And you think I'll rip it to shreds to get even."

"I know you wouldn't do that."

"Oh, and you know that because you're such a *keen observer of human nature.*" By this time I had stopped so I could shriek directly into his face. "Is that why you know I'm not going to send your rotten six pages around all of publishing with a Post-it that reads: 'Avoid like the plague.'"

He gestured weakly to the steps of the New York Public Library. "Could you . . . could we sit down? And talk?"

"Are you going to vomit?"

"I don't think so."

"Too bad."

But I sat. After which, he sat. And said, "I have something to confess to you."

"Okay."

"Two things, actually." He coughed.

"And they are?"

"One," he raised a finger. "I find you a very frightening person."

"Considering what I think of you, I would hope so."

"Not to sound Stalinist, but it makes me very nervous to think that you have any power in publishing." He chewed at his thumbnail. "Are you offended?"

I thought about it, then shook my head. Someone like Ivan would think something like that about someone like me—it was only natural.

"Okay." He exhaled. "Here's the second thing . . ."

"You're a post-op transsexual."

"No. That would be easy to tell you. This is hard."

"Go ahead."

"The second thing is, I find you attractive."

"Oh."

"I've discussed it in therapy, but it's not working. And even with everything you've told me this evening, I'm still finding it hard to overlook the fact that you have just the amount of baby fat on your body that happens to be my particular kink—"

"And I work in publishing," I interrupted. "And I'm about to read your book."

"Believe me, that's a drawback at this point. So, I figured the best thing to do was tell you, let you laugh at me, and . . ."

"Is that what usually happens? When you tell women you're attracted to them?"

"Usually."

"Sounds like you've propositioned some awful women."

"No," he said defensively.

"What kind of person would laugh at something like that?"

"Well, I'm sure you're about to."

"I'm not."

"You're not?"

"No."

Fact!

```
It is not a good idea to become romantically
involved while you are in recovery.
```

Fact!

```
Ivan was cute.
```

We went to a quiet spot. We talked. We ate. We had another beer. Then Ivan begged me to read the six pages. Because, he said, he couldn't stand not knowing what I thought of him *and* not knowing what I thought of his book, so I took them out of the envelope and read them. Six pages of tiny type, single-spaced, with no margins.

It was rotten. Not putrid, but rotten.

I handed them back. Ivan said, "You can't be finished."

"I'm a fast reader. I'm known for it."

"So?"

"I can't tell anything from that. It's just six pages."

"Did you notice I put in the dog?"

"Page three, fourth paragraph. I noticed."

"Would you be interested in another half dozen oysters?"

"Ivan. Look. I can't do anything for your book. Honestly. B. Arthur is not looking for original material by unknown authors."

"I know." He looked hurt.

"So?"

"I just wanted to know what you thought of it. If you liked it at all."

And that's when I knew I kind of liked Ivan Feiffer. Because the book was rotten.

But I said I liked it.

Ivan was no dummy. Looking skeptical, he said, "Really?"

"Yeah, really." I can't look you in the eye and say it, Ivan, but I really, really like it.

"I think you're just saying that."

"Why would I just say that?"

"You wouldn't just say it?"

"No, of course not." If you were ugly, I'd never say it.

"Okay." He nodded, then broke out in smiles all over. "Great. Amazing. That's . . . that's so great. Thank you." Okay, Ivan was no dummy, but he was a writer.

"Don't mention it." Ever.

"You want to read another chapter?"

"Let me digest this one."

"Sure. I understand. Wow. Can I kiss you?"

"Here?"

"Sure. I'm a good kisser. I'm known for it."

And for once, Ivan was right. I'm not sure how the bartender felt about it, but it worked for me. I was almost ready to say I would read the next chapter, when I heard something on the television that distracted me from all matters literary, romantic, or otherwise.

"A stunning development on the opening day of the Lylo Wingate trial . . ."

Breaking free of Ivan, I gestured to the bartender. "Could you turn that up, please?"

Giving me a strange look, he hit the remote. ". . . the mystery woman who was in the car on the fatal night that ended Buster Rosen's life came forth today to make an incredible announcement . . ."

Ivan said, "God, I'm sick of this fucking case already."

I shushed him, then strained to hear as the solemn announcer continued: "Dinah Sharlip now claims that she was behind the wheel when the SUV swerved that tragic night, killing beloved deli owner Buster Rosen. Sharlip claims it was *she* who sped from the site of the accident without calling. She says she thought she could call later from her cell phone. But, tragically, the batteries were dead."

"Yeah," said the bartender. "Just like that poor sap Rosen."

CHAPTER ELEVEN

FAME AT LAST

*O*F I look back on the events that immediately followed Dinah's "stunning announcement," it's hard to describe them in linear, sequential fashion.

I do remember falling off the stool.

I do remember Ivan yelping in pain as I stepped on his foot.

And I do remember asking the bartender for a fairly stiffish drink.

I stared at the television, stunned by the sight of Dinah hurrying down the courtroom steps, pursued by a pack of press and some schleppy guy in a raincoat. The newscaster, who looked like he had just popped the biggest boner of his life, explained that court had been recessed until tomorrow morning. (At which time, they would presumably lock Dinah up and throw away the key.)

"Who's the guy with the raincoat?" Ivan wanted to know.

"Her lawyer," said the bartender, because bartenders know everything.

The Wingate family fortune at her disposal, and Dinah had as her lawyer someone who looked like he exposed himself to preschoolers? Looking again, I thought there was something vaguely familiar about Mr. Raincoat. Was it possible? Had I myself encountered him in a lonely isolated playground?

Sorry, folks, it's not that dramatic.

A memory did surface, but it wasn't of isolated playgrounds—it was graduation and embarrassed introductions. The schlep in the raincoat was Dinah's cousin Marty. Cousin Marty who'd been rejected from twenty-three law schools before finally getting into Wabash University and who was currently employed, if memory served, in his uncle's menswear store.

Lylo loves Dinah and he lets Marty of Menswear stand between her and the pokey? Nuh-uh.

But I have to give Marty of Menswear credit—he did do one thing right. He got Dinah a good bail bondsman. As the newscaster informed us, Dinah couldn't be formally charged until an investigation took place, but thanks to Cousin Marty, she wouldn't have to sit behind bars while they kibbitzed over chair vs. lethal injection.

And that's when it occurred to me—Dinah would be home any minute. Frantic, I tore out of the bar, hurling apologies at a somewhat bewildered Ivan—who did not, after all, know that his newly squeezed squeeze was sharing a room with the most infamous murderess in town—and flung myself into the nearest cab.

Remember how Dinah had moved back into my apartment because I lived in such a nowhere neighborhood, the press would never in a million years look for her there?

Wrong.

Wrong, wrong, *wrong*.

My first clue was when I couldn't find my building. Why, you ask, could I not find my building? Buildings do not just disappear; they are large, generally easy to spot. I could not find my building because it was covered in media. Everywhere you looked, trucks with network logos on them, microphones, lights, isolated TV reporters in trench coats, and fat guys eating donuts. People I had never seen before were calling themselves neighbors and giving interviews. At the corner, I spotted poor Mr. Papagalou, surrounded by microphones, waving his hands and saying he knew nothing, he only wanted to get home to East Islip. Sal was desperately trying to get the more aggressive reporters off the front steps. Meanwhile, Norm was snarfling through donut boxes, waddling up to the cameras, and generally being a big, fat ham.

Here it was: the Press, up close and personal. Red in tooth and claw does not begin to describe it. I stood gape-mouthed, taking it all in. My heart was going a mile a minute. I had a funny buzzing sensation in my fingers. There was a roaring in my ears. I was vaguely aware that I was panting and my palms were sweaty.

A camera guy brushed past my shoulder and I completely lost it.

I burst into the crowd, shrieking, "Friend of the accused, friend of the accused. Guys, please, guys, no interviews, please, back off boys, give me room. I'm a friend of the accused, Dinah needs me, guys, I gotta get to her, let me through, you gotta let me see her, she's in a fragile state, she could do something crazy, come on, I'm a friend of the accused!"

It wasn't until I reached the stoop that I realized not a single person was listening.

Except for Sal, who said, "Why are you yelling?"

In a quick face-saving gesture—or at least a pathetic attempt at distraction—I hauled Norm's snout out of a wax paper bag. (Have you ever tried hauling a basset hound away from something near and dear to his heart, i.e. food? There are easier things in this world.) Then I made my way upstairs, drenched in humiliation and shame, Sal's question echoing in my ears: "Why are you yelling?"

Yeah, why were you yelling? No one listens to you.

They listened to Mrs. Lipinski. Mrs. Lipinksi who has seen Dinah maybe once.

Yeah, but she's better than you.

Why? Why better than me? I'm a friend of the accused.

Some friend. You didn't even know she was going to plead guilty.

My hand was on the doorknob, when I heard something—

someone?—stir inside the apartment. With great trepidation, I inched the door open, fully expecting a thousand cameras to go off in my face at once.

They didn't. There was someone in the apartment, but it wasn't Dan Rather. It was Dinah.

"Hey," she said.

"Jesus . . ." I slammed the door shut. "How did you get in here?"

"Mrs. Delgado from upstairs. She got me in through the basement while Sal was shooing them all off the steps. Some zoo, huh?"

She was hideously calm. And she had no right to be. I had just been ignored within an inch of my life, the least she could do was be mildly hysterical.

But now she was rummaging around the refrigerator. "Do we have any diet soda?"

"Dinah . . . the words 'beside the point' are flashing in my head. Will you please tell me what is going on?"

"Hey, you watch the *Ten O'clock News*." She shrugged. "That's what's going on."

"I'm going to say one thing to you," I announced, "And that's—"

Then I stopped. I had more than one thing to say to her, and I wasn't sure which should go first: Stop lying? Get a good lawyer? A good agent?

"Are you out of your fucking mind?"

Okay, it probably wasn't ideal, but you have to figure, thoughts are governed by Darwinian law: in times of stress, the most powerful emotion will be expressed first.

"Lylo's making you do this, isn't he? He told you to get up there and testify that you were the one driving that night."

"No, he is not making me do this. Jesus, you do read too many tabloids. Haven't you quit yet?"

I said something to the extent that no, I had not quit, because I was no longer in the happy position of reading about the trials and tribulations of strangers, but instead now read the tabs to learn the crucial events in the lives of my nearest and dearest.

"And why was creepy Cousin Marty with you at the hearing?"

"Creepy Cousin Marty is a *lawyer*." Now she was defensive. "You remember Marty; he came to graduation."

"Yeah, I remember Marty at graduation. Where I don't remember Marty is standing next to Bill Kunstler or Johnnie Cochran, winning those big high-profile murder cases. Why, with all of Lylo's billions, do we have Cousin Marty as a lawyer?"

"Could you forget about Lylo for a minute or two?"

"No, I cannot forget about Lylo for a minute or two. Because I can't think of any other reason you would say you did something that I know you didn't do."

"You don't know that at all," she said blithely. Blithely! I ask you, the woman is about to join a chain gang, and she's blithe!

"I want to help," I said. "Tell me how to help."

"Stop worrying," she said. "That's how you help."

But Dinah, I wanted to tell her, I'm a Great Bit Player now. I worry! I help! I fix things!

Only I couldn't for the life of me figure out how to fix this.

Maybe, I thought, maybe there was something I was missing. A motive besides love of Lylo. Once I figured out what it was, maybe I could persuade Dinah it wasn't worth it. (And maybe I could achieve world peace by breakfast.)

We were brushing our teeth, just two gal pals getting ready for slumber land—one who had no life and one who had taken life—when I had an idea.

I said, "It's publicity, isn't it?"

"What do you mean?"

"I mean, it's all a scam. And you're going to admit it, only you're waiting for everything to reach complete fever pitch, and then you're going to announce to the world that, in fact, Lylo was driving his moronic SUV when it ran into Rosen, and you're innocent of everything except perjury and other small unpleasantries."

And then you'll come home and be a nobody again, like the rest of us, right Dinah? Right?

"Wrong." Dinah gargled. "Hey, you know that chick . . ."

"No, I do not know that chick, which chick is this?"

"The um, the . . . agent. Book agent. W . . . something. W. Pinkerton?"

"Webby Peterson?" I admit it, my knees buckled slightly. I worked in publishing, I couldn't help it. At the name of Webby Peterson, you either cross yourself or genuflect.

"Yeah." Dinah spit. "She called me about some book project. My true story, and so on . . ." Hawk, spit. Our next Emily Dickinson, ladies and gentlemen. "But I don't really like writing. It's boring. I thought maybe that writer you know might be able to help me out. What's his name, Boris something."

"Ivan," I said coldly. ("Boris something," indeed.)

"Yeah, Ivan. So?"

"Ivan is already engaged in several projects," I said loftily. (Like mine, Dinah. You're not the only one with a book project around here!)

THE AEROBICS OF *Celebrity* SPOTTING

THE POGO
When on a crowded street and a celebrity is spotted up ahead. Rise onto your toes. Launch self into the air. Repeat several times. But continue walking and try not to get arrested.

Dinah gave me a look. "Well, if *Ivan* ever gets tired of 'projects,' tell him I have a gig that pays."

And that's when I knew I had to get Dinah acquitted. As an ordinary slob like the rest of us, she had been bad enough. As a celebrity murderess, she was a total pain in the ass.

"Come on," said Danny, when he came home later that night to find the city's new public enemy number one sleeping on our couch. "Are you really surprised?"

"That she lied?"

"That she did it."

"But she didn't do it, Danny. Do you really think she did it?"

Danny thought for a long time, then sighed. "As much as I'd like to believe otherwise—no, I don't think she did it."

Take it from yours truly—it is a very strange thing to see your friend's face splashed all over the front page.

As I stood on the subway platform on my way to work the next morning, I was surrounded by the following:

SHE DID IT!

I DID IT—DINAH!

DINAH DROVE THEM TO DOOM!

I KILLED BUSTER!

You remember that children's book *What Busy People Do All Day?* Dinah was now what unbusy people did all day. Suddenly, all these people who had never met her knew her inside and out.

Columnists and letter writers took up their positions. Dinah was the wild child, the cold-hearted party girl, a sign of the times, a misunderstood young woman who was doing it all for love. Every single aspect of her life and character was examined for clues. The amount of ink expended on the significance of her wardrobe would drown an elephant.

What made the whole thing almost funny was the fact that not a single one of these opinions was offered by anyone who knew her. One guy she dated for three seconds in our sophomore year wrote an "exclusive" profile of Driven Dinah. "She was determined to be famous," he wrote. "And now, I guess she has what she has always wanted—although I have to wonder what price she may have paid."

In a single subway ride, my estimation of tabloids plummeted. For the first time, I could see the gulf between what they printed and the truth. I mean, I almost started believing that movie stars lead perfectly ordinary lives, never do drugs, or cheat on their spouses.

Lila Rosen, I noted, had very little to say about Dinah's "confession," preferring instead to talk about her plans for an upcoming citywide event called "Be a Deli Man for a Day." As a tribute to Buster Rosen, people would be encouraged to sign up to volunteer their time to a number of charitable and community organizations.

"I would like the people of New York to focus on the good my husband did in his lifetime," she said, "rather than the manner in which his life ended."

Around noon, Ivan called me at the office. He was confused—and who could blame him? How many dates end with the girl bolting out of the bar when her friend becomes headline news for killing the nicest guy on the planet?

I explained the situation and apologized profusely. Ivan was suitably impressed.

"Wow," he said.

Then he said, "Would you mind if I asked a selfish question?"

"Not at all."

"What did you think of the kiss? Not to change the subject or anything."

"I liked it."

"Yeah?"

"Yeah."

"Enough to do it again?"

"Absolutely."

"Again in the soonish time frame?"

I hesitated. Soonish would definitely be preferable, but I had to ask: what right did I have to be plunging into the sea of love when my best friend was about to be sent up the river?

I explained my dilemma to Ivan, who said he understood. He sounded a little hurt, but I figured that was all right. Writers are perpetually insecure; bow to their every little whimper, and you'll throw your back out.

"I'm not saying we can't see each other."

"No, I know you're not." But I could hear the pain in his voice. In revenge, he would probably turn me into a character in a story: the vampish editor with four-inch heels who trifles with the affections of a naive young scribe, then dumps him after his first bad review.

I was debating whether or not to insist he get rid of the heels when I realized he was asking me something.

"Sorry, what?"

"I said, maybe we could have dinner sometime next week."

"That would be great, I'd really like that." Although, who knew what I would be doing this time next week. ("Ivan darling, I have to cancel. They're putting Dinah into the electric chair, and she wants me there to hold her hand.") But I really didn't want Ivan thinking he was getting the brush-off.

So, Ivan hung up all happy—no doubt on his way to the laptop to jot down a few notes on his new character: the wonderful girl he was going to rescue from her degrading job in publishing. Which left me to wonder how the hell I was going to rescue Dinah from her degrading job as Lylo's fall guy.

I started by absorbing everything I could about the Lylo Wingate case. Then, three days later, I sat back and considered what I knew.

I knew for a fact that Dinah wasn't guilty. (Well, no, Your Honor, I didn't know it for a fact, but I *strongly suspected* that Dinah was not guilty. Primarily because I *strongly suspected* that Lylo was. Because I knew *for a fact* that he was an asshole.)

But that was all I knew for a fact. Other things remained maddeningly unclear—primarily, why would Dinah say she did it when she didn't? Was she really willing to say that she ran Buster Rosen over to save the butt of Lylo—the Most Hated Man in New York?

Or was Lylo beside the point?

Was the front page and a book contract worth incarceration?

What would Charles Manson say?

I needed advice, the perspective of someone totally outside the situation. Here I had a problem. No one I knew was willing to be rational on the subject of Dinah Sharlip. Danny was impossible; he seemed to feel that even if Dinah wasn't guilty of this, she would probably be guilty of something at some point, and therefore the whole thing could be viewed as a social preventative. And as far as Ivan was concerned, this was all just another reason he wasn't getting sex or his novel read. So he wasn't kindly disposed toward Dinah either.

Just when I was trying to figure out how to write to Dear Abby without giving the game away ("Dear Abby, My friend has just confessed to murder. I think she is lying for her boyfriend. What should I do?") the perfect solution hit me. When in need of someone completely unspoiled by knowledge of real life, go to my mother. The woman didn't read newspapers, watch television, or move the radio dial past the classical station. (And is it any wonder I am the mess I am today?)

Oddly enough, the last time I had seen my mom was when I made amends to her for my celebraholism. So, over sesame noodles, I sat in my mother's kitchen and brought her up to date on my recovery and my new path in life.

Not surprisingly, my mother was puzzled at first by the concept of the Great Bit Player. (Guilt, I'm sure, played some role in this.)

"A great bit player?"

"That's right." I nodded. Nodding helps a lot in these situations, allowing you to reinforce the point and let the other person know you are not annoyed by their inability to get it.

"Why would you want to be a bit player?"

"Not *a* bit player," I corrected. "A great—"

"But a bit player. In someone else's life."

"Ma . . ."

"I mean, why not have your own life?"

"It *is* my life."

"You're a bit player in your own life."

"The bit player concept is relative, Ma. It essentially signifies that we don't all have to be stars. I think that's healthy, don't you?"

"Oh, absolutely. It's the relative part I'm not getting."

"How do you mean?"

"Where you're relative to everybody else."

"Everybody's relative, Ma. Everything is relative . . . Einstein said it. It must be true."

"Look, you're five-foot-three, right?"

"And a half."

"Are you five-foot-three relative to me? Or if I don't stand next to you, are you suddenly not five-foot-three anymore?"

"You're talking precise measurements. I'm discussing subjective values. For example, I'm five-foot-three—and a half—whoever I stand next to. But I am short or tall, depending on whether I stand next to you or a dwarf."

"No, you're not."

"Yes, I am."

"No. You're still short. You're just not as short. But you're never going to play in the NBA."

Okay, so my mother wasn't getting it. It was time to move on to other subjects.

Namely, Lylo Wingate and Dinah. I outlined the whole story as I understood it, then said, "So, what do you think?"

My mother tilted her head this way, that way. "I think Dinah's a strange person."

"So you think she might be saying she did this because she loves Lylo and thinks this is the way to get him."

"No, I'm saying she's perfectly capable of running the man over."

"Ma . . ."

"You wanted my opinion, I gave it to you. Although . . . although . . ."

"What?"

"I noticed something on TV the other day. Billy had it on." Billy was her assistant at the dance studio. "The news was near the courthouse, and Lylo was there. Everybody was out on the steps, and Billy said something like, 'Oh, Miss Dinah's not going to like that.' Something like that. And I thought, My God, she's become one of those people that people talk about like they know them.

So I said, 'What? What's she not going to like?' And he showed me, on TV."

"What, Ma?" I was practically screaming now.

"That girl. She was with what's-his-name . . . Lylo. Blonde, expensive clothes, real East Side type. She wore sunglasses," said my mother, as if this told me everything I needed to know.

"And she was with Lylo?"

"She kissed him on the mouth. Is that 'with'?"

"That's with."

Leave it to my mother—one of your more clueless individuals, and she comes up with what Perry Mason would call a very convincing motive for Dinah's sudden guilt.

At first, Lylo had attended all the legal hearings, armed only with his lawyers. But in the past couple of days, a new player had emerged on the scene. A blonde had started to accompany Lylo on his arduous journey through our legal system. She was tall, rich-looking, and had those pouty lips that look so sexy under a pair of sunglasses.

Her name was Bethany, and at first I assumed she was just another Wingate. Like a cousin, showing up á la Kennedy to support the guilty-as-hell relative—*once*—and then scram. I remember Dinah once muttering darkly of trust-fund babies and mafia moll wanna-be's, but I never made the connection.

Now I rethought. This girl had everything—money, looks, meager IQ—that Dinah couldn't offer Lylo.

So what could Dinah give him that she couldn't?

Acquittal.

Later, as I got ready to leave, my mother said, "About this celebrity addiction . . . did I have something to do with that?"

For a moment, I was surprised she'd taken it in at all. "No, Ma."

"You feel I neglected you?"

"No, Ma. You were earning the rent." I shrugged on my coat. "I think this is one we have to lay at Dad's door."

"Because he left?"

"No, because he's a goof." I didn't ask if we'd heard from him. Every once in a while, I get a postcard from some bum town the Broken Leg Theater Company is playing.

My mother laughed. "Okay, whatever you say."

She still couldn't handle the truth. It was sad, but she had tried, so I smiled, gave her a hug, and left.

Sal was sitting out on the front stoop when I got home. He didn't say hello the way he usually did, but I was so preoccupied with Dinah that I didn't really notice. It wasn't until I got upstairs and Danny asked if Sal was still out there that it even occurred to me that Norm hadn't been in his normal, drool-dampened spot.

"I guess he told you," said Danny, peeking out the window.

"No, what?"

"He lost Norm."

I stared at him. "What do you mean he *lost* Norm?"

"The agency took control."

"What does that mean?"

"It means, they took over. They said Sal wasn't caring for Norm in a way that protected their investment. They have points in the contract pertaining to Norm's care. The agency can take possession of Norm if Sal violates the terms of the contract."

"What do you mean, Sal wasn't taking care of Norm? That was the most spoiled, beloved basset I've ever seen."

Danny made a frustrated noise. "I didn't say he wasn't taking care of Norm, I said he wasn't taking care of their product. Norm was gaining weight."

I moaned. "That's not Sal's fault—Norm just can't resist bak-

192 • EMMI FREDERICKS

eries. And everyone in the neighborhood feeds him, for God's sake."

"Well, there's also the testical issue." I must have gone pale, because Danny said quickly, "But they're holding off on doing anything about that, because they're worried about the bad publicity."

I whispered, "But Norm still lives with Sal?"

Danny shook his head. "The agency gave him over to a dog handler."

"They can't do *that*. Who the fuck read this contract?"

"No one. When they offered Sal the deal five years ago, Sal didn't know from contracts. He thought the agency represented him and Norm; it never occurred to him that they would be pitted against each other. So he never had an outside lawyer read the contracts, and now he no longer has Norm."

"There's got to be something he can do. Animal rights groups, someone . . ."

"He tried them."

"And?"

"They said he had been exploiting Norm all along and that Norm deserved to divorce him legally, so that he could make his own business decisions without interference from Sal."

"Oh, man . . ." I stood up, wobbled, then sat down. "Poor Sal."

"Poor Norm," said Danny, thinking, as always, of the actor. "Jesus, it's a fucking ugly world."

And then he said, "Oh, by the way, Dinah left. She's moving in with her cousin. She said to tell you she's fed up with your interfering—whatever that means."

CHAPTER TWELVE

CRASHING AND BURNING

WELL, THERE was no way we could just leave Sal sitting out there Norm-less and bereft, so I went downstairs and dragged him back to our place. Danny opened a bottle of wine, and we let Sal pour out his pain.

"I don't care about the snip, snip," he sobbed, to Danny's acute discomfort. "But that diet's going to make him so unhappy."

"They're not going to put him on a diet," I said, bravado courtesy of three glasses of red. "And there's not going to be any snip, snip. You take my word for it, Norm's going to be back drooling on your lap in no time."

Sal tried to give me a brave smile. But his lip trembled, which made his neck wobble, which made him look like Norm, which made *me* start crying.

"You watch," I said. "We're going to call everybody we know." (Like we knew anybody—Norm was the most influential person we knew.) "And we're going to write letters. And we're going to—"

"Call advocacy groups," said Danny, who was thinking a little more clearly than the rest of us.

"And people. Important people. Like . . . fat people. Fat people advocacy groups. Making Norm lose weight—it's blatant discrimination. It's prejudice."

"He gets all these letters from kids," Sal said sadly. "I don't know where to send them now."

It was three-thirty in the morning when, with promises of letter campaigns, phone banks, and federal intervention, we got Sal back to his apartment—now poignantly emptied of bassets. He moaned at the sight of Norm's food bowl, but Danny hustled him off to the bedroom and threw a blanket over him.

"Poor guy," said Danny as we headed back downstairs.

I nodded grimly and mentally added another goal to my Great Bit Player list.

6. Get Norm back. (With nuts.)

"We'll start a letter campaign," I said to Danny. "Get a picture of Norm, put together some provocative copy, tell everyone to write in to the agency."

"Schools," said Danny. "All those kids who write Norm. Animal rights groups. Dog-walking groups."

"You get the lists," I said. "I'll write the letter."

And would you believe it, I did?

From Sal, I got a picture of Norm at his most sloppy and adorable, and underneath, I put in big bold letters: REPOSSESSED BY CORPORATE AMERICA!

Then below, in smaller type:

This is Norm, of Good Friend Life Insurance. Norm has been taken away from his friend and owner Sal Marchap because of corporate greed. He is to be starved and castrated. Please save Norm! Tell Big Business they can't come between man and his best friend. Write to:

And then the address of the agency.

Thanks to the Bickerstaff Books copier, I had 1,000 flyers ready by the time Danny had the list of potential Norm-Savers ready. So one Friday, when I was feeling just a tad flu-ish, I skipped off work and stuffed envelopes.

And stuffed . . .

And licked . . .

And stuffed . . .

And licked . . .

And as I stuffed and licked, I started thinking. Other than paper cuts and a very sore tongue, I didn't feel I had a lot to show as progress on my Great Bit Player goals. Dinah had disappeared. Ivan thought my book was depraved, and I was still coming up short on ideas on how to make Danny the Next Big Thing.

Which meant that any day now, Danny could decamp to Duluth and Dinah could be the property of a gal named Big Sue.

But, my friends, it was no accident that I happened to be home on that Friday. On that Friday, a vision came to me.

That vision was *Florinda!*

Everybody knows Florinda. Right? You either hate her or you love her, think she is a sign of the coming apocalypse or your personal savior. There are those who claim they have never seen her show. I don't believe these people, but just in case you're one of them, I'll give the brief on *Florinda!* Or Flo*rin*da! as she is announced each and every weekday afternoon.

The country has gained and lost weight with Florinda, they have gotten divorced with Florinda, overcome rape with her, and fallen in love with her. She is their best friend. But she's also their great champion, a defender of the righteous. Cheating boyfriends, deadbeat dads, and slutty sisters get no mercy on Florinda's show. They might as well just shoot themselves before coming on the air and avoid the grilling they get from the audience. Even when the show is light and girlish, such as the time Florinda devoted an entire show to that actress who keeps losing the Emmy, passions inevitably ignite, tempers flare, and the people's voice is heard. On that particular show, Florinda showed clips of the winners for every year this sinfully overlooked actress lost, and asked the audience, who did *they* think was the winner? By the time it was all over, three of those Emmy-winning actresses had applied for orders of protection.

Florinda gives a voice to people who can't get heard in their own home. They come on TV, and suddenly the whole country is listening to them. We might think they're brain-dead morons, but we do listen, and that's what counts.

I don't usually watch the show, being the gainfully employed type. But as I was home, I was feeling more than up to a little gladiatorial screaming bout. I'm not sure what that show was about, but it was a confrontation scenario, with everyone up and screaming and pointing fingers, and generally having a rip-roaring time. The people who turn up on *Florinda!* are, by and large, women, with some men thrown in for segments that require them. ("Cheating Boyfriends," "My Husband's a Woman," that kind of thing.)

The audience had just about reduced the guest victim to pulp when Florinda gave the woman a hanky and cut to a commercial. The camera drew back . . . and that's when I saw it, flashed on the bottom of the screen:

"DON'T HATE ME BECAUSE I'M BEAUTIFUL. Too gorgeous for your own good? You could be a guest on an upcoming Florinda."

Before I even had a clear vision of the complete plan, I was dialing numbers. All I knew was that they were looking for beautiful people on TV and that Danny needed to be on TV, and that somehow, these two realities had to meet and make magic together.

After floating on hold for an obscenely long time—apparently, a lot of people feel they suffer from being too beautiful—I finally got on the line with a bored operator.

PRIMARY RESPONSIBILITIES OF THE FOC (*Friend of Celebrity*)

Kiss ass.

I announced, "Your producer got this idea when she saw my friend, Danny."

"Uh-huh," she said, and gave me the time and place for the auditions.

I lay back on the couch, giddy with excitement. Everyone in the country watched *Florinda!* And after this particular show, this is what all of America would want to know: who is that amazingly gorgeous guy and how do I get in touch with his agent?

I could see it all now:

News flash! An amazingly gorgeous man appeared today on Florinda! *Audience members ripped each other to shreds trying to get to him.*

. . . Love letters and proposals of marriage continue to pour in for Danny Beale, the stunner who captivated America with his appearance on Florinda! *last week.*

. . . Hunk of the Decade Danny Beale met with some of the biggest players in Hollywood last night, signing a record three-picture deal with Paramount. Danny is seen here at Spago's with his dear, dear friend, the woman who has single-handedly managed his career into its current supernova status.

And when he had made it really big, Florinda would have him back on the show for old time's sake—and a boost in her ratings.

But . . .

But . . .

I'm sure by now we've all spotted the flaw in my scheme.

Danny. And his artistic integrity.

I meditated: what was the best way to get someone of utter integrity to do something sleazy? I was on deadline here. The first round of *Florinda!* auditions was a mere two weeks away. For a moment, I contemplated telling Danny that I had a fatal illness, and that my final dying wish was that he should appear on the *Florinda!* show—but the show was taping next month, and my continued existence might pose a problem.

'—Fact!
Sometimes, even a Great Bit Player must ask for help.

What I needed was someone who was interested in Danny and his problems. Someone who knew a lot about how the entertainment world worked, who could give me some expert advice on how to herd a nervous stallion through the flames of television exposure.

I thought about it for two seconds, and then I called Julian.

At first he pretended to be none too excited to hear from me, but I could hear the quickened beat of his heart over the phone.

As *Cyrano* was well into rehearsals, I asked, "How's our Christian doing?"

There was a long pause. "What does Danny say?"

"Oh, not that much." Not much good, anyway. "But I'm sure that's just a concentration thing—you know, he's letting the performance slumber in its chrysalis, until it emerges in full, gorgeous butterfly form. Danny's like that."

"So he always stinks in rehearsals."

No, I thought, he stinks in performances, too, but you're the one who got all hot and bothered over his "rare and special qualities."

"He doesn't rush his interpretation," I said, a chill in my voice.

Julian snorted. "Oh, look, I knew the guy was a stiff when I hired him. He was comatose in the audition. I asked around, I know the story."

I was mildly irked. It was one thing for me to call Danny a stiff, but it was a bit much coming from a guy who hadn't even gotten to first base. "Funny, I didn't have you pegged as a guy who lets his delicates dictate."

"I don't," he snapped. "I wouldn't have had a shot at hiring him, except that Magalda liked his 'awkwardness.' She thought she could do something with it."

"Well, now what does she think?"

"Not much. But it's okay, the audience never expects anything out of Christian. I'm just surprised, because what I had always heard is that the guy tried too hard. He's just sleepwalking through this show."

"He's been a little depressed recently," I said in a smallish voice. "He's not going to get fired, is he?"

"No. But he's not going to make headlines, either."

"I've been thinking about that," I said. "And I've got an idea."

I outlined the scheme and waited for his reaction.

Julian thought a while, then said, "It couldn't hurt. But I don't think one *Florinda!* appearance is going to catapult him into Hollywood's tentacles."

"Are you kidding? You're telling me that the moment the American viewing public gets an eye-load of Danny, we're not going to be fielding offers of expendable sidekick all over town?"

"Oh, right," said Julian. "And every producer in Hollywood will just happen to tape that particular show."

"With a title like that they might."

"Maybe," said Julian. "Maybe."

"But I do have one teensy problem . . ."

"Danny doesn't want to do it."

"You're not the man in charge for no reason, Julian."

"And you're telling me this . . . why?"

"Because I thought with your background in theater, if you told Danny it was the right thing to do, he would do it. He thinks I'm a crass commercial opportunist."

"It's nice when friends know each other so well."

"So, will you?"

"No."

"Why not?"

"Why should I?"

We were poised at the bargaining table.

"Because," I said, "because this is not something you could tell Danny over the phone."

"It's not?"

"No, it's definitely a face-to-face kind of conversation."

"Which means what?"

"Drinks?"

"I don't drink." He was smiling, goddamn it. I could hear the glee over the phone.

I parried lamely. "Pellegrino is a perfectly acceptable social alternative. I'm surprised you didn't know that."

Julian yawned. "I better hear an offer of dinner fast, or this phone is going to be back on its hook."

It's amazing what threats can do. In an instant, all thought of how I would get Danny to agree to dinner with Julian flew out of my pretty little head. I told Julian that the next time I called, I would have an invitation.

"In a decent restaurant," he said. "No starving artist specials."

So, great, one problem solved, four hundred and fifty to go. Numero uno: how to get Danny to dinner without arousing our romance-phobic ingenue's suspicions of a setup?

Problem numero dos—the fact that I had promised to see Ivan next week—gave me the answer.

Fact!

It is easier to get nice people to do something for you than it is to get them to do something for themselves.

"Danny, I think I'm in love." (Not strictly true, gentle reader, but necessary for our purposes.)

"That's wonderful." Big smile over the breakfast table. "I am so happy for you."

"I really want you to meet him."

"Great, name a day."

"I thought we could go out to dinner."

"Swell. Just not Thursday or Tuesday or weekends. Rehearsals," he said sourly.

"There's something else . . ."

"Dinah's not coming, is she?"

"No, no. The thing is, Ivan is trying to write a play."

"Terrific."

"And I thought it would be good if he could get some career advice from that guy from the Magalda Bernadin group." Danny froze. When someone freezes, it's a sign to talk fast. "I forget his name, Julius, Jonah . . . Anyway, the guy is just so busy, you know, his schedule is so crazy, I thought, well, we should just get everything out of the way in one evening."

After some persuading, Danny agreed, but he said, "Promise me . . ."

"Anything."

"That this is not a date."

"Of course it's not."

"Because I'm not interested."

"No way. Actually, I think Julian's seeing somebody. I think last time I talked to him he said something about some guy."

"As long as he understands that I am not interested."

"Of course he does, Danny. And why would he care when he has this fabulous relationship going?"

Ivan was an easy sell. He was even willing to play the hopeful playwright—anything for love. He was big on the subject these days.

"Can I show you my apartment afterwards?"

"Yes."

"Will you look at my etchings?"

"Gladly."

"Read twenty more pages of my book?"

"Ten pages."

"Fifteen."

"Two."

"Eight?"

"Deal."

Generally it's best for those in recovery to move beyond bad memories, but in the interests of general knowledge, I will now take you step by step through Julian and Danny's first date.

Frankly, the memory stings even now.

Even before the big night, problems began to present themselves. Most of them derived from Danny's suspicions—perfectly justified—that this was a setup. He didn't like the choice of restaurant. ("Why so expensive?") He wanted to dress casual. ("No one's going to be looking at me . . . right?") He didn't want to come, period.

"Honestly," he told me the night before, "I think it would be better if I meet Ivan under different circumstances."

"No, it wouldn't be."

"I'm going to be really uptight. There's something about Julian that makes me nervous." (A good sign. A good sign that could screw the whole thing up, but a good sign.) "Ivan'll think I'm a jerk."

"No one would ever think that of you, Danny."

Ah, if I had known then what I know now.

I, of course, had my own anxieties. This was for all intents and purposes my first real date with Ivan, and there wasn't one genuine, sincere factor in the whole deal. What kind of relationship were we creating, I wondered as I dressed that night. One based on lies and manipulation and commerce . . . and what, exactly, was the problem again?

After a last-minute dicker over birth control (bring, don't bring, oh, bring, for God's sake), I presented myself to Danny.

"Lovely," he said.

"Yeah?"

"Yeah. Really nice."

I looked him up and down, and asked, "Is that what you're wearing?"

"Why?"

"No reason," said I. As we left, I thought, at least the good Lord gave him cheekbones.

PRIMARY RESPONSIBILITIES OF THE FOC (*Friend of Celebrity*)

Remove incriminating evidence and/or body fluids.

Ivan, Danny, and I met at Fido's after work. Then we met Julian outside the theater. There was no very good reason for this, other than I wanted to remind Danny of all the good that Julian might do for him.

Big mistake.

Julian emerged from the stage door, and there was much greeting and more introducing of Ivan—who was, after all, so keen on the theater and playwriting and all that—and then we proceeded to walk to the restaurant.

"What's the name of the restaurant?" asked Julian, who already knew.

I told him.

"Nice place," he said. "Good wine list."

So this is how it worked. Try to envision it: I am trying to hang back and talk to Ivan. Danny is also trying to talk to Ivan, and Ivan is trying to talk to me, while Julian is trying not to talk to Danny, but get his attention, if you know what I mean.

Danny inquired politely after his boyfriend, and Julian said, without batting an eye, "It's over. We had trust issues."

The trouble started, as so many things do, at a bus stop. At a bus stop maybe three doors down from the restaurant that was our destination. On the side of the shelter, there was this advertisement for some clothing store. It had these two guys, holding hands and walking down the beach together with some kind of dog running behind them.

Nice, right? Progressive, right? Just the thing everyone wants to see breaking down the barriers of old?

Everyone, it seems, except Danny and Jesse Helms.

"Look at this." He pointed. "Look at this."

I looked. "Great."

"Great? Look at how dumb they look. Look how . . . they look like they have *rocks* in their head."

Julian said, "I know that guy, he does have rocks in his head."

Danny stalked back and forth in front of the ad. "I mean, now it all starts, you know? Now we're acceptable, we have credit cards, we use them. People want to sell to us."

I said, "Did I miss the tragedy?"

"They want to sell to us, which means they want to sell us. Package us. We've joined the great media ionizer. Zap. In goes a person, out comes instant male nurse." He shook his head. "Sometimes I wish we were still fucking invisible."

"Strange," said Julian. "Exactly *not* what I was thinking."

"But we are invisible, who we really are. I think when you're . . ."

"Closeted?"

"No, just not *out* there, big, larger than life, you have some privacy. Some sense of yourself that's not defined by this media monster."

"No," said Julian. "No, *stop*." Julian put a hand over his heart. "Advertising demeans people with stereotypes. I just do not believe it, I am about to faint. I am going to pass out, right here, on the pavement. Did you know?" He addressed a terrified elderly passerby. "The media is taking control of our minds! It's taken over our very souls!" This to a young woman walking a Schnauzer "Run!"

And then to pretty much anybody within a five-block radius: "The media controls our minds! The media controls our minds. Run! If you have no mind, run! Flee! Get away while you can!"

PRIMARY RESPONSIBILITIES OF THE FOC (*Friend of Celebrity*)

Always remember that they are never older than thirty-five if they are women, forty-five if they are men.

There was a pause. No, call it a silence. One of those long, painful silences that could easily end with somebody dead. Julian began to calm down. Danny fumed. I tried to imagine what Thelma Ritter would do in such a situation, and—you know?—failed utterly. Finally, Ivan suggested we go into the restaurant, and we all agreed that that was the best thing to do.

At this point, I must make a confession: I had an ulterior motive in choosing the restaurant I did. Restaurant reviews can be just as name-droppy as Liz Smith's column. For weeks, I had been reading that the new place where the hoi polloi grazed was Furuncle's, owned by Bobby Floggit.

The minute we passed through the clouded, lead glass doors, all thought of Danny, Julian, and Ivan evaporated. *They* were here. I could smell them, the perfume of rich, pampered skin under layers of Armani and Versace. I inhaled, nearly fainted. After abstaining so long, the scent of real live celebrities was almost more than I could bear. I took little breaths, terrified to blink, as we were escorted into the dining area. Then, with the utmost delicacy, I let my eyes travel right and nearly shrieked. I looked to the left, almost fainted. Recklessly, heedless of the consequences, I did a mad, rolling eye survey of the entire room while Handel's "Hallelujah Chorus" resounded in my head. They were here! I was here! We were all here together! Waiter, my chicken paillard and Chardonnay!

In fact, I was so dizzy with celebrity intoxication, it took me about five full minutes before I realized Danny was kicking me under the table. Hard.

"What?" I looked in his direction, then slightly—I'm sure Danny didn't notice—over his shoulder. Oh, my God! Oh, my God, oh my God. Oh, my gods!

"I thought you said Ivan was interested in theater."

"He is interested in theater. Insanely interested," I said, busily figuring out if I could ask the waiter to send a drink over to table four.

"Then why doesn't he know who wrote *The Glass Menagerie*?"

"He's very poorly educated." I dragged my eyes away from the director at table four. "For God's sake, Danny, that's why I wanted him to meet you and Julian. He knows absolutely nothing, and he needs guidance."

"Why does he want to go into playwriting? He's an extremely talented novelist."

"How do you know?"

"He told me."

I looked to Ivan, who was keeping Julian entertained with stories of Sheriff John and company. In fact, they were imagining a screen version. An X-rated screen version. Okay, so Ivan was not coming off like an acolyte of Arthur Miller's.

"Darling?" Ivan perked in my direction. "Didn't you want to ask Julian some questions about the theater?"

"Well, I thought I'd wait until we'd at least bought the man a drink."

"This is such a good man," said Julian. "I like this man so much." He hailed the waiter and the wine list.

I said to Julian, "I thought you didn't drink."

"Whoever told you that?"

After Julian had spent my 401K on a bottle of wine, I said, "Julian, maybe you should tell Ivan just how hard it is to get noticed by the right people."

"Very hard," said Julian, twirling his glass to watch the legs form. "Very, very, very hard."

"And about the unorthodox methods one might have to resort to, in order to attract the attention of all those right people."

"More unorthodox, the better," said Julian.

"You might also," said Danny, "want to tell him how important it is to maintain your integrity and creative focus."

"I might," said Julian, "but why?"

"Because success isn't very meaningful without it."

"Ivan knows all about maintaining his creative integrity," I said. "What he doesn't know is how to get people in a position where they want to compromise it."

"And that," said Julian, glancing at Danny, "shouldn't be a big problem in his case."

"There should be loads of people just dying to compromise him," I said.

"Tons."

"Millions."

"At least two or three," said Julian. "Are people having appetizers?"

I strongly believe that in a work of life guidance, failures must be chronicled along with successes, in order to give people a full picture of the obstacles they face. Believe me, if it weren't for this particular ethic, I wouldn't hesitate to skip the details of what followed.

One of the main obstacles you will face on the road to becoming a Great Bit Player is willfulness. Out of a misguided sense of pride and self-respect, people will refuse to do what you want them to.

In the time it took us to consume the portobello mushrooms and mesclun salads, our pheasant with cranberry, and our grouper Milanese, I completely failed to bring the conversation back to the subject of Danny's Success. (Never mind mentioning the boundless opportunities of appearing on *Florinda!*) No matter what conversational gambit I used—self-esteem, creative opportunities, free parking—nothing worked.

I had help. Julian was perfectly happy to talk about Danny, and all Ivan wanted to do was make me happy, so they too tried to steer the dinner chat around to the appropriate topic. But Danny was a veritable Wall of China; there was simply no way around him. He didn't partake in the discussion, either to object or agree. For about three quarters of the evening, his only contribution to the conversation was, "Pass the Pellegrino."

But just when it looked like the night was going to be a complete and utter flop, Danny turned to Julian and said, "Don't you think people have to work for their own self-respect?"

"That kind of self-respect can give you hairy palms," said Julian. "It also has been known, on occasion, to bore audiences."

"I think if you're good, and you work hard, it happens for you eventually."

"I think if you want to sell something, you put it in the front window."

"I don't want to sell something, I want to work."

"And you know how many people just want to work?"

Well, after that, Danny was quiet for a while, but not quiet like he had been earlier in the evening. It wasn't until we ordered dessert—Julian finding it necessary to order a cognac along with his espresso—and Ivan wondered aloud whether it was harder to be a writer or an actor in New York that Danny spoke, saying writer, just as Ivan said actor.

PRIMARY RESPONSIBILITIES OF THE
FOC (*Friend of Celebrity*)

Tell a post-plastic-op celebrity that you would never, ever know they had anything done.

210 • EMMI FREDERICKS

"Why would you say writer?" asked Ivan uneasily, like there was some kind of gulag for novelists no one had told him about.

"How long have you been working on your book?" Danny asked him.

"Three years."

"And what happens if it doesn't get published?"

"It will get published," said Ivan, because naivete is the true gulag of all novelists.

"How do you know that?" Julian asked.

Ivan shrugged. "Because it's good." He looked at me. "It has a lizard in it."

"On the off chance," Danny persisted, "that it doesn't, some-how, find a publisher . . . what does that mean? You've spent three years working intensely on something no one will ever read."

"So?"

"So you don't find that painful?"

"No. Because I can write whether or not anyone reads me. You can't act unless someone's watching."

"My point exactly," I said.

"And," said Julian gently, "there's no age limit for success in writing."

It was a blow. Danny would never admit it, but I could tell he was upset. I opened my mouth to say something and then shut it. Part of being a Great Bit Player is to know when it's time for the principle players to take over, and this was one of those times. Danny was dragging his fork through his raspberry coulis in a way I can only describe as despondent. Ivan was looking worried that he'd hurt Danny's feelings, and Julian was just waiting for Danny to crumble so he could pick up the pieces. There's no getting away from it. Love, like the pursuit of success, has its predatory ele-ments.

But I didn't know how predatory until Julian said, "You know who I ran into the other day?"

We all looked at him. What acquaintances were we going to have in common? Meryl Streep? Mel Gibson?

Julian smiled. "Roger Kelton."

Danny looked up. He didn't have to say a thing. The panting, desperate curiosity of rejected love was all over his face.

Still, he swallowed, and managed to get out a series of words that sounded something like, "What's he working on these days?"

"Oh, didn't you know?" Julian looked surprised. "He's out on the coast."

"San Francisco."

"No," said Julian patiently. "Hollywood? You have heard of Hollywood, right?"

"Is he doing some kind of independent film?" Danny got excited. "Are they doing *The Idiot*?"

"Only in the Hollywood sense. He's directing *Fangland*. Part Four."

There was dead silence at the table. Finally broken when Ivan said, "*Fangland Three* sucked."

"I assume that's why they're calling in someone of Roger Kelton's stature for the next installment," said Julian.

"I don't believe it," said Danny, who had turned just the teeniest bit pale. "You must have the title wrong."

"*Fangland Four: Incisors of Doom* is not a working title you forget," said Julian.

And it was at this point that I made what seemed like my chief Boo Boo of the evening. "Danny," I said, "do you think maybe if you called Roger, he might get you a part?"

Now, the reason some people would call this a miscalculation is that Danny got up and abruptly left the restaurant. But no sooner had Danny left Furuncle's than Julian bolted after him. (Not before, I might add, throwing down a wad of cash sizable enough to make me think that if Danny didn't want this guy, he had, well, rocks in his head.)

The whole thing was so dramatic that it was some time before I noticed that something highly irregular had occurred.

The drama was over, the principles had exited, and the Great Bit Player was still onstage.

How, you may ask, do you define being onstage? Well, in my case, it can be defined by sitting in an extremely nice restaurant, a big wad of cash in hand, and a reasonably good-looking gentleman next to me, who was looking like two empty seats at the table was his idea of a Good Thing.

Ivan said, "I like Julian a lot."

"Yeah," I said, fingering the money. "He's a nice guy."

"I liked Danny, too."

"You didn't see him at his best."

"Well," said Ivan, "I hope it works out for them."

"Me, too."

I don't know if you've ever been in this particular situation, where the scene suddenly shifts, and you can't think of a thing to say. Here was Ivan, who I was fairly accustomed to treating in a manner that bordered on abusive. And yet, without Danny and Julian to focus on, he was making me uncomfortable to the point of speechlessness. Help! Give me a line, somebody. Tell me what to say. Tell me what the plot is here. Ivan kept looking at me like there was something to be said, and I couldn't for the life of me think of what it was without a TelePrompTer.

Darling, don't rely on other people to do things so you can have something to watch all your life!

All right, Ma. I get your point. Now tell me what the fuck to say.

PRIMARY RESPONSIBILITIES OF THE
FOC (*Friend of Celebrity*)

Lie for them in court when necessary.

But Ivan said it first. (And so he should, being a writer. He gets paid to come up with the dialogue.) "You want to get out of here?"

So all I had to say was "Yes."

Ivan, being the writer, also made up the plot. He decided it would be nice if we kissed on the corner while waiting for a cab. I didn't argue—it was his story. He decided the cab should go to his house. It made for a nice change of scene, a new dimension to the story so far. And he decided there shouldn't be a whole lot of talking once we got to his apartment, and that frankly the audience shouldn't see a whole lot of it, because the lights never got switched on.

I was just the editor. I made a few suggestions here and there. But overall, I let him do what he thought best.

Which, as it turned out, he did very well.

Sometime in the middle of the night, Ivan whispered, "Now will you read my novel?"

"No."

He stirred slightly. "How come?"

"Because I might not want to do this again if I did. And I want to do this again."

The next morning it was bagels. It was whitefish salad. It was coffee with whole milk. And anybody who doesn't know how bagels and whitefish translate romantically, well, you have no soul, so

214 • EMMI FREDERICKS

why bother explaining. The whole thing was perfect, and not a thing about it made sense. It was the worst case of miscasting I had ever seen. The Great Bit Player becomes the Ingenue. But it was also sort of fabulous, and I didn't feel like arguing with the script.

Paradise lasted right up through the last kiss on the corner before I went down into the subway. ("Call me?" Kiss, kiss. "Tonight." Kiss, kiss, kiss . . . If it weren't me, I'd be sick too, but it was me, so suffer.)

Not a lot of romantic idylls survive the New York City subway, this is true, but this was even more brief than most. Oddly enough, the first emotion that came to me was . . . guilt.

Yes, guilt. Guilt over abandoning Danny in a moment of extreme emotional distress. Guilt over forgetting that Dinah was perhaps days away from being convicted of the crime of the week. For ten hours, neither one of them had even entered my mind. What kind of friend was I? What kind of Great Bit Player was I?

Danny would never forgive me, I realized as I left the train station. He would never forgive me for lying to him, for setting him up with Julian in such an underhanded way. Oh, he would never say so. He would say nice things like he understood, and he was sure I meant well. And then in about six months, he would be off to Duluth, and I'd never see him again.

And then Dinah would go to jail, and I wouldn't see her again

PRIMARY RESPONSIBILITIES OF THE FOC (*Friend of Celebrity*)

Never, ever sell your story (until the benefits of the sale outweigh continued friendship with said celebrity).

until she deposited herself on my doorstep ten years later with who knew what godawful habits picked up Inside. Julian would not be likely to hang around without Danny as an incentive, so that left me with Ivan.

Ivan . . . who was creative.

Ivan . . . who had written a novel.

A coming-of-age novel.

But, as that other great heroine decreed, I wouldn't think about that now. Now, I had to return home. To Tara. (Or the fourth-story walk-up that serves as Tara in this story.) With every step, I thought of different ways I could apologize to Danny. Maybe I could blame it all on Julian, say that I had no prior knowledge and that the whole rotten scheme was his idea. Danny didn't like him anyway, so what was to lose?

You can imagine my surprise when I opened the door, and there was Julian sitting on the couch, reading the paper.

CHAPTER THIRTEEN

THE RISE OF A GREAT BIT PLAYER

Fact!
Even a Great Bit Player can be surprised by a plot twist.

IN SPITE of all my efforts to create just such a scene, I was shocked at the sight of Julian sitting nonchalantly on our couch, in a way that did not suggest he had just dropped by for coffee. As far as I was aware, he did not moonlight as a meter man, so the only plausible explanation for his presence was that Danny had invited him. For purposes unknown and hopefully nefarious.

"Have a nice evening?" asked Julian.

"I did. Thank you. And you?"

"I had a nice evening myself."

"I'm glad to hear it."

"I thought you would be."

We sat for a while longer as I tried to figure out how to ask all those tacky questions without sounding, well, tacky.

"Danny's out," Julian said. "He's running a quick errand."

"Does it involve putty or fright wigs?"

"I don't think so."

"So," I said casually, "can I presume we're going to be seeing more of you?"

Julian stretched. "I think you can assume that."

"Do I get the filthy details or not?"

I did. Apparently, Julian had gone no more than a block before he found Danny spinning helplessly on the corner, looking very much like a man who meant to go directly to Penn Station and buy a train ticket to Duluth.

I sat up, visions of Danny Duluth-bound flashing in my head. "That's not where he is now, is he?"

"Oh, no."

"How do you know?"

"Because I don't think Danny wants to go to Duluth anymore."

"Why not?"

"Because I was born in Duluth," said Julian.

There, on the corner, Julian had told Danny all about his little hometown. By the time he was through, Danny was no longer laboring under the illusion that Duluth was an oasis of Real Theater. Through the power of Julian's descriptive skills, it was now an uninhabitable backwater, where only malls and garden gnomes flourished.

"I told him about Maison Du Popcorn," he said. "I think that's when he realized what he would be getting himself into."

"So, then what?"

"Well, then he thought Newark. He had some notion of returning to his roots, bringing culture back to his homeland—he wasn't very coherent." Julian sighed with the resignation of someone in thrall to the beautiful and unbright. "But I persuaded him that something as important as the rest of his life needed some more in-depth thought, and why didn't we talk it over somewhere more hospitable than a street corner?"

"Have I ever told you how much I admire you, Julian?"

"No, you haven't."

"Well, consider yourself told. Then what happened?"

Fearing seduction, Danny wouldn't go to Julian's house, but

due to the fact that neither of them had any cash—Julian because he had given it all to me, and Danny because he never has any—they had to go somewhere that didn't require money. There are no such places in New York, and so Danny agreed that Julian could come back to our place, where he would lend him the cash to go home.

"Did Danny really think you were going to cab it home after coming all the way here?"

"Sure."

"Why?"

"He thought you would be here." Julian smiled.

"And then I wasn't."

"That's right."

"I see." I smiled. "Well, that all worked out well, didn't it?"

"Even better than you think." Julian smiled. "I told him."

"Told him what?"

"You know, about . . ."

But just then we heard the rattle of the key in the door, and Danny came in with a paper bag in hand. My mood slumped. "No putty or fright wigs," indeed. Julian had a lot to learn about Danny. I couldn't even imagine what grotesque had taken hold of Danny's fancy in such a short time. Quasimodo? The Ancient Mariner? Mistress Quigley? What made it all the more rotten was that Danny was looking even more gorgeous than usual. He had that hair-flopping-shyly-over-the-eyes look of postcoital defenselessness. And in a few hours, it would all be covered in glop and powder.

He grinned. Clearly all was forgiven. "Hi."

"Hi."

"Welcome back."

"Why, thank you."

He hesitated, slightly thrown by the first friend–inamorata combination. Julian got up first. "I'm going to shower and all that good stuff," he said, and left us.

I said, "You don't mind if I gloat a little."

Danny shook his head. "It's your right."

"Gloat, gloat, gloat . . ."

"That's enough."

"He's nice, isn't he?"

"Yes, he is."

"I was right, wasn't I?"

Danny nodded. "You were." He held out the paper bag. "Look inside."

I looked inside, inhaled sharply.

"Danny . . ."

"What do you think?"

"Danny . . . *The Reed Report*."

"Uh-huh."

The Reed Report, for those of you who habitate under rocks, is the weekly published listings of all casting calls in cable and network television. To see Danny with a copy was like seeing a Baptist with a book on Satanic worship.

"I can't believe it."

"Yeah, there's a residual sense of skin crawl, but . . . there it is."

"The key word here is *residual*. Oh, Danny, I think I'm going to cry." I opened the book, said in a small voice, "There's the listing for the *Florinda!* show."

"Julian told me about your idea. For me going on the show and wowing the viewing public. What do you think, am I too late?"

"What? You could never be too late. Oh, Danny, I'm so excited. You watch, you watch . . . the minute that show hits the air, you'll have producers crawling at your feet begging you to do Ibsen in the park." And action flicks, and best friend parts, and even—oh God, dreams couldn't go too high now—maybe even *a sitcom.*

I tried to pull back, compose myself. *It's Danny's dream, it's Danny's life.*

No, it's not, it's my dream, it's my life.

Cut it out. Repeat after me—it's Danny's life.

Yes, okay, it's Danny's life, but it's my limo, my luxury hotel suite, my power lunch . . .

I was debating free Versace vs. free Donna Karan, when Danny said, "Look, I have some not so good news."

Dinah. It was Dinah. Oh, God, in my mad foolish excitement over Florindas and Feiffers, I had forgotten all about poor Dinah.

"Is it Dinah?"

Danny looked surprised. "Dinah? No, it's Sal. They had to take him to the hospital. He collapsed last night."

"Oh, my God." This was much worse. Sal was a really nice person, whereas Dinah was, well, not. "What happened?"

"He fell on the stairs this morning. Mrs. Rosemount found him and called the ambulance. Apparently, he hasn't been eating since they took Norm away."

I looked at the pile of flyers, bearing Norm's picture and the slogan: REPOSSESSED BY CORPORATE AMERICA. We'd only sent out a hundred so far. But there was no sign that people were giving up, say, saving the whales to save Norm.

Who was I kidding? Did I really think average Americans were going to take time out of their busy lives to do anything about Sal and Norm? With things like Lylo and Dinah and J.J. and Fuzzy to distract them?

And even if they did, did I really think the agency would listen? No, on both counts.

But the plan did have one point in the plus column: I couldn't think of anything better.

So Danny and I spent the rest of the day stuffing and licking, stuffing and licking, stuffing and licking . . .

Strangely enough, even though he had played a crucial role in getting Danny to agree to the auditions, Ivan couldn't see the point of it all.

"Why do you want him to go to these auditions?"

"So that he can get on the show," I said. We were sitting at Willy's Noodle Shop, which, if you're ever in Midtown, is not at all a bad place.

"Is that a good thing?"

"Yes, it is," I said, speaking very slowly. "Because if he gets on the show, he can be seen."

"He can be seen if he takes his clothes off in Times Square at rush hour."

"Not by as many people."

"But *Florinda!* is so . . . so . . ."

"What?"

"Degrading."

Can I ask? Which generation was it that men made the transition from manly meat-eaters with the refinement of a billy goat to the delicate, morally aware aesthetes of today? When did men start using words like *degrading*? When did they stop being rank opportunists ready to sell their grandmother for a buck? Are mere morals and aesthetics what made this country great? Who *raised* this bunch of ninnies?

I made a note to myself: Suggestion—"Girly Men, and Why" on the next *Florinda!*

Maybe Ivan and I could appear on the show.

As we parted on the corner, Ivan said, "Hey, what's your friend Dinah doing?"

"Potentially? Twenty-five to life."

In the three days leading up to the *Florinda!* auditions, Julian and I joined forces to create what we saw as the perfect Danny Beale. It was an excellent partnership—a combination of the eyes of love (Julian) and the eyes of the female heterosexual (yours truly) who made up the bulk of the *Florinda!* audience. The results, if I may say so, were fantastic. We scrupulously tailored Danny's look to be a perfect evolution of that casual drop-dead gorgeousness he habitually wore into something that would translate well across America. Danny showed a certain amount of apprehension throughout the process, but budding love was doing wonders for his passivity.

Danny did put his foot down on one point, however: only one of us could come with him to the audition. (Actually, at first, he said neither of us could come, but I said that the audition was likely to be strenuous and that he needed a gofer to fetch mineral water and power bars—which was a lot better than telling him the truth: that I simply didn't trust him not to do a last-minute bunk out.) Julian, who probably sensed that his presence would only make Danny more nervous, graciously stepped aside and let me be the gofer.

On the big day, Danny was quite calm. (I, on the other hand, had the evil jitters, but being on the verge of a complete life change will do that to some people.) The *Florinda!* studios are located on the West Side, in the mid-seventies, in a surprisingly nondescript structure for a building that houses one of the top-rated shows on TV. As we made our way up the block, I stayed close to Danny, trying to deflect cigarette smoke and grungy passersby who might soil him. And Danny seemed to be taking it all in stride. But just before we proceeded through the revolving doors that would spin us into fame and fortune, he balked.

I had anticipated something like this and did not panic. Instead, I gave him a gentle push, but he resisted, saying, "No, wait, just hold on a minute . . ."

Danny slowly backed away from the building. I wondered if I should throw a shawl over his eyes, slap him on the flank, and shout, "Yah, mule!"

"I just have to prepare."

Preparation turned out to be a certain amount of pacing up and down the pavement, accompanied by swallowing nervously. If Danny had been "preparing" to play a nervous wreck, we would have been in fine shape.

"Think beautiful thoughts," I told him.

"I think I'm going to throw up."

"That's nerves."

"No, I think it's ethics."

"Danny, you're an actor. You don't have ethics, you have publicly attractive causes. Any twinge of morality you are currently experiencing is the result of half a grapefruit and five cups of coffee. Take a deep breath." He did. "Better?"

"Not really."

"Take another breath."

He took one, nodded, and took another.

"Now ready?"

A pained look crossed his face, but I took that as a yes and pushed him through the revolving doors while he was still exhaling.

It was just as well Danny had done his breathing exercises outside, because otherwise he might have bolted at the pandemonium inside. It's a scary thing how many people in America think people hate them because they're beautiful. The line for the auditions stretched down one very long corridor, turned a corner, and kept on going. And this was just to get an interview.

Danny went pale at the sight of so much competition, but mine was the clearer head, and all I saw was a bunch of plug-uglies with serious delusions of grandeur. Lots of stars of tomorrow wanna- bes. One guy kept saying to anyone within earshot he was only there because his agent sent him, while the brunette next to him wildly sprayed herself with some toxic chemical. Lots of people who would have sent back grilled cheese sandwiches because they had cheese in them.

I noticed a few of them visibly lose heart at the sight of Danny. Good. He was striking terror into the heart of the opposition.

I maneuvered him into place on line, gently adjusted his shirt collar, and placed a lock of hair over his eyebrow.

"You look great," I told him.

He smiled weakly. "I know you're right, and that this is some- thing I have to try."

"Good boy."

"Just, right now, I'm imagining that I'm Quasimodo."

"Whatever works for you, Danny."

It soon became clear that not everyone on line was going to get into the preliminary interview. I have to hand it to the *Florinda!* people. They were models of ruthless efficiency. A representative of the show—a short, thin woman with enormous glasses—was making her way down the line, surveying the possibilities, and cutting the weak members from the herd with a curt, "Thank you, we're not interested." I could hear sudden gasps and tears throughout the corridor, and steeled myself.

As the studio Torquemada approached us, I noticed that Danny was doing strange things with his mouth. I gave him a sharp elbow and told him to cut it out. "It's a relaxation tech- nique," he whispered.

"It looks like you're rearranging false teeth."

"I wish."

Having delivered the bad news to a nearby redhead, the *Florinda!* flunky cast her appraising eye upon Danny. I stepped aside so as to not spoil the picture and held my breath.

She motioned Danny to step forward. He didn't, so I pushed him. Walking around him—presumably to get a posterior view—she inhaled deeply, and said, "Okay, oh, yeah, now this I can do something with."

Through clenched teeth, Danny mumbled, "I am not a this."

The woman took a step back and pointed a lethal fingernail. "Yeah, and you're not an animal. You are a human being. A beautiful, gorgeous human being who—I am willing to bet—shows up great on film." She handed him a card with a number on it and told him to go inside to the waiting room.

"What happens there?" I asked anxiously, visions of casting couches (and side exits) dancing through my head.

"Our producer will chat with him, make sure he's not a total moron, see how he shows up on film, that kind of thing. Now you"—she spoke to the woman standing behind us—"go and get your teeth straightened and a decent dye job. Next!"

They didn't let me go into the interview with Danny, so I was forced to wait outside, worrying for three and half hours.

For about an hour, I tried to cut down the competition by going up to the prettier candidates and saying things like "I hear the beauty thing is just a setup. The show's really called, 'My Best Friend's a Jerk—and I'm Going to Tell Him.'"

"My friend's a casting agent, and she says she'd never cast anyone who appears on this show."

"I knew someone who went on *Florinda!* She got herpes."

But these people were diehards. Little things like humiliation and herpes were not going to deter them. So I wandered aimlessly down the block, until a huge headline at a newsstand caught my eye: LYLO TO TESTIFY!

Throwing two quarters at the guy, I grabbed the paper and tore it open.

> *"Rap sensation Lylo Wingate announced yesterday that he will tes-tify in his own defense. Wingate, son of Bubble King Lyle Wingate, Sr., is charged with reckless driving and vehicular manslaughter in the death of deli owner Buster Rosen. The announcement comes a week after Wingate's companion, Dinah Sharlip, claimed that she was at the wheel the night of the fatal accident . . ."*

I read the article all the way through, then bought two more papers, desperate for a comment—preferably expletive-laden—from Dinah. But there was nothing. Only this from Marty the Schlep: "We are fully confident that Mr. Wingate's testimony will shed further light on the events in question."

Good one, Marty. That'll have Dinah making license plates in no time.

And of course, everywhere, there were photos of Lylo with the beauteous Bethany.

Just as I was racking my brains, trying to figure out how to get to Dinah before she ruined her life and/or got a movie deal, Danny emerged, pale and shaken, from the audition room. I rushed up to him, threw my jacket over him, and rubbed his shoulders. (Hey, they did it in *Rocky*.) "How did it go?" I asked as we made our way out of the building. "Do they want you on the show?"

"They want me on the show," he said in a dull voice.

I leapt into the air, then came down to earth—at least halfway. "Did you meet Florinda?"

"What does Florinda look like?"

"Large. Loud. A cross between abusive and maternal."

Danny nodded. "I met Florinda."

I went out of my mind with excitement. Barely able to breathe, I gasped, "What was she *like*?"

Danny thought a moment, then said, "I think she was the most awful woman I've ever met in my life."

To reward Danny (and myself) for a job well done, I splurged on a cab home. I was feeling pretty smug, if you want to know the truth. But I wasn't so full of myself that I didn't notice Danny wasn't exactly blooming. He didn't say much on the ride home. I wasn't sure what to make of it—maybe he was one of those people who can't be comfortable with success. Or it could be—and this is what he said it was—that the whole thing had made him sick.

"Think of the future," I told him.

"I am," he said cryptically.

"You're not thinking of backing out, are you?"

"Oh, no."

But he sounded resigned. Not happy. Not upbeat. Not like the Star of Tomorrow.

That evening, Julian called to see how the audition had gone. Danny talked with him for a little while, then said he was exhausted and went to crash out.

I got on the phone to say hi, and Julian said, "He is not sounding thrilled."

"Aftershock," I said breezily. "He'll feel zippy in the morning."

Julian made a noise of skepticism, then said, "You know, don't get me wrong, I'm as opportunistic as the next guy . . ."

"But," I said warily.

"But I'm wondering if maybe we're deciding what's good for Danny when we should be letting him make the choices himself."

"That's the kind of thinking that has Danny living in a rattrap with me instead of in a penthouse with you, Julian."

"I take your point. But I don't know, I'm feeling . . . guilty."

"There are drugs for that kind of thing, Julian. Go take them. Good night."

I repressed a snort. First Ivan, then Danny, now Julian. What was going on with these men? What was this hideous outbreak of funk? Ivan and Danny—well, you expected a certain amount of wispiness and flimse, but Julian?

However, doubts and second-guessing aside, Danny was now set on the road to Fame and Fortune. Now it was time to turn to Goal Number Two. It was time to think about Dinah.

I needed to know more about Lylo's announcement that he would testify, needed to see how it was playing. Surely, by now, people were wondering. Surely they could see that Dinah's "confession" was merely the act of a desperate woman in love—and that she was being ruthlessly exploited by a heartless, uncaring pseudostar? I mean, how stupid were people?

Answer: pretty stupid.

I turned on the television to find that as far as the viewing public was concerned, Dinah was not the Woman Done Wrong but the Woman Gone Wrong.

In fact, it only took about two seconds to find an entire program dedicated to the subject of Dinah Sharlip. Why she did it, what it meant, who she was, and who we wanted her to be. The show started with a selection of Dinah clips: a baby picture they got I know not where, her yearbook photos (the one from college had to have parts blacked out), pieces of her art (also with parts tastefully blacked out), and excerpts from all the key moments of the case, culminating, of course, with her "confession."

JUDGE: Do I understand you to say that you were at the
wheel the night Buster Rosen was killed?
DINAH: Yes, Your Honor.

The courtroom montage faded, and the host, a very serious-faced woman, stared into the camera and said, "Joining us next to examine this subject in depth, the author of the forthcoming study *The Deadlier Sex: The Violent Femmes.*"

She swiveled in her chair and said, "Doris, thank you for joining us."

"Thank you, Jennie," said Doris the Hack Quack.

I nearly shit myself.

There, on my television screen, was Doris Byrd, aka Doris the Hack Quack, aka Doris the Fraud, aka Doris the Complete Fucking Loon.

How the hell had she gotten on TV? I could just imagine the phone call. *Oh, yes, Jennie, I am fully qualified. I studied at Yale and Johns Hopkins, and I'm currently conducting a study, to be published in the fall, on women who kill. I also have a private practice. Do I take referrals? Absolutely, Jennie . . .*

Now Jennie was asking, "Doris, can you give us any insight into the mind of women who kill, women like Dinah Sharlip?"

"Oh, absolutely, Jennie. You see, women like Dinah Sharlip feel *invalidated* by today's society. They feel *marginalized* by the still-narrow parameters placed on feminine behavior. And so they *strike out* against what they perceive to be a biased gender construct."

"But how do they choose their targets? What makes them snap?" asked Jennie, bringing it all right back to basics for the folks at home.

You might think that would stump old Doris, but no. Without a blink of an eye, she said, "It's extremely difficult to ascertain the dynamics between the latent hostility and the object of transferal that then serves as the projected recipient of that hostility. And rage," she added as an afterthought. "I find the presence of a car quite significant."

Yes, as the instrument that flattened the said object of transferal, Buster Rosen, I think we could all agree that the car was significant.

"You sound as if you sympathize with women like Dinah Sharlip," said Jennie.

Well, Jennie, as Dinah Sharlip is a marginalized murderess and I am stark raving mad, yes, I can say that a certain sympathy does exist. Except that I am much, much crazier than she is.

Doris said, "Jennie, I think all women can sympathize with Dinah Sharlip. Don't you?"

End with sad, sympathetic smile and Jennie saying, "Provocative words from Dr. Doris Byrd"—(Doctor? *Doctor?*)—"author of the forthcoming study *The Deadlier Sex: The Violent Femmes.* Next we'll talk to uber-agent Webby Peterson, who's fielding the many offers for Dinah to tell her side of the story. Webby, do you agree with Dr. Byrd that many women feel a need similar to Dinah's to strike out, as she put it?"

"Absolutely, Jennie. I'm anticipating widespread interest in this project for just that reason."

As I switched the television off, I realized that I now knew two very important facts:

1. The whole world had lost its mind.
2. Dinah was going up the river.

Why? Because it was what everyone wanted to happen. You know how studios screen movies and then change the ending if the audience doesn't like the one they have? Well, for a while, we had an ending with Lylo going off into the sunset in chains—an

THE AEROBICS OF *Celebrity* SPOTTING

THE BUMP AND BRUSH
For experienced celebrity spotters only! *When in a room with a reported celebrity, but celebrity has his/her back to you and neither the Sideways Lean or Sidestep is possible. Take several steps toward the celebrity. Take one step too many. Apologize profusely. Avoid legal entanglements.*

---

ending that was just swell by me but didn't seem to really work for anyone else.

Look at how many people had a stake in Dinah's guilt . . .

The American public wanted Dinah to be guilty because they were tired of Lylo being guilty.

Doris Byrd, because she had told talk shows she was conducting a study on women who kill. If Lylo were guilty, she would have to change her study to Rich Assholes Who Kill—which didn't sound nearly as snappy.

Webby Peterson, because she was going to score a book deal for Dinah.

Lylo's lawyers, because they were Lylo's lawyers.

Danny, because he still hadn't forgiven Dinah for horning in on *The Idiot.*

Ivan, because then he wouldn't have to meet Dinah, which he didn't want to do—even if he didn't know it yet.

And of course, Dinah herself.

So the only two people who were on Dinah's side were me and my mother, who couldn't care one way or another.

Which left me to conclude one thing . . .

Dinah was going up the river.

I would have to get a visiting pass to Sing Sing.

Unless . . .

Unless . . .

Unless someone came forward with new evidence that proved she was lying.

Minor glitch . . . no such person seemed to exist.

Glimmer of hope . . . I knew she was lying.

Glitch . . . I hadn't seen the accident.

Glimmer . . . maybe I didn't need to.

I began to ponder furiously. And as I pondered, a plan took shape. No, I can't call it a plan. It was more than that. Nothing so petty as a scheme, so meager as an idea, it was the *Magnificent Seven* of plans, something worthy of Steve McQueen, carried out in this case by a Great Bit Player, because only a Great Bit Player could pull it off.

CHAPTER FOURTEEN

ORDER, ORDER IN THE COURT OF PUBLIC OPINION

*H*ERE'S HOW I pictured it.

The time: The day of Lylo Wingate's testimony.

The setting: A high-ceilinged, oak-paneled courtroom. A fan twitches lazily overhead. The air crackles with tension. Every seat in the courtroom is filled. People crowd into the balcony, stand at the back of the room. The press is out in full force, pens poised on notepads, fingers at the ready on their laptops.

Every now and then, someone cranes their head, trying to catch a glimpse of Dinah, sitting near the front of the courtroom. Dinah tries to look composed, but her trembling chin betrays her terror. She anxiously searches the room for a sign of Lylo, as Marty picks at a hangnail.

The judge would emerge from his chambers, the courtroom would rise, and the sound of a gavel would crack in the silence . . .

The judge—who, if I had my way, would look something like Paul Scofield—fixes Dinah with a sorrowful yet stern look. (Deep down, he knows of her innocence, but he is hampered in his pursuit of justice by her mad desire to destroy herself for love.) He instructs the defense to call their witness. A rumble of excitement is heard in the courtroom. *He's coming, he's coming . . .*

On cue, Lylo enters the courtroom. A squeal of excitement from the female and impressionable. He ignores poor Dinah, whose eyes follow him, pathetically hoping for solace, and takes his place in the witness stand.

The Wingate stooge oils up to the witness stand and asks, "Isn't

it true that the night Buster Rosen was killed"—at the mention of Buster's name, all heads in the courtroom would bow—"you were too intoxicated to drive?"

Looking down at his Gucci loafers, Lylo would whisper, "Yes, sir."

"Were you aware at the time that you were intoxicated?"

"Yes."

"And did you get behind the wheel of your car while intoxicated?"

Lylo straightens up, apologetic geek turned model citizen. "No, sir, I did not."

"Then is it safe to say that at the tragic moment that Buster Rosen was struck and killed"—again, all heads in the courtroom bow at the mention of Buster's name— *"you were not driving?"*

"Yes, sir." Lylo's lip trembles with indignation.

The Wingate stooge moves in for the kill. "I ask you, *who was driving?"*

Lylo would bite his lip. "It was . . ." he would say in a fake choked-up voice. "It was . . ."

But before he could falsely accuse Dinah, I, bursting like a thunderclap in the courtroom, would leap from my seat and shout, "Your Honor, I object!"

Paul Scofield would glare at me—he does not tolerate outbursts in his courtroom—and say, "Young woman, I do not tolerate outbursts in my courtroom."

And I would say, "I understand and apologize, Your Honor, but I have evidence that must be heard."

The crowd would start murmuring and buzzing (because that's what crowds are there for) until the judge raps on the desk several times and bellows, "Silence." Then he would motion to the bailiff to bring me forward. As I leave my seat, Dinah would whisper, "Don't do it. Don't tell them anything."

But Paul Scofield would tell her to be quiet and instruct me to come closer.

"Now then," he would say, "what is this piece of evidence you have to offer?"

"I have evidence that proves that *this woman*"—here I would point to Dinah—"is lying when she says that she was driving the car that claimed the life of Buster Rosen." (All heads in the courtroom bow.)

"And why would she do such a thing?"

"To protect *that* man." My finger, now the sword, if you will, of justice, would swing to Lylo, followed by an audible gasp from the crowd.

"And how do you know this?" the judge would ask.

"Because *she* told me, Your Honor."

It was perfect. No matter how many times I ran through the scenario, I couldn't find a glitch. Dinah would be free, Lylo would go to jail, the tabloids would have their story, and Paul Scofield

TOP TEN THINGS *NOT* TO SAY TO A *Celebrity*

I've loved you since I was five years old.

would sleep better at night, knowing he hadn't sent an innocent woman to jail. The only person who would know I was lying was Dinah, and who would listen to a low, amoral cow like her?

But there was something else . . .

Something even better than truth, justice, and the American way.

It would be the triumph of the Great Bit Player.

The fact was, I had spotted a slight flaw in the Great Bit Player gig—and that was that people tended confuse you with the furniture. You were overlooked, ignored, unseen. And while I couldn't remember exactly what the underlying purpose of the Great Bit Player was, I knew it wasn't to be the same old unseen schlub you had been before. Hey, even Eve Arden and Thelma Ritter got a laugh now and then.

I got all fizzy just thinking about it. What a debut—and not just on any stage, but on the stage of Public Opinion. At the height of that month's Trial of the Century, I would nail one of the most hated men of tabloid newspapers. Despite the energies and devotion of so many, it would be me who finally fingered Lylo Wingate, Jr., son of Lyle Wingate, the Bubble King.

I decided not to tell anybody about my plan. Right now, the only people who would know I was lying would be Dinah and me—and I wanted it to stay that way.

I did tell Danny and my mother that on the day of Lylo's testimony, I would be there to lend moral support.

They had exactly the same response: "Why?"

Danny said, "How can you lend moral support to someone with no morals?"

My mother said, "I think you're deluding yourself, honey. But it's a nice delusion."

Ivan, on the other hand, was a sweetheart. Was very touched

that I wanted to be there for my friend in her hour of need. Said he'd never dated someone so warmhearted and giving. That, in fact, if I was going to support Dinah, he wanted to be there to support me.

Which sounded great to me, because what's the point of making your big debut with none of your nearest and dearest there to witness it?

"You're sure your friend won't mind?" he asked. "It's got to be a pretty emotional day for her."

If he only knew.

The Monday, Tuesday, and Wednesday before Thursday were the longest three days of my life—followed by the longest six hours. The hearing was scheduled for two o'clock. I debated calling in sick but decided against it when I realized the story wouldn't exactly hold water when I turned up on every front page the next morning.

 TOP TEN THINGS *NOT* TO SAY TO A Celebrity

Why haven't you come out yet?

But it was hard to act normally in the office. I was suffering from considerable pre-celebrity jitters. (It's no small burden, let me tell you, knowing that within the next twenty-four hours you might become a Trivial Pursuit answer.) And my nerves only got worse when I ran into Felice in the ladies' room.

"Oh, hey," said Felice as I came out of the stall. "You want to do the Lylo pool?"

"The what?"

She waved a batch of paper at me. "The Lylo pool. You know—you can bet guilty or not guilty. Then you have all these, like, bonus levels. Not guilty because that chick did it, not guilty because the jury thinks he's cute. I even put in a total long shot: not guilty because Buster Rosen never died and he walks into the courtroom and there's a mistrial. You want to play?"

I looked at the betting slip. "You really thought this all out, Felice."

Was it possible, had I ever been this pathetic? Thank God, this dreadful anonymity would soon be a distant, painful memory.

"I did the table on my computer." Felice offered the sheet of paper. "It's five bucks."

I grabbed a paper towel and washed my hands in a highly pointed way.

I said, "It's very distasteful to profit off others' unhappiness, Felice," and left the ladies' room.

I was in an extremely tetchy mood when I met Ivan for lunch before we made our way to the courthouse. I hadn't had nearly enough time to go through my speech. I tried to run through it over corned beef on rye but most of the time I couldn't remember anything more than "Your Honor."

Ivan, I'm sorry to say, was getting on my nerves, too. He kept yakking away like it was any normal day. Like somebody we knew wasn't going to be famous by the six o'clock news. At one point, I

TOP TEN THINGS *NOT* TO SAY TO A *Celebrity*

Gosh, you look worse in person.

TOP TEN THINGS *NOT* TO SAY TO A *Celebrity*

Your second wife seemed so nice. Whatever happened to her?

kicked him in the shins under the table, but I pretended it was a random muscle spasm.

Being a writer, Ivan was heavily into What Ifs. Like what if Lylo proposed to Dinah on the stand? What if Lila Rosen whipped out a gun and blew Lylo away? What if Dinah was halfway to Tijuana right now?

"Maybe she has a sack of unmarked bills and a forged passport stashed somewhere."

"Ivan."

"Don't get mad. I'm just making up scenarios. Daring daylight escapes and stuff. It's what happens when you write *Days of Dust* for a living."

He patted my hand. An apology for defiling this somber occasion with childish fantasies. For some reason—maybe my own childish fantasies—this irritated me. Pulling my hand away, I said, "Dinah's not going anywhere; she's getting a book deal, for God's sake."

A longish pause. Then Ivan said, "She is?"

"Webby Peterson signed her up."

"Webby Peterson?" Ivan's voice had gotten very, very small. "Webby Fuck-You-Pay-Me Peterson?"

"Yes," I said testily, "Webby I-Only-Represent-Books-People-Will-Read Peterson."

Ivan flinched.

Half meaning it, I said, "I'm sorry, Ivan."

"No, no, it's okay."

But I could see that it wasn't. Not really.

And I would have done something about that, I swear, except for the fact that I was experiencing a full-fledged attack of stage fright. As we approached the courthouse, I kept telling myself it wasn't *Hamlet*, that the audience had no idea what I was supposed to say, and that if I flubbed a line here or there, it would all get cleaned up in the tabs the next day. I was delivering headlines, not the Gettysburg Address.

We got within sight of the courthouse and Ivan said, "Wow."

Which pretty much summed it up. The press was everywhere. And despite my raging nerves, I was gratified to see the dangling microphones, the zooming cameras, and reporters practicing their patter. I gloated for a moment. They would have to rework in a hurry once they got an earful of what I had to say.

Ivan and I bustled up the steps. But then I heard a roar from the press and turned to see Lylo making his entrance. He smarmed his way through the crowd, the ever-present Bethany beside him turning and pouting as if she were on a runway, and not on some courtroom steps with trash clinging to her heel.

I didn't want to come into contact with a man I was about to prove guilty of manslaughter, so I hustled Ivan along until we got to the metal detectors. Some people hate metal detectors, but I have to admit they always give me a little thrill. They mean you're going someplace where there are people important enough that someone might want to kill them.

We found our way into the courtroom and took our seats in the area reserved for spectators. ("My days as a spectator are over," I almost said to the bailiff, but didn't, as the poor man would have had no idea what I was talking about.) Ivan was trying to look everywhere at once. And by this time, the excitement was starting

TOP TEN THINGS *NOT* TO SAY TO A *Celebrity*

How's the trial going?

to get to me. I was having trouble breathing. Even "Your Honor" had gone right out of my head. All I could imagine now was leaping to my feet and shouting "I object!"

I wanted to go to the bathroom, pee, and compose myself, but I was terrified they wouldn't let me back in. The courtroom was filling up. Dinah wasn't there yet. Neither was Lylo. But I did catch sight of Lila Rosen as she came in. She was wearing a beige suit and a big button that said BE A DELI MAN FOR LIFE. I tried to catch her eye, but she was busy fishing a Kleenex out of her bag.

I started to worry that, despite the foolproof nature of my scheme, things weren't going to work out as I had planned. The fact was, I was feeling strangely out of sync with what should have been my Big Moment. Part of it was Ivan—he was so awed by the proceedings, and it was hard to feel like a jaded insider when your date has turned into Shirley Temple. Nor did the courtroom have the floor-to-ceiling windows I had imagined, the ones that were supposed to give the impression that the Holy Light of Truth was shining into the Darkness of Ignorance at just the right moment in my speech. Instead, there were crummy plaster walls painted a bilious orange. The chairs were covered in scratchiti, and the ceiling was too low. Nothing could ring out triumphantly or bellow defiantly in this chamber. This was a room built for droning.

The judge, when he arrived, was not Paul Scofield—who I didn't really expect—but a small, balding man who appeared to be getting over a cold.

Nor, frankly, were the jury members what I had had in mind.

Instead of the charming cross section of urban America—the grandmother who knits, the cab driver who clears his throat compulsively, and the earnest college student—we had an assortment of gum chewers and fidgeters who looked like they would rather be anywhere than where they were. They did not look like a group of people dying to hear what I had to say.

Basically, the whole thing was all too real. Which made me feel real. Which meant not like the kind of person who leaps up and delivers shocking new evidence that makes headlines.

My inability to turn heads was underscored with Lylo's arrival. He entered the courtroom, greeted with the kind of murmuring and humming I had anticipated for myself.

I felt myself becoming a Spectator again, the creeping chill of irrelevance stealing across my soul . . .

No, no! Fight it! You are a Great Bit Player!

Deep breath. Rehearse speech. *"Your Honor, I object!"*

Then it was Dinah's turn to come in, followed by Marty. There was an even busier buzz as everyone tried to see how she reacted to Lylo, but nether of them looked at the other. Except for one time, when she pretended to be fixing her contact lens and glanced in Lylo's direction. If he noticed, he didn't show it. No thumbs up, no insincere smile, nothing. Bethany just yawned.

Dinah couldn't see me. Which was just as well. If she'd known I was there, she probably would have told the bailiff I was deranged and demanded that I be removed from the courtroom.

The judge took a hanky out of his robes and wiped his nose.

TOP TEN THINGS *NOT* TO SAY TO A *Celebrity*

I hope you don't mind me saying so, but your last movie/CD/book stunk. *(No points for honesty, ladies and gentlemen. Celebrities hate honesty.)*

TOP TEN THINGS *NOT* TO SAY TO A *Celebrity*

What's Letterman really like?

Then he croaked, "The People of New York State versus Lylo Wingate will now proceed. Is the prosecution ready?"

"Yes, Your Honor."

"Just a moment, Your Honor!"

That wasn't me. In case you were wondering, it was not me. Not a word had passed my lips. Just for the record, it wasn't Marty either, who was sticking by his guns and remaining an ineffectual schlep to the very end.

Startled, I searched the room for the person who had stolen my line. But nobody was standing up. Whoever it was had obviously decided they could do without the jumping up part.

There was an outburst of murmuring and buzzing (my murmur! my buzz!). The judge banged his gavel (my bang!). "The court is about to hear testimony from Lylo Wingate. The courtroom will please give him the courtesy of silence."

"I'm going to give him more than that, Your Honor." A middle-aged woman in the third row got to her feet. Frantic, I wondered if I still had a chance here. Could I, even now, lay claim to fame?

Jump up! Speak! "Your Honor, I object!"

Didn't. Couldn't.

The judge rapped the gavel a few times. He was really starting to feel that head cold. But the good woman was not to be deterred. Raising her voice to be heard above the banging, she said, "My name is Mrs. Sheila Hobsbaum. I've been in Florida for the past few months, and so I apologize for coming so late to the proceedings—"

"Madam, you can't—"

"But . . ." Mrs. Hobsbaum silenced the judge and his gavel with a look—like how could he be so rude and who had raised him? "I just wanted to say that I was home the night poor Mr. Rosen was struck, and if you want to know who was driving, I can tell you. That's all."

And she sat down again. But not before she gave Lylo a very dirty look that didn't leave a whole lot of room for doubt as to what her testimony would be.

There was a split second of silence (my split second!), then more buzzing and murmuring. I looked over at Dinah, who was shaking her head, like she didn't care what Mrs. Hobsbaum had to say. Lylo was looking at his lawyers like they had seriously fucked up when they forgot to give Mrs. Hobsbaum the Rosen treatment down in Florida. And in his excitement, Marty the Super Lawyer actually rushed the judge, who started banging frantically and yelling for a bailiff.

TOP TEN THINGS *NOT* TO SAY TO A Celebrity

When are you going to stop wasting your talent on cheap commercial ventures and do something with real quality?

Lylo's lawyers started to object all over the place. The prosecutor said that she had had no record that this witness was scheduled to appear, and as such, there had not been due notification.

"I didn't know, either, Your Honor," said Marty the Super Lawyer, eager not to be forgotten.

At this point, the witness herself spoke up. "I tried to contact them, but all I got was voice mail, and I have a rotary phone."

There was a lot of laughter over that one. (The next day, the tabs would scream, PRESS ONE FOR GUILTY!) By now the judge was completely fed up and ordered all the lawyers, plus Dinah and Mrs. Hobsbaum, into chambers.

Panicked, I jumped up and waved my arms to get Dinah's attention. She might need a character witness. She might need someone to make a phone call, someone to get her coffee . . . But Dinah never looked back and never saw me. She just went off into the judge's chambers, where everything that was important would take place, leaving me behind to read about all it in the morning papers.

Again.

Ivan couldn't understand why I was so upset. He interpreted my bottomless depression as anxiety over Dinah's fate. I let him think this for a while because the truth was just too humiliating.

But after a few hours of being earnestly consoled, I decided I couldn't take it anymore and confessed. You know, it's a wonder they never tried earnest consolation in all those World War II movies where the Nazis are trying to get Gregory Peck to confess. "Oh, dear, it must be so very difficult to be an American commando. You must feel very misunderstood and underappreciated." It's so irritating you'll do anything to get the person to shut up.

So there in a downtown park, amidst crapping pigeons, I explained the entire plan, too dispirited to care if telling Ivan blew my chances for credibility on the appeal.

Ivan, I have to say, was a little slow on the uptake.

"You were going to lie," he said.

"Yes. But for the sake of truth, justice, and the American way."

"And you're upset because you think the judge isn't going to believe Mrs. Hobsbaum, and her testimony will somehow have a bad impact on your testimony?"

I took a deep breath. In relationships and in recovery, honesty is essential. "Yes, but not exactly."

"Not exactly how?"

"Not exactly in the sense that yes, I am upset that the judge might not believe Mrs. Hobsbaum, in which case, Dinah goes to jail." Ivan smiled, looked relieved. "But . . . I am also upset because I had this whole plan to electrify the courtroom with my surprise testimony, thereby not only rescuing Dinah from the clutches of the law, but rescuing myself from the depths of obscurity and nonentityhood."

"And now you can't do that."

"And now I can't do that."

"But it's, like, seventy percent depression over Dinah and thirty percent depression over the nonentity thing."

"No, it's more like the reverse."

"But your friend may go to jail."

"But my friend can become a TV movie, and frankly, she was never that great a human being."

Ivan frowned. "What kind of human being are you?"

"More common than you know, Ivan," I said. "More common than you know."

And that's how I wound up losing my chance for fame and fortune and my boyfriend all on the same day.

CHAPTER FIFTEEN

AN OBJECT LESSON

STRANGELY ENOUGH, Ivan's reasons for breaking up with me were similar to Alvin Schremmel's.

According to Ivan . . .

I was disgusting.

Well, no, not disgusting, but he was disgusted.

Well, not disgusted, but really, really disappointed.

Or, not so much disappointed as . . .

"Ivan," I said finally, "quit being a nice guy and say whatever it is you want to say."

"I know I'm probably being a jerk," he said miserably. "But I just can't deal with your world view. I'm really sorry."

I would like you, the reader, to take note: Ivan said it, he said "jerk" first. And if Ivan said it, I saw no reason not to agree with him. Wholeheartedly, in fact.

In one of those pissy little fits of anger where you say everything wrong but in just the right words, I said, "This has nothing to do with me—you're just upset that Dinah has Webby Peterson as an agent and that Dinah's going to get a book published before you. Which is to say before *never*."

There was a long pause. Then there was another one. Then Ivan said that actually, maybe he was the slightest bit disgusted with me, hurried into the nearest subway station, and disappeared.

I sat there for a minute, feeling awful. There were so many things I should have said—anything but what I had said. And after a minute, I jumped up and said them.

"You're going to be sorry," I yelled after a long-gone Ivan. "You're going to be sorry when my friends are famous, and I'm living in Beverly Hills with a pied-à-terre in New York. You're going to be sorry when I know tons of famous, influential people who could not only get your crummy book published, but have it drastically rewritten so it makes a halfway decent movie. You're going to be sorry when you're pathetic and unpublished and I'm famous and fabulous. You're going to be sorry, Ivan Feiffer!"

But the only people who heard me were a few pigeons who flew off in a panic to relieve themselves on someone's head.

I went home, minus one friend and one boyfriend, to find a huge stack of my Norm appeals returned for wrong addresses.

Danny was watching the evening news. As I came in, he said, "Hey, great news about Dinah."

"What? Why?"

He gestured to the television. "Lylo pleaded guilty. Dinah's off the hook—didn't you know?"

I stared, stupefied—and not for the first time that day. "No, I didn't know."

"But I thought you were there. Lending 'moral support.'"

Oh, sure, Danny, rub it in. Take a big, sharp piece of glass and shove it straight into the old vena cava. It's all right, I can take it.

"They threw all the little people out before the big scene," I said bitterly.

Danny gave me a very odd look and switched off the TV. "Are you okay?"

"I'm fine," I said.

"By the way, someone named Sheila Karpfellner called for you. She left a number."

I had no idea who Sheila Karpfellner was, and given how today was going, I had no wish to find out. Whatever it was probably involved death or taxes, or both.

Wanting to steer the conversation toward bright and future plans, rather than past and failed ones, I said to Danny, "So, are you all ready for *Florinda!*?"

Danny sighed. "How ready does one have to be?"

I suppressed a stamp of the foot, and said, "Danny, you seem hesitant."

"What do you mean?"

"Not sparkling. Minus the glitter in your eye, absent the sunny smile. You lack the joie de vivre one likes to see in the stars of tomorrow."

"I'm sorry." He let his head hang a little to let me know he meant it. "I guess I'm still feeling a little queasy about tomorrow." Frustrated, he dropped his hands into his lap. "I don't know. Just . . . none of this feels right."

Fact!

When confronted with willfulness, Great Bit Players may experience the urge to leap upon the willful subject and pummel them with intent to damage.

These impulses are counterproductive and must be suppressed. When confronted with willfulness, adopt a gentle yet firm tone and speak in vagaries about "choices" and "feelings."

Which is what I did.

In my most patient voice, I said, "Moving forward, taking risks, always feels strange."

"But it doesn't feel like moving forward," said Danny. "It feels like giving up."

I inhaled. Then inhaled again, wishing I had something to inhale. "Look, think about Julian," I demanded, my teeth just a hair more clenched than would have been ideal.

"What about him?" said Danny.

"I bet your relationship feels strange at times, even frightening."

"Sure."

"Getting to know someone, getting to trust them, is a tricky process."

"Yes, it is."

"And . . . you know, you're always a little afraid that it's not going to work out."

"Yes, you are."

"That they'll dump you over some dumb, trivial thing, and you'll be left all alone . . ." For some reason, my throat was getting all tight and it was hard to talk. "And you won't have any idea why, and you'll feel like shit and be convinced no one will ever love you again."

Danny looked at me. "Are you okay?"

"I'm fine. I just have to go to the bathroom for a minute."

For a long time, I sat on the toilet with a damp towel pressed to my eyes and asked myself a few questions. Like, what was happening to me? Why were so many people telling me to get lost? First Dinah, then Ivan . . .

Was I really becoming a horrible person?

No, you just did what everyone told you to do, dummy. You got a life.

Yeah, but what's a life without my friends?

The same friends who thought you were so boring you constituted a public health menace? Good riddance.

I was standing in front of the mirror, really, really wishing I could take back what I said about Webby Peterson, when Danny knocked on the door, and said, "Anything I can do?"

I looked around the bathroom—an act that took all of five seconds because our bathroom was smaller than a roach motel and less hygienic. I thought of Bickerstaff Books, of Ivan's dreary novel, of Dinah disappearing on me, and called out, "Yeah."

"What?"

"You can knock 'em dead on *Florinda!*"

Danny was going to be beautiful and hated whether he liked it or not.

That night, I had a dream. In it, I was surrounded by a sea of reporters, all of them asking questions, their cameras focused on me, their microphones poised to catch my every word.

"Is it true you're responsible for reuniting Norm and Sal Marchap?"

"How did you manage to save Norm from Corporate America?"

"Did Norm howl in gratitude or just slobber on you?"

I saw myself at City Hall, Norm wagging his tail and dripping saliva on the mayor's shoes as the mayor gave me the key to the city. Then we were in a Cadillac, rolling down Fifth Avenue, with streamers cascading down. Norm ate a few, then puked them on the floor of the Caddy, but nobody minded.

Then me in a nice Donna Karan–ish outfit, being asked by Barbara, "What gave you the courage to stand up to the Big Guys and get Norm back for his friend and owner?"

"Well, Barbara, sometimes, there's a right thing to do and a tasty way to do it."

No, rewind . . .

"Well, Barbara, sometimes you just have to do what's right." Manic applause from the audience.

"I hear you're also responsible for getting Danny Beale his big break in movies."

"Oh, no, Barbara. I have to give Danny credit there. He's the one with the talent."

"But if you hadn't pushed him to go on *Florinda!* he never would have been noticed by Steven Spielberg."

"Well, we're just lucky that Steven happened to be home with a head cold that day and saw the show."

"Of course, you have known your share of tragedy. Your friend Dinah Sharlip is, of course, serving fifteen to life for vehicular manslaughter."

"Sadly, we can't help everyone, Barbara."

"But they did arrest that young man who was stalking you?"

"A very troubled soul. A would-be novelist."

"Well, I'm sure we all look forward to your new book, to be published later this month, *How to Be a Great Bit Player.* Can you tell us, is it true you were paid the highest advance in the history of publishing?"

"Money means so little to me, Barbara, it's all about helping others."

Me in a palatial town house by the park, me at Café des Artistes gossiping with Woody, me courtside at Madison Square Garden, me in *Vanity Fair* . . .

And then I woke up and it was time to get ready for *Florinda!*

Julian supervised the perfection of Danny's appearance, and I was called in to give final approval, which I did.

Julian laid a hand on Danny's shoulder. "Earth to star, earth to star . . . come in, star."

"Here," said Danny with a sigh.

"You look fantastic," I told him.

"Well, don't hate me for it."

Julian couldn't stay with us for the show, but he wanted to at least come with us to the studio. He even bought us a cab ride so Danny would arrive pristine and unrumpled. In the car, Danny let Julian hold his hand. That was okay. I mean, it was nice. And he smiled when Julian made little jokes. That was nice, too.

He didn't talk to me much. But that was okay.

No, really, it was.

But when we got to the studio, Julian barely had time to say good-bye and good luck before a swarm of handlers swept Danny off into makeup.

"What do you think?" Julian asked me. "You think he'll be okay?"

"He'll be fine," I said firmly, feeling that it was time for Julian to butt out. He had only been worrying about Danny for a few months, whereas I had been a nervous wreck over Danny for years.

No sooner had Julian exited stage left then I was pounced upon by a *Florinda!* gofer, who asked me, "Are you someone?"

"I'm a friend of one of the guests."

"Oh." Big phony smile, big phony voice. "Then you'll have to sit right over"—a hand clamped on my arm and yanked me toward a seat somewhere north of Siberia—"here, where she can see you." *And absolutely no one else can.*

The Big-Toothed Gofer had put me all the way to the side, and about as far back as you could get and still be in the studio. For a moment, I seethed. How long, oh Thelma, how long was I to be relegated to the Siberia of Nobodyville? Seated far from the bright lights and friendly eyes?

The studio was starting to fill up now. People were starting to clap and whoop like it was a rock concert, gearing up for a good old misery-fest—a competition in psychic trauma where the most fucked-up wins.

Dinah would have had a blast.

Except Dinah wasn't talking to me.

Ivan would have loved it.

Except Ivan wasn't talking to me, either.

Well, who needed Dinah, who had been ready to throw her life away on Lylo Wingate? And who needed Ivan, who wrote novels less commercial than a phone book in Sanskrit?

The stage crew was clearing the way for the star's arrival. The crowd was totally revved up. People started stamping their feet and chanting, "Flo-rin-da! Flo-rin-da! Flo-rin-da!" Heartache was on the way, and no one wanted to miss a second. The cameras started moving in, and the stage door lights went on. The crowd erupted into a complete frenzy as the Empress of Angst bounded onto the stage and proceeded to give a rotten imitation of someone who was shocked, just shocked, to find so many people here . . . and all applauding little old her.

Before us was a sweet, shy hamhock of a Southern belle. We had the widened eyes, the hand clapped demurely to the bosom, the dip of the head, the intentionally ineffective wave of the hand for silence. Of course we would not be silent—the sign for APPLAUSE was still flashing madly, for one thing. We stood and cheered our heroine, who laughed; it was just, so, so dear of us all to make such a fuss.

But finally, Florinda raised both her hands and said, "Wow! Okay!" A last whoop from a group of diehards in the back. "Okay, today . . . today we're going to be talking to some of the most hated people in the world." A lusty cheer from the crowd. "These people have never committed a crime, they haven't killed anyone, and in real life, they happen to be very nice people—some of them anyway." A wink to the audience—don't worry, folks, you'll get your bloodshed.

"Who are these outcasts? They're beautiful people—and they say their beauty is ruining their lives."

The audience went batshit. It was just the combination *Florinda!* crowds crave: privileged and whiny. The mistresses who moaned that their married lovers wouldn't leave their wives, the credit card addicts who complained they never had enough money, the spoiled rotten kid who bitched that his hard-working mom and dad just didn't understand. This was the core appeal of *Florinda!* The public's chance to cut the malcontents down to size.

It was at this point that I experienced a vague twinge of misgiving. The tone of the event was a little . . . off. This crowd seemed unlikely to take one look at Danny and fall at his feet—unless it was to gnaw at his ankles.

But I quickly dismissed these defeatist thoughts. I had come too far to second-guess myself now.

Florinda was bringing her guests onstage now. Danny brought up the rear, looking extremely nervous, but I was encouraged by what I saw. His competition was nil. A lot of hard-looking faces, buff bodies, and dye jobs. Only Danny looked like someone you'd want to talk to, let alone share saliva with.

"So," said Florinda, addressing the five human sacrifices before her, "you all feel that being beautiful has created real difficulties in your lives."

A lot of nodding. Except from Danny, who looked nauseous. Florinda walked up to one blonde woman. "Candace, tell us how has your beauty affected your life."

"Oh, Florinda!" Big sigh, like, where to even *begin*? "Well, it is impossible to have women friends."

A rumble from the crowd. I couldn't blame them; I hated her, too.

Sensing a prime target, Florinda tipped the microphone closer to Candace. "How so?"

"Women just totally can't deal with me."

"You mean they get jealous."

"Well, not right away. Actually, some women will try and be friends with you so that, you know, they can have your leftovers. You know?" She appealed to the audience, like we had all tried to attach ourselves to beautiful people to get dates and should now feel guilty. "They try to be nice, but after a while, the envy just . . . I don't know, they just feel like they can't talk to me or be with me. I don't know." And she gave a pretty little shrug.

Florinda chatted with a bodybuilder for a few seconds. He shared with us the pain of having all his friends' girlfriends fall in love with him. Florinda asked him if he didn't think he had some control over that. He said he didn't think so. Then we cut to a commercial.

During the beak, Florinda took a heavy-duty slug of mineral water, while the crowd wondered if it was time to attack yet, then decided not. The signal had not yet been given by the goddess.

When we came back on the air, Florinda turned to Danny. I leaned forward. Here it was, his big moment . . .

She asked him what he found so tough about being gorgeous. "I mean, how much of a problem can it be to be a beautiful actor?"

Danny had been looking a little catatonic, but her sarcasm provoked him into speech. "It is a problem," he said.

The first giggles from the crowd. "It is," he insisted. "Nobody takes you seriously."

Florinda composed her face. "You mean, people don't consider you for certain roles."

"That's right," said Danny.

Now the bodybuilder wanted to say something. "I gotta agree here, I think there is an overall insensitivity to beautiful people. A lot of people think I don't have pain."

Danny said quickly, "That's not what I meant . . ."

But Florinda said, "Oh, do they?"

Now the blonde wanted in on the discussion. "Yeah, like, if you're gorgeous, you don't have problems or . . . you know, they don't realize how much worse it is for someone like me."

"Uh-huh."

"I have a million problems ugly people never have to deal with."

"Uh-huh, wow."

Danny was trying to say this wasn't at all what he meant, but no one wanted to hear it.

"Definitely discrimination," said the bodybuilder.

"Oh, yeah . . ." Now four heads were nodding.

"Nobody takes you seriously at all."

"Nobody."

"Nobody."

"Like, you know, if you have this, then you can't have that."

THE AEROBICS OF *Celebrity* SPOTTING

THE ANAL DIVERSION (aka THE FART)
Startles the celebrity into changing his/her position vis-à-vis the spotter, thus allowing for a better view. Many celebrities will also turn their heads in order to determine "who dun it," providing the opportunity to "spot" from several angles.

"Looks and brains. At the same time." This was Florinda clarifying for the benefit of those watching at home.

"Right." They all nod, say "Right." Florinda is there, she understands them, she is getting it.

At this point, Florinda announced slyly that it was time for a commercial break. The dumb bunnies on the stage sat there smiling. Meanwhile, the crowd was gleefully withdrawing the verbal tomatoes for a full-scale pelt-fest the second we got back from break.

I tried to catch Danny's eye, but he was staring at the stage door. Had he looked in my direction, I might have conveyed through the use of eye signals and sign language that I was sure the audience liked him. That they saw he was in a completely different class from his fellow guests. That it was all going exactly according to plan . . .

But he didn't look my way. So I didn't have to lie.

Then came the moment I had been waiting for—the call to arms, the sound of the trumpet, the bay of the hounds. Florinda hopped up and said brightly, "Wow, okay, we're back, and we're going to take some questions from our studio audience."

Immediately a thousand hands went up.

In a rare flub, Florinda chose poorly for her first question. The man was your fire-and-brimstone, today's-show-represents-the-end-of-civilization-as-we-know-it type. Mindless worship of beauty was causing a whole bunch of things to go wrong—ecology, the government, you name it. No one wanted to deal with the global repercussions of moisturizer, and we quickly switched off to a woman who knew what was needed: straight-out abuse.

"I just have to say," she began, like we were all twisting her arm, shrieking, *Speak, woman, speak.* "You all are the most self-obsessed *losers* I have ever seen."

First blood! The audience cheered. The woman said, "I would

like to ask Candace, in particular, does she ever think of anyone but herself?"

Candace replied that she certainly did. "I have, like, a lot of sympathy for other people."

Somehow, the audience didn't buy it and gave her a big raspberry. Candace sat back, shattered. Her lipstick was smudgy and everything.

Florinda prowled the floor, microphone in hand. She gave it next to a man who said he didn't see what was so bad about people liking the way they looked. The crowd made short work of him, and he sank back into his seat, looking like he would never speak again.

Florinda continued to prowl. I was torn: pleased that Danny hadn't been singled out for torture but anxious because he hadn't had much of a chance to make an impression. I was just thinking of raising my hand and asking him how he managed to be such a good-looking guy but obviously such a fabulous inner person as well, when a guy toward the back stood up and said, "I'd like to ask Danny the actor something."

He sounded halfway normal. Both Danny and I looked up hopefully.

"What makes you think it's because you're handsome that you don't get roles? Have you ever considered that maybe you're just no good?"

Danny's face went dead white, as Florinda announced cheerfully that was all the abuse we had time for. Up came the closing music and frenzied applause. Before Florinda could even shake Danny's hand, he dashed backstage.

We had said we would meet at the stage door, so I started making my way outside, fighting a happy, exhilarated crowd as I went. Sure. For them, it had been a great show. Every guest—completely totaled.

Only from my perspective, it was a crash-and-burn fest.

I didn't see Danny right away, so I leaned against the building and brooded. By all the signs, I hadn't saved Danny's career. I mean, how likely was it that some talent scout had watched the show and thought, "Zowie, gorgeous, sullen, and no talent. Just what I want for Spielberg's next picture."

And not that it was Danny's fault, exactly. But I couldn't help thinking that his preshow vapors had contributed to his lackluster performance. He had taken the whole thing too seriously, that was the problem. He should have been light. Urbane. Upbeat. George Clooney. Not . . . the Blob.

I was lost in sulks when someone shoved past me and nearly dislocated my shoulder. Rubbing it resentfully, I peered down the street for a glimpse of my assailant, and spied Danny, hightailing it down Seventh Avenue. Apparently not at all perturbed that yours truly was not with him.

Moving after him, I shouted, "Hey!"

Danny did not slow down. If anything, Danny sped up.

I broke into a gallop (okay, loping jog). "Hey, Danny!"

Finally, I caught up. Gasping, I said, "Hey, aren't you that wonderfully handsome guy I just saw on *Florinda!* Gee, would I love your autograph . . ."

Here is what I expected: a laugh, maybe a little smile. A light punch in the arm, maybe, but overall, friendly affection tinged with an understandable I-Want-to-Kill-You-But-Won't-in-Light-of-Our-Many-Years-of-Friendship vibe.

Here's what I got. No laugh, no smile, and a look that said If-I-Punched-You-Now-I-Wouldn't-Stop-Until-You-Were-a-Bleeding-Mess-Begging-for-Mercy.

Then he just started moving again.

Trotting along behind, I tried to figure out what had him so pissed at me. I mean, yeah, he had bombed; yes, he had been humiliated—but he had to bear *some* responsibility for that. It wasn't all my fault.

I said, "I hope you're not upset by what that jerk said at the end of the show."

"Oh, no," said Danny.

"Well, good."

"I was long past upset by the time we got to the jerk at the end of the show."

"Oh."

"Who, by the way, was not a jerk. Who, by the way, was the only sane, rational person there."

I let this pass. Danny was having a fit. You don't argue with stars when they are having fits. It's a good way to get slapped.

I tried changing the subject. "You know, I think this could help your performance as Christian. Give it a whole new depth and resonance."

"That's great. Too bad I'm quitting the show."

"Danny." I stopped him from crossing the street. "Slow down and talk to me. What is this about?"

"What is this about?"

"What's the plot here? What's your motivation?"

"My motivation," said Danny, "is that I will be moving out of the apartment. My motivation is that I don't want to be friends with you any longer. My motivation is that I feel humiliated, used, manipulated. To sum up, like an asshole. Does that sufficiently cover my motivation?"

"I know you're really angry—"

"No, I'm past angry. I'm just really sad."

That stopped me. It wasn't so much the words—it was the voice. I hated his voice. Because he was right, it didn't sound angry at all. Angry people change their minds. Sad people don't.

Carefully, I asked, "Why are you sad, Danny?"

"Because I thought you were my friend, and that what was important to me was important to you."

I started to say one thing. Then I started to say another thing. Then something else, and then I gave up. I just stood there and tried to swallow this very large lump in my throat.

"I finally got it. Sitting through that hell. I finally realized just how little you think of me." Danny stepped closer. "You think I'm stupid. You think I'm naive. First you thought it was sweet, how I wanted to be a serious actor, even though I wasn't any good. Now you're just annoyed because I'm not the big star you thought I was going to be."

I didn't know what to say. I tried and tried to think of the right sentiment, the words that would make Danny forget that I had just trampled all over his dignity, made a joke out of his aspirations, and generally treated him like a backward child.

And while I was thinking about all this, Danny walked to the corner, hailed a cab, got into it, and disappeared.

After that, there wasn't a lot left for me to do.

Except go home.

So that's what I did.

I climbed up the stairs, put the key in the door, and walked into the emptiest apartment I had ever been in.

I went to the bathroom.

I got something to drink out of the fridge.

I wandered into my bedroom.

Wandered out again.

Went back, remembered why I left, and came back to the living room.

I sat on the couch.

Thought how if it were much more silent I would lose my mind. So I turned on the television.

I don't really remember too much about the days that followed. I think there were three of them, but it could have been four. After the second day, I lost all track of time. The television schedule might be tattooed on my synapses, but if you had asked me what time it was, I couldn't have told you. Measurements like two o'clock or five-thirty meant nothing to me anymore. It was time for *Oprah* or time for *The Price Is Right.*

After the third day—I think it was the third day—I couldn't tell if I was awake or asleep. If I was dreaming or watching TV. I dreamt that the president got shot and thought it really happened. Fuzzy Winterspoon broke off her engagement, and I thought it was a dream.

I ate almost nothing. Getting off the couch was too much of a hassle. On the first day, I called Bickerstaff Books and told Felice I was having surgery and wouldn't be in for a while.

I forgot to listen for the sound of Danny coming home. I forgot to listen for the telephone. I stopped wondering if I should call someone.

Why should I need to call someone?

Who would talk to me anyway?

On the fourth day, I thought about moving, then thought, Nah. I just couldn't see any reason to. Why shouldn't I just sit like this for . . . well, the foreseeable future? It wasn't like I would have to eat a whole lot—how many calories could be necessary to maintain this lifestyle? If a spare muscle started to atrophy, well, I'd watch an exercise program, do a few kicks. My one worry was that I would run out of batteries for the remote.

I had spent so much time and energy trying to get a life.
And where did it fucking get me?
Right back where I started.
This was a life, I thought, zapping away with the remote.
This was a very good life.

CHAPTER SIXTEEN

THE END OF THE JOURNEY

O H, MY God, what the fuck is this?"
I was dimly aware of cigarette smoke. This was an irritant. Someone was breathing. Air was moving in the room. Dust motes were being disturbed.

I was being disturbed, goddammit.

I croaked into the darkness, "Go away."

"No problem, believe me." The sound of something being kicked across the room. I flinched. Activity. Energy. Bad, bad, bad.

"*Ugh.* I just came by to get my stuff."

More noise. Doors being opened and shut, things being moved. The sounds hurt my head. This would not do. The invader must be repelled.

But with the minimum amount of energy expended.

Dinah entered the light of the television. I blinked, not entirely sure if she was the real thing or a figment from the television.

"What's wrong with you?"

"Nuh . . ." Ooog. My throat was dry. I groped along the floor for a mug I dimly remembered putting down a little while ago. Or was it yesterday?

"I wouldn't," said Dinah, as my hand closed on the mug.

"Why?"

"You don't want to know. Hold on." She stomped off. Then a light went on in the kitchen. (Ooooch, ouch. Light, very bad thing.)

She came back with a glass of water. "Here. Drink this. Maybe you'll live."

"I don't think so," I gasped.

"Why not?" She sat on the arm of the couch. With some trepi-dation, but I guess I couldn't blame her. Now that I thought about it, it was a tad smelly in the old homestead. Despair will do that. I bet Dostoyevsky's digs didn't smell like roses either.

"I can't live. I don't have a life."

"You sure don't now." Dinah aimed a mild kick at the couch. "Get up."

"No. I'm meeting my fate with stoic dignity."

"Oh, please. Get up."

"No," I said, and was surprised at the force in my voice.

So was Dinah, as it happened. Intrigued, she stepped back (no doubt to get a full perspective on the whole disgusting picture). She stared at me for a long moment, then bent down and picked up the television remote.

"Don't do it," I said.

"Do what?" Her thumb hovered over the button.

"What you're thinking of doing. Don't."

"You don't know what I'm thinking. Anyway, what are you going to do to stop me?"

"I'll . . . I'll . . ." Oh, God, movement was tough when you had committed yourself to complete inertia.

"You'll nothing," said Dinah cruelly, and switched off the box.

For a moment, I watched, stunned, as the light died.

"Is that so bad?" asked Dinah.

"Yes. Turn it back on."

"No."

"I'll only turn it on when you go. You haven't proved anything."

"I might not be leaving, so there."

"Yes, you will be leaving, you'll be going to prison, for perjury and dating jerks and things."

"I'm not going to go jail for perjury and I'm not dating a jerk. At least not anymore," she said.

"Ha," I croaked. "So, Prince Charming dumped you for not taking his place at Rikers?"

"Lylo's not going to Rikers," she said irritably. "He's going off to some health farm for the rich and unstable."

"Oh." That didn't sound so bad. I wondered what tax bracket you had to be in to get in.

"But he did dump me. If that makes you happy."

I was about to say that it did. That it served her right for having a life and being famous and leaving me out of it all. That I bet it felt really rotten to fall out of the spotlight and back into the cold light of day with the rest of us losers.

But then I noticed that Dinah was blinking more busily than usual. She was a woman who had loved well, but not wisely, and I didn't have the heart to be cruel. Something that probably explains my perpetual failure and anonymity, but what can you do? I'm a fuckup for the good of mankind.

"I'm sorry, Dinah."

"No, you're not."

"Well, no, I'm not. Lylo's a jerk, there's no getting around it. But hey, look. At least you have the book deal."

Dinah made a harsh, abrasive noise. "Webby what's-her-name dumped me, too. She's doing a book with Lylo instead. So I hope you didn't get your friend's hopes up."

"My friend?" It had been four days of straight television; my mind was not at its keenest.

"Boris."

"Boris?"

"Boris." Dinah made an impatient gesture.

"Ivan."

"Whatever." Dinah, I could see, was going to be much happier with me not having a life again. Me with a life meant she had to remember names and faces and other bummy things not directly related to her.

"Boris dumped me," I told her. "He said I was disgusting."

"Because of . . ." She gestured to the couch.

"No, this was before. He said I was disgusting because I had this plan to jump up and announce at the trial that you told me you were going to lie about driving the car."

"You were?"

"I figured you would be free and I would be famous. It was a dumb idea."

"It is a dumb idea."

"Yes, I said so, I don't need affirmation."

Dinah stood up and said, "So, are you getting up or what?"

"Why? Am I doing something?"

"Yes, you are. Unless . . ."

"Unless what?"

"Are you still doing that recovery bullshit?"

I thought a long moment. "I think I've moved into a new phase." I put my feet on the floor. "Dinah?"

"What?"

"I'm glad they didn't send you off to some place for the rich and unstable."

"I'm not. I wanted a fucking vacation."

A long time ago, when Dinah and I first moved back to New York, we were heavily into spas. We would go whenever we had some spare cash, so that for two hours, we could entertain the fantasy that our faces and bodies were economically viable and worth pampering to the tune of $150. Dinah even wrote it off on her taxes.

Which is how I found myself once again flat on my back in one of the city's less pestilent relaxation salons. Side by side, Dinah and I lay prone in the darkness. Delicate slices of cucumber refreshed my screen-sore eyes, while milk of magnesia gently leeched the impurities from my pores. Exotic, soothing scents wafted through the air. Somewhere, a Tibetan bell rang. I thought of cows and world peace.

This is why you always have to have people around you who knew you when. Because these are the people who know that when you have been stupid and self-indulgent, the only answer is to go out and be even more stupid and self-indulgent.

For a moment, I wondered if I ordered a smoked salmon pizza from Spago's, would someone go get it for me. Probably not.

"Dinah?"

"Mm?"

"Do you really think I'm boring if I don't talk about celebrities?"

"No. I think you're boring when you're trying not to talk about celebrities."

"Oh."

"Does that make sense?"

"Yeah. Dinah?"

"Yeah?"

"Did I do a horrible thing to Danny?"

A long pause.

"I'm thinking," said Dinah.

Oh, God. A person who lied in court about squashing harmless geriatrics thought I was immoral. I peeked from under my cucumber slice for a sign that Dinah was kidding, but her face was perfectly composed.

"Here's what I think," she said finally. "You either did a crappy thing for good reasons or a good thing for crappy reasons. I can't figure out which."

"But not a crappy thing for crappy reasons."

"No."

"Dinah?"

"Mm?"

"If Lylo called you tomorrow from jail and wanted you back, would you go?"

There was a long silence. Then: "Nah." Then another longer pause. "Although, if that Manson guy called, I could be available."

"Dinah?"

"Mm?"

"You're kidding, right?"

"Yes."

"Dinah?"

"Mm?"

"I'm not sure about something here."

"What?"

"Have we learned a lesson or haven't we?"

"I have."

"And?"

"Never date guys from Westport."

"That's not applicable to my situation."

"Yeah, well, I'm a person, not a fortune cookie."

And so it was back to the land of the living for yours truly.

It was a shock, I have to say. On that first day when I went back to work, everything seemed very loud. People moved too fast, there was talking, and headlines, and signs. It was all a little too much to absorb, particularly that first subway ride. Whenever possible, I shut my eyes and thought of big, fluffy sheep.

As I walked down the street, toward the hallowed halls of 1265 Avenue of the Americas and Bickerstaff Books, bagel and coffee in my hand, I wondered: is this a life?

Was I cured?

I felt a lot better than I had three days ago.

I figured that was cured enough for now.

It felt funny to be around people. Dinah was the only human being I had talked to in a week. Danny still hadn't come home. But I kept telling myself he had to come back sometime—even if it was only to pick up some clothes and extra putty.

But as I got off the elevator and headed to my office, I felt a completely irrational surge of hope.

Because maybe, just maybe, Ivan had called.

However, the first individual I ran into was not Ivan bearing roses and darling-can-you-forgive-me's. It was Felice the Tabloid Queen.

"How was the surgery?" she asked listlessly. Felice was feeling pretty down. Her Lylo pool had been a complete bust, because she had forgotten to put down a box for Plea Bargain and a lot of people wanted their money back.

"Peachy. Stitches come out next week." By then, I figured, I would want some more time off. Dinah was making noises about a trip to Atlantic City that sounded promising. Perjury could probably get you a free hotel suite, at least.

"Hank Laufler's coming in today," Felice told me. "He wants to drop off the last of the manuscript. I said you'd be in."

Oh, God. More wrangling over vegan virgins and buff barbarians. By now, Hank had probably turned Raymond into a civil engineer with a thing for wildflowers.

"Anybody else?" I asked hopefully.

"Nope, that's it." Sure, Felice, crush the feelings of a woman who's just had surgery.

As I headed down the hall to my office, she called, "Oh, by the way, we're bidding for the Lylo book."

So, surprise, surprise, there wasn't any message from Ivan on my machine. And Danny hadn't called either. There was, however, a message from Sheila Karpfellner, leaving yet another number and asking me to call her back.

I didn't really want to think about the people who weren't calling me, so I did.

"Oh, hello," she said excitedly, when I said who I was. "I just had to tell you I got your flyer."

My . . . flyer? I had sudden hideous visions of a card with the number 1-800-DO-ME-NOW on it. What flyer was she talking about?

"The one about Norm. The basset hound."

"Oh. That's great."

"And I wanted to tell you that my fifth-grade class—I'm a teacher—is going to send letters to the agency."

"That's . . . wonderful." Great. Now I had gotten a classroom full of innocent children to partake in my madness. "I'm sure it'll help."

"I certainly hope so," said Sheila the Teacher, and hung up, leaving me feeling guilty and morose.

At ten-forty-five, fifteen minutes before Hank was due, I crossed my fingers and said a quick prayer that everything was fine, and that Camelia and Raymond's passion had progressed along the usual tortured lines before reaching its sublime—but appropriately married—conclusion.

I knew something was wrong the moment Hank walked in.

Primarily, because his hands were empty. Writers dropping off material generally carry it with them, in the telltale brown envelope.

I jumped to the safest and most obvious conclusion: "Twinge of writer's block, Hank?"

He straightened in his chair, all three chins rising along with him. "It's more than a twinge," he said.

"I'm sure it feels like it's more. I'm sure it feels like a big painful spasm in your creative colon, but Hank, believe me, the best writers get blocked from time to time, and I know you're going to get through it."

"No, I won't."

"You will."

"No, I won't, you see, because I'm quitting the *Days* series."

I was stunned. Not so much by his decision, but by his decisiveness. When did Hank sprout a backbone?

"Hank, why would you do that?" More importantly, why would you do it now? Today? Not to mention at this stage in Camelia and Raymond's romance. What were they supposed to do? Live out their existence half finished, in a permanent state of literary coitus interruptus?

"What about Raymond?" I asked. "What about Camelia?"

"I don't care about Raymond," Hank said bitterly. "He's just another piece of overblown barbarian beefcake."

Not a very complimentary way to describe supposedly the dishiest Saxon since Errol Flynn donned tights, but Hank was in no mood to be argued with.

"But Camelia," I said softly. "She was coming along so well. She was really developing into a breakout character for you."

This moved him, I could tell. He struggled for a minute, then cried, "No. No, you're lying. I can't do it anymore. I can't do it to *her.*"

He reached for his handkerchief and blew his nose. "I'm sorry, I just can't. It hurts too much."

"What does, Hank?"

"Treating her this way."

"Treating . . ."

"Camelia," he said simply. "I'm simply too close to her."

"I see."

"So, you understand why I can't write this book."

"Because you can't let her marry Raymond."

"No, because I can't write her as another ninny with a super-model's body and a squirrel's brain. I'm sorry. I know it all must seem very self-indulgent."

Crackers would have been my choice word, but he was the writer.

"No, not at all."

"Have you . . ." He toyed with the hem of his jacket. "Have you ever created anything? Something you've written or painted?"

"No, I haven't, Hank."

"Well, maybe when you do, you'll understand. Sometimes, if you're very lucky, you feel a connection, a kinship, to your subject. A character or . . . story. And you just know what they have to be. You know what they would do and what they wouldn't do. And if someone asks you to make them be something they're not, well . . ." He swallowed. "*Compromise* is the first word every writer learns, but there's a time when you start to disgust yourself."

"I'm sorry, Hank." I was, too. In spite of all rational thought, I was feeling pretty low that I had tried to come between him and Camelia.

"I can compromise myself, but I can't compromise her. Does that make any sense to you?"

"We're still talking about Camelia the fictional character . . ."

He smiled. "Yes, we are."

"Then it makes a lot of sense to me."

Hank was so happy about this, he took my hand and said, "People have a core—even fictional ones—and you can't make them what they were never meant to be. We aren't meant to be endlessly reinvented and repackaged. Just so we can be sold."

And not all of us aren't meant to labor in painful obscurity and die unknown. But Hank, I reminded myself, was a writer. A writer who believed in his characters more than he believed in himself. It wasn't his fault. You could think of this kind of gentle goofiness as sort of genetic preconditioning. The kind that, hopefully, by the time I had children, they would be able to test for and eradicate in the womb.

"So," said Hank, "I hope you understand."

"I do, Hank." You're a sick man; you can't help yourself. What sort of person would I be if I judged you as a capable, functioning human being?

"And you're not angry."

"No, I'm not angry, Hank."

And I wasn't. Call it hangover from my breakdown, but I wondered if maybe the world wasn't a better place for a few Hank Lauflers on the premises. Not a richer place, not a more successful place, but in some indefinable way, better.

He smiled gratefully and got up to go. But just before he left, I got an idea.

"Hey, Hank?"

He turned.

"You know what you should do?"

"What?"

"Write your own book. With the kind of heroine you want and the kind of story you believe in."

Hank got very excited. "Do you think Bickerstaff Books would be interested?"

"Sure," I said, "you never know." Which is Croatian for Never in a Million Years, but Hank didn't need to know that.

Hank Laufler left Bickerstaff Books possibly a happier man than he had ever been in his life. For about two minutes after he left, I was a happier woman than I had been in two whole weeks. Then

I checked my machine, and there was still nothing from Danny or Ivan, and I felt rotten all over again.

I couldn't believe it. How could Danny still not be speaking to me?

You made him go on Florinda! *You trampled his dreams.*

I did not trample his dreams.

He said you did.

Well, they were dumb dreams.

And you wonder why he's not speaking to you.

I was about to point out that I did not make Ivan go on *Florinda!* when my phone buzzed and I jumped. In the process, I knocked the receiver off the hook and heard the voice of the lobby receptionist.

Ivan Feiffer was here.

Did I want to see him?

I said, "Sure," and hoped that Ivan, if he was listening, could hear in that, *Come back, darling, all fat-headedness is forgiven.*

But what did Ivan want, I wondered as I searched my office for something resembling a grooming tool. (Or a sedative.) Did he want my forgiveness? Or was this to be a time of recriminations? Or worse, grist for his mill, to be recycled in his next novel?

Squaring his chin, Berkley strolled with studied nonchalance into the lair of his nemesis: the woman he had once loved above all others, the temptress who had set his mind and body aflame, even as she spun spurious dreams of publishing fame before his dazzled eyes . . .

Or . . .

Squaring his chin, Berkley rushed with frenzied haste to the bower of his beloved, his darling whom he had so cruelly wronged. Was

there time? Oh, let there be time, he thought, to tell her that he had
come to his senses, that at long last, he was giving up his dreary
coming-of-age novel to write that hit summer beach read that
would at last make him worthy of her.

"Uh, hello?"

I blinked. Somehow Ivan had gotten into my office.

"Hi."

"Hi."

For a moment, we were silent, each weighed down by poignant memories of whitefish.

I said, "Sit down."

He did. Nervously. "They said you had surgery."

"Oh, that."

"Are you okay?" Was I wrong, or did I hear a hint of anxiety in his voice?

"I am . . . now," I said, looking deeply into his eyes, trying to convey that if he had news of hit summer beach reads, I was receptive

Ivan returned the gaze for a moment. Then looked away. "I read about Dinah."

"Oh, right."

"It's great. That they let her off."

"Well, there was some arson thing in the Bronx. People are tired of Lylo; they want something new."

"I thought it was that the judge showed leniency."

"Yeah, that, too." Ah, Ivan, my sweet innocent scribe.

"Well," he said, digging into his briefcase, "I have the last chapters for *Days of Dust.*"

This, I had not expected. "Oh . . ." He put them on my desk. "Um, well, it's going to take a while to . . . peruse these, I'm sure there are problems, and you'll have to . . ."

"Mr. Bickerstaff looked through them. He thought they were okay." Ivan, my darling, B. Arthur couldn't read a matchbook.

"Also, I told him I wasn't interested in working on another."

I yelped. "Why not?"

"I want to devote more time to my novel. And . . . and . . ."

"And?" I was half out of my seat.

"I don't know, it was just sort of a painful experience," he said sadly.

"But a great experience, too," I said, desperately. There had to be a way back. Something I could say that would push Ivan right over the edge and back into my arms. *Rhett, I love you.* No, that wasn't it. Hadn't worked for Scarlett, wouldn't work for me. *Loved Rebecca? I hated her.* No, not quite the thing, either. *The Force will be with you . . . always.* Argh.

Then, I thought of it.

"Say, Ivan?"

He looked up. "Yeah?"

"I was wondering something."

"What?"

"What happens to the dog?"

"What dog?"

"The one in your book."

"I made him a lizard," he said in a chilly voice.

"Oh."

"You said you liked lizards."

"Well, you could make him back into a dog. Dogs are good."

"I already did."

I smiled. "Showing that artistic integrity again."

"That's right."

"I like that in a man."

"No, you don't."

Ook, stalemate.

I swallowed. "I could learn to live with it."

"You could?"

A glimmer of hope in his eyes. It was time to deliver the coup de grâce.

"Say, Ivan? You think you'd let me read more of your book?"

He got up, came around to my side of the desk. "I might."

"I just gotta find out what happens to that dog."

After Ivan and I had explored all the joyous reunion stuff you can reasonably explore in the confines of an office, we took ourselves off to Willy's Noodle Shop and expressed mutual remorse over lo mein. Then we embarrassed ourselves in the Lobel-Schrafft lobby and parted with promises of future defilement. Ivan joyfully agreed to come back on the *Days* series. I didn't tell him about Hank's quitting. Primarily, because Ivan was a fellow writer, and likely to say something idiotic like, "Gosh, quitting a steady gig for your artistic principles—what a swell idea!"

Not much could have improved the day.

Except a phone call from Danny.

Which was what I had on my office voice mail. It told me to meet him at a bar on Forty-fourth Street after work.

And so I did.

He was sitting at a booth, the most gorgeous companion a pint of beer could have outside of a corned beef sandwich. For a moment I hesitated by the door—what if he was feeling vengeful and threw the beer in my face? What if Florinda was hiding in the bathroom, ready to film the whole thing? " 'Friends Who Trample Their Friends' Dreams'—on the next *Florinda!*" But Danny smiled, and that gave me the courage to slide in opposite.

For a moment, I played with one of those cardboard coaster thingies. Then I took a deep breath and let it out on, "Danny, I don't know how to tell you how sorry I am."

"You could get all the tapes of the show and have them burned."

Horrified, I looked at him. His face was absolutely straight. I said in a choked voice, "I'll certainly try . . ." Maybe I could pretend I was Danny's mother and part of some religious cult that forbids TV appearances. The only way to save my son's immortal soul would be through a ritual cleansing (read bonfire) of the tapes . . .

"Be awful hard," said Danny, taking a sip of his beer.

"Well, it would, but I'm willing to try." Picket lines. I'll hire some extras, throw a few sheets and bangles on them. We'll make it work. Anything, Danny, just come home.

But then Danny said, "Nah, I don't think it can be done."

"Oh."

"So, I guess I'll just have to accept your apology."

"I can grovel, make little kissy noises around your feet."

"But I have one condition," he said.

"Anything."

"Don't say 'anything' until you hear what it is. You know your problem? You're too impulsive. 'Repossessed by Corporate America.' " He rolled his eyes. "Cute idea, but you didn't think it was actually going to work. It didn't, did it?"

"No."

"You're not to blame. You're probably borderline something or other."

"Gosh, thanks." I suppose in these groveling scenarios, it's necessary to take a little shoe leather to the teeth, but that didn't mean I had to like it.

I sniffed. "I guess that's what Julian says. That I'm *borderline*."

"No. As a matter of fact, Julian was the one who told me I owed you an apology."

"Pardon?" Trust Danny; he never sticks to the right script.

Danny smiled. "Much as I'd like to think you ruined my life by making me lower my artistic standards"—I winced. I didn't mean to, but some words just hurt—"after I thought about it a while, I realized it wasn't fair to blame you."

"That's sweet, Danny, but I was the one who brought *Florinda!* into it."

A brief shadow passed over his face. "Yes. Yes, you did. But—I shouldn't have done it if I didn't want to." The smile was back. "The truth is, I was getting a little desperate in my career."

"I know. I should know. I exploited your desperation. I'm really sorry."

"You're forgiven."

"Was that your condition?" I said hopefully.

"No."

"Oh."

I started imagining. Kick Dinah out of the house, one. Give me the bigger bedroom, two. Have Florinda assassinated, three . . .

"You have to accept something."

I guessed immediately. "You're moving in with Julian. That's fabulous. Name a housewarming gift and it's yours."

"I'm not moving in with Julian."

"Oh."

"I'm giving up acting."

I tried to say oh, didn't quite manage it.

"Are we still friends?" Danny was watching me very carefully.

Shocked, I drew myself upright. "Of course we're still friends. Don't be dumb."

282 • EMMI FREDERICKS

Danny nodded. "So you do actually like me for something besides my future in action flicks."

"Danny, for God's sake."

"Okay, I just needed to be sure. Sorry."

I brightened. "Then you're not giving up acting?"

"No, I am."

"Oh." A slight dim on the brights.

"Look." He took my hand. "Remember when that guy at the *Flo*—" He couldn't quite say the name and coughed over it instead. "That guy in the audience who said maybe I didn't get the parts I wanted not because I was good-looking but because I wasn't very good?"

"That guy was so stupid, Danny, you can't listen to someone who goes to the *Florinda!* show, for God's sake." Said I, conveniently forgetting I had also been in the audience.

Danny patted my hand in a gentle signal to shut up. "The guy wasn't stupid, and he wasn't wrong. And that's why I'm quitting."

"Danny, how can you quit? You love theater so much."

"I know. I'm not quitting completely . . ."

A glimmer of hope on the horizon. Directing? Producing, even?

"I'm going be a teacher."

I wobbled but maintained a firm grip on the table. The glimmer was gone, replaced by something I can only describe as a long, dark tunnel into oblivion. After several ragged breaths, I said, "But Danny . . . think of what you're doing. The risks, the dangers."

"I know."

"The ten-year-old mumblers who think they're the next DeNiro. The teenage vamps ready to scratch your eyes out when you pass them over for Juliet. The dreadful parents who think it's your job to get their squint-eyed no-talent into Yale or Julliard. Danny . . . I'm not sure you can hack it."

What I said gave him pause, I could see it. But he squared his shoulders manfully—probably a gag he was working on for *Cyrano*—and said, "I'm going to find out."

"Danny, I beg you, think what you're doing. Remember the rotten pay, the gyms with no acoustics. Remember how we treated our teachers. Think of *high school talent nights* . . ."

In my heart of hearts, I thought that would do it. I thought the prospect of endless renditions of "I'm Just a Girl Who Can't Say No" and thirteen-year-olds doing Noel Coward with bad British accents would turn it around.

Danny said gently, "It can't be any worse than *Florinda!*"

I knew I was beaten. So I said, "I think that's wonderful, Danny." I said it very fast, so I didn't actually have to hear myself say it, but I said it.

Danny smiled. "You think it sucks."

"I don't, Danny, honestly."

He laughed. "Yes, you do."

"Danny, I don't believe this. I am absolutely thrilled for you. You're ending one part of your life, but you're moving on in a positive, mature way, and using your passion to inspire others. I am very happy."

He paused. "You are?"

"Yes," I said firmly, doing a far better acting job than Danny Beale had ever done in his life.

But actually, I was happy for him. A part of me. A very small part of me. A very small part of me was happy for Danny.

And for me.

I looked at it this way. Danny might not be the next big third-reel sacrifice, but at least he was coming back home. Dinah might not be the next Squeaky Fromm, but she was out of jail. And Ivan might not have a stranglehold on the bestseller list, but he had a very nice grip in other areas where it counted.

And I would never have to see the movie of Roger Kelton's *The Idiot.*

But the best thing of all?

For twenty-four hours, I hadn't had a single thought about a celebrity.

It probably couldn't last. But it was a start.

CHAPTER SEVENTEEN

WHERE ARE THEY NOW?

*D*ANNY WAS sensational in *Cyrano*. Twenty-five people saw him be sensational, then he hung up his wigs forever.

Danny and Julian did wait before they moved in together. About six months. Then they got an apartment in Park Slope. Danny started his degree in special education. In two years, he will bring the light of theater into children's lives. All his premieres will be held in school auditoriums from now on.

I've promised to buy tickets to every one.

Julian, in order to finance Danny's passion, quit theater and went to Wall Street. He's doing very well.

Several things happened as a result of the Buster Rosen case. In no particular order of bizarreness, they are:

Soon after the trial ended, the Rosen family held the first annual Be a Deli Man for a Day. It was a huge success. This year, they held the second annual Be a Deli Man for a Day, but turnout was down. By then everyone was wearing ribbons for Billy the Stunt Pig. Billy had died of a heart attack while filming an action sequence. You could buy the ribbons for a dollar, and the proceeds went to NO PAM (No Pig Abuse in Movies). People liked wearing ribbons more than they liked working in soup kitchens, so Billy won out.

Doris the Hack Quack got her own television program. It was an immediate hit and is even now edging up on *Florinda!* in the ratings. She called me and asked if I wanted to come on. I said no but thanks anyway.

Having finally admitted that he was the one driving on the fatal night, Lylo Wingate, Jr., sobbed before the TV cameras and said how sorry he was, how badly he felt, and how he had wanted to confess all along, but his lawyers had advised against it. Some people were moved. Others thought it was a pile of self-serving crap. (I was on the side of self-serving crap, myself.)

He served a year in a Supportive Environment for the Rich and Unstable. He came out more popular than ever, finally possessed of the "street cred" that had eluded him when he was just another rich white boy (instead of something really, you know, cool, like a rich white boy who had run someone over).

But Lylo played it cool. He said he was working on a new album, attended a few quiet parties. At one of those parties, he met Fuzzy Winterspoon.

They're planning a June wedding.

Hank finished his novel, *The Unseen Heroine*, the story of a medieval novice who cultivated roundwort in her garden and smiled gently at a passing knight every third year.

It's been on the bestseller list for three months now.

Ivan also finished his novel. It was rejected by forty-seven agents. Then it was rejected by eighteen publishers. Ivan has now started a new novel.

But it's okay. I love him anyway.

Dinah did not write a book. But she did sell her story to the *Enquirer*. (I have the cover framed in my bathroom.)

The trial worked for her in other ways, too. For one thing, everyone became very interested in Ms. Sharlip's body parts. It was only for a little while, but she managed to make several sales and now has a nice cushion of cash. I asked if she minded selling off all her work, but she said she was through with art for good.

"That's not where the power is," she told me.

World, meet Dinah Sharlip—agent.

And what of Norm and Sal? There, too, I'm pleased to report a happy ending.

Remember Sheila Karpfellner? The teacher who got my Norm flyer? Well, she and her fifth-grade class were a little more motivated than I thought. With the letters, they got some local news attention, then went national, and before you knew it, letters, faxes, and e-mails were coming in from all over the country, bombarding Good Friend Insurance with calls for justice. Within a month, Norm was back with Sal. Proving that sometimes, the boring, repetitive lick/stuff crap actually works.

Sheila Karpfellner, wherever you are, you are a Great Bit Player.

Okay, so Danny is in love at last and fighting the good fight in our schools. Dinah is on her way to fulfilling her rightful destiny as an evil exploiter of other people's talents. Ivan is scribbling away in joyous anonymity and enjoying his first happy relationship, with yours truly. (Hey, I might tell him his novels stink, but I laugh at his jokes and pay for my half of the Chinese takeout.)

So, could we be any happier?

Yes, we could be.

And we are.

Since I first started this book, I am happy to announce that there has been a big change in my life.

Oh, my God! As a result of your involvement with the Florinda! *show or the Lylo Wingate trial, somehow you have actually become . . .*

A CELEBRITY!!!

Not exactly.

But not exactly not, either.

Here's what happened:

After his ordeal with the agency, Sal went through a crisis over whether he wanted Norm involved in show business anymore. In the end, he decided yes, because more people than ever were writing to Norm, and Norm loves the attention and fuss. But Sal felt he couldn't handle the business side. He was sick of being Norm's manager—he just wanted to be Norm's friend. (Plus, he wanted to go back to calling him Ulysses, which he was contractually forbidden to do as his manager.)

So now Norm and Sal live happily and at peace in Sal's apartment, which is still right above my apartment, which is a very convenient thing since I am Norm's new manager.

That's right.

I have entered Great Bit Player Nirvana.

I work for an extremely famous star.

I am very well paid.

Norm has no wife, no girlfriends, no significant others. I have to keep him out of embarrassing entanglements with the odd leg now and again, but other than that, the risk of paternity suits is slight.

Norm is not addicted to drugs or alcohol. He is addicted to danish, but it's fairly easy to limit his intake for the simple reason that he cannot go to the bakery by himself.

Norm is a perfect

All I have to do is

mercial shoots and gu

has water and kibble. I

not feel up to answering

him. If he takes a dump, I

Norm is a beloved citiz

where. With Norm, I have l

(not me personally, but I v

Norm were interviewed), and

den.

And last month, Norm was c   ᵣ ꞁnagazine's
25 Most Beautiful People.

It's not just a life. It's the perfect life.

So, that's my story. And a few other people's, as well.

But are you cured? Do you still think about celebrities?

Of course I do. Everybody does. Just last week, I was watching the news. Forty people dead in a train derailment. Sextuplets were born in Cleveland. Forty people only famous when they're dead, six famous from birth. This is our world, readers. This is America. Everybody's a commodity here, not just Sara Lee. Those aren't squares or circles or triangles on our flag. They're stars.

But I don't have to be one. As a matter of fact, if being a star means having to marry people like Lylo Wingate, I'd just as soon not. Backstage at Letterman is good enough for me.

And I've come a long way from the shuddering, weeping, guilty mess Dinah discovered with the remote in her hand. I said I wanted a life, and now I have one. Maybe thirty-five people in the world know my name, but hey, by and large, they're the people I like.

.ogram Danny made up for me?
.it into the world and tell others what

.e.
.r listening.